DIVISION 5

The Makanza Series
Book Four

KRISTA STREET

FREE E-BOOK!

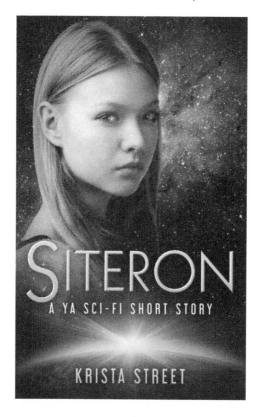

To Lizzie and Jesikah, for your continued support, friendship, and enthusiasm throughout the making of this series.

And to my dad, for all of your help, thank you.

1 – HOME

"Meghan, you can't go to work with a gunshot wound!" My mother stood in the doorway of my childhood bedroom with her arms crossed. One of her blond eyebrows arched in disapproval.

I struggled to get my shirt on and grimaced. My mother didn't try to help. It was the first time in four days she hadn't stayed at my side, helping me with every little thing.

"Mom, I have to go to work. You heard Bethany. I can't leave her in that state if she's going to be miserable for the rest of her life. I need to help her."

I turned my back so she wouldn't see how much it hurt to put clothes on.

Janine Forester frowned.

I knew she did even though I wasn't looking at her. I also knew she was studying me. I could feel it. Like someone was holding a burning poker to my neck.

Her exasperated sigh followed. "There's no reason you can't return in a few weeks. The doctor said you're supposed to rest, take short walks, take your pain medication and antibiotics on schedule, and not lift more than ten pounds for at *least* six weeks. Not to mention, you're not supposed to drive."

I finally turned around to face her.

My mother's fingers drummed on her bicep. Glittering hazel eyes met mine—eyes that mirrored my own eye color.

"Mom, I'm leaving. It's not up for discussion."

Searing pain shot down my right arm when I tugged too sharply on the sleeve. I carefully put my arm back into the sling. The sound of ripping Velcro, when it took several attempts to get the straps right, filled the room.

Thankfully, my pants were already on. Now, it was a matter of packing the rest of my clothes one-armed before I headed back to Sioux Falls.

It was crazy to think my recent physical limitations had begun only a week ago. That was when I'd woken up in the hospital after my former boss shot me in Mobridge, just outside Reservation 1 in northwest South Dakota. Dr. Roberts had been waiting near a building beside my vehicle. I had no idea how he'd found me. I could only guess that he'd followed me when he spotted me driving through the streets.

And when I'd returned to my vehicle with Davin, the twins, and Sharon, Dr. Roberts had raised his gun to shoot Davin. Without considering the consequences, I'd lunged in front of the only man I'd ever loved.

So now, a still-healing bullet wound marred my upper chest. But it had been a week since the incident, and I'd spent the entire weekend in Vermillion at my parents' home recovering. And while my mother was right, I wasn't 100%— far from it—I couldn't stay here any longer.

For multiple reasons.

My hand stilled over my suitcase as those reasons pummeled my mind. It had been four days since I'd seen

Davin Kinder—the Kazzie infected with strain 11—the man I'd been in love with since I started my job at Compound 26 over a year ago.

Davin was free now. He was no longer a prisoner in the Compound or on Reservation 1. All of the Kazzies were free. The Post Wave Rehabilitation Act ensured that despite Senator Douglas' promise to overturn the law.

White-hot pain squeezed my heart, an ache that had nothing to do with the bullet wound. It felt like someone had taken my soul and clenched it between their hands, wringing the life right out of me. Not only had I been shot by my former boss, the same man who'd tormented Davin and my friends for years, but I'd also made a startling discovery about Davin only four days ago.

Unbeknownst to me, he'd been in communication with his former girlfriend, Jenna, during his time on Reservation 1. Weeks ago, I'd found letters from her under his bed. They'd agreed to meet in Rapid City if Davin were ever freed.

When I'd found those letters, I hadn't wanted to believe what I was reading. It hurt too much.

For so many months, Davin had pushed me away despite our feelings for each other. He'd been adamant that a relationship would never work with someone on the outside. So when Jenna showed up at the hospital four days ago, looking for Davin, it became apparent his rule had only applied to me—not her. The only explanation for her arrival was that he'd cultivated a relationship with her long-distance while he'd lived on the reservation.

The flash of guilt I'd seen on his face, when Jenna had arrived at Reservation 1's hospital, had confirmed my suspicions. That guilt seared itself into my memory like a deeply embedded tattoo. There was no removing it. It would forever haunt me.

I bit my lip hard enough to make me wince. My eyes squeezed shut as the feeling of betrayal fired inside me. I didn't want to know any more about Davin and his ex. I'd chosen to walk away from him four days ago. It hurt too much to stay in his life knowing he had chosen her over me.

You have no choice but to move on now. You need to forget him.

"Meghan? Is there any way I can talk you out of this?" My mother's voice snapped me back to the present. Her arms rested against her sides, her disapproving expression in place.

I shook my head. "Sorry, Mom. I'm going."

Her eyes dimmed, but she nodded.

I was still trying to wrap my head around the change in my mother. For the past few days, she'd been attentive and caring. Considering the mother I'd grown up with had been as aloof and cool as the clouds above, I was still halfway convinced she'd become possessed or an alien had taken over her body.

As I made a move to lift my bag, she rushed to my side and pushed my hand away. "At least let me carry your things."

The air rustled around her as she hoisted the long strap onto her shoulder. It dug into her thick sweater, but her head stayed high and her back straight. As always, my mother exuded poise and elegance. Even in jeans and a sweater, she looked immaculate. She'd always been that way. Growing up, nothing seemed to faze her.

Before she could turn, I placed my hand over hers. It felt strange to touch her—we'd never touched or been affectionate in my family. But as strange as it felt, she didn't pull back.

"Thanks for your help this weekend, Mom. I'm sure I'll be fine back at my apartment."

The tightening of her mouth was her only response before she nodded curtly and strode through my bedroom door.

With a sigh, I followed her.

The worn carpet in the hallway shuffled beneath my soles as we headed to the stairs. Jeremy's empty bedroom lay across the hall. The door was closed. I knew if I opened it his room would be exactly as it had been seven years ago. Posters of rock bands on the wall. A navy blue comforter on the bed. Clothes strewn about the floor. A scarred desk with comic books in the corner.

Neither of my parents had cleared out his room after he died. At this point, I figured they never would. In a way, I was glad. It was one of our only reminders of my dead brother.

I stepped carefully down the stairway, my good hand holding tightly to the railing. Even though I'd been taking pain medicine regularly since leaving the hospital, certain movements still hurt.

Snow danced outside the living room window when I finally reached the main floor. Since it was the beginning of winter, it was freezing out. I eyed my coat in the entryway. *I wonder how long it will take to put that on.*

My mother slipped on her boots and opened the front door. "I'll load your things in the car. Be right back."

A strong gust of cold air swirled inside. The wind blew long locks of brown hair around my face before she closed it.

Lifting my good arm, I pulled down my winter jacket. Only a slight twinge of pain followed when I wrangled it on and pulled it over my shoulder. Even though my wound had started to heal, I was still weeks away from a full recovery. It was something my mother had constantly reminded me of during the past twenty-four hours—ever since Bethany, the Kazzie who could fly and wanted *Makanza* eradicated from her body showed up unannounced on our doorstep.

Just as I slipped on my boots, my cell phone buzzed in my

back pocket. Pulling it out, my heart stopped when I saw the caller.

Davin.

It was the third time he'd called today. So far, I deleted all of his messages and texts without listening to or reading them. My decision to move on meant accepting a life without him.

Completely without him.

Tapping the ignore button, my hand shook when I shoved my phone back into my pocket. Pain from the movement shot through my wound, eliciting a groan from me.

Just as tears formed in my eyes, my dad rounded the corner. I hastily blinked them back.

"Hey, kiddo. Where you headed?" With brown hair and brown eyes, my father looked like an older version of Jeremy. I imagined if my brother had survived, he would have been the spitting image of my dad.

My cheeks heated when I gingerly zippered my jacket up. "Um… back to Sioux Falls."

His eyebrows rose. "Now? But I thought you were staying here for a few weeks. You know, until you get back on your feet."

I shrugged, not able to meet his gaze. "I was going to, but then…" With a firm pull, I got my hat on. "Well, you heard how upset Bethany was yesterday. I can't leave her like that, and I'm not getting anything done down here."

My dad continued to frown as I wound a scarf around my neck. He leaned against the wall and crossed his arms. "The Compound's not going anywhere, Meg. You can go back to work in a few weeks."

I managed a smile. "You're beginning to sound like Mom."

His eyes dimmed. "About that… You know she was really looking forward to you staying here."

I cocked my head and was about to respond when he said in a rush, "She's been working really hard on a few things. You wouldn't know since we see so little of you, but she's been trying really hard to connect with people more. Ever since your brother died—" His words cut off as pain entered his eyes. And if I didn't know better, tears did as well.

I stood frozen as I stared up at my father. *Reach for him, Meghan. Say something!*

But nothing happened. It was like I'd seized up.

Clearing his throat, he crossed his arms again. "Anyway, she's trying, Meg. She really is. And I think almost losing you last week has done something to her. I've never seen her cry like she has in the past few days."

"Mom? *Cry?*" The stunned word left my mouth just as the front door opened.

My mother, in her faded winter jacket, eyed us curiously when she stepped into the entryway. Closing the door, she stomped the snow off her boots. "Bill, would you mind collecting the rest of Meghan's things? She'd like to get on the road."

My dad pushed away from the wall. His frown stayed in place. "Sure thing."

I watched his retreating form as my mother and I stood awkwardly beside one another. For a moment, it felt like it used to. Stiff. Formal. The complete opposite of a warm, loving relationship.

Clearing my throat, I said, "Maybe you and dad should come up to Sioux Falls to visit soon?"

My mother's eyes widened for the merest second before she tentatively smiled. "That would be nice."

My dad appeared a minute later. He helped me out the door while carrying my remaining bags. Together, he and my mother buckled me into my car, like I was a toddler being put to bed. They fussed around me. And while it was embarrassing, it was also kind of nice.

Once again, I was reminded of what Davin had been telling me for months. My parents really did love me. It was simply our past that we had to overcome.

The thought of Davin brought another stab of pain into my heart and, for the first time in four days, I questioned if I'd overreacted by jumping into the back of my parents' car and speeding away before he could explain himself. But then I remembered the letters and the guilt on his face. Betrayal once again fired inside of me.

Just forget him, Meghan.

After awkwardly slipping on my mittens, I stared at my parents through my open window. Cold wind blew inside my car, but I didn't make an attempt to roll the window up.

"Well, I guess this is goodbye."

My dad stuffed his hands into his pockets. "Yeah, kiddo. We'll see you soon."

Clasping her hands in front of her, my mother addressed my dad. "Meghan has invited us to Sioux Falls. Perhaps we can join her next week for an outing?"

My dad grinned. "Really? That would be great."

I finally waved goodbye as we all promised to see each other soon. Even though my dad hadn't bothered to put on his jacket, they both stood in the driveway watching me go until I rounded the corner and disappeared from view.

It was only as I began the hour-long trek back to Sioux Falls that I felt Sara trying to make contact. We'd spoken every day since I'd left the hospital. Despite her being my best friend, I hadn't told her what had happened between me and Davin. She didn't even know about the letters I'd seen. No one did.

The scratchy feeling filled the back of my mind, like a cat pawing a door open. It was soft and hesitant. Lately, Sara had been walking on eggshells around me.

I opened up our telepathic link. *Hi, sorry. Did I just give off a weird vibe?*

No, that's not why I wanted to talk.

Since the twin and I shared a telepathic connection, it was easy for us to get into contact with one another regardless of where we were. Sara and Sophie were currently living in Rapid City with Davin and his mother, Sharon. In other words, Sara had up-to-date information on everything Davin was doing.

All I knew was that Davin had seen Jenna twice in the past few days when Jenna had stopped by their home.

It was two times more than I wanted to know about.

What's up? I tried to sound casual as I drove down the neighborhood streets toward the interstate.

Have you been crying again?

Me? Crying? A hysterical laugh bubbled up in my mind and drifted to her. *Why in the world would I be crying?*

Meghan… I could tell she wanted to broach the subject. The subject we'd both been carefully avoiding all weekend. *I know how you feel about Davin.*

Sara—

Let me finish. I've seen how you look at him, and I've seen how he looks at you. This is silly. Jenna doesn't mean anything to him. Not anymore.

Once again, self-doubt filled me as I questioned if I'd overreacted, but as always happened in my life—logic prevailed. *Is that why she showed up at the hospital? How could she know that's where he'd be unless he'd told her? They'd obviously been talking. He could have at least told me.*

Before Sara could respond, I added, *And how do you know*

Jenna means nothing to him? You were at the hospital. You saw how he looked at her, and Davin's free now. He's finally free to live in public. He's no longer a prisoner within Compound 26 or Reservation 1. He can do as he pleases, and he should. I want... My voice shook in my mind. *I want him to be happy, and if Jenna makes him happy then...*

I couldn't continue.

I loved Davin more than anything, and I did want him to be happy. But the truth was, what I'd really wanted was for him to be happy with *me.*

Yeah... She suddenly didn't sound as convinced in her words. *But you should see him right now. He's a wreck.*

I bit my lip harder as snowflakes fell on the windshield. *But you also said she's been to their house twice in the past few days. Maybe he's only a wreck because he feels guilty, not because I'm gone.*

Maybe, but... Ugh, Meghan. I just really don't think that's the reason. I wish you'd talk to him.

The thought of talking to Davin made my breath catch.

Sara sighed. The soft sound billowed through my mind like a summer breeze before she said, *I'm still not convinced he wants her. I think her showing up at the hospital caught him off guard. And regardless of what you think, I don't think Davin knew she was going to do that.*

Leaning back in the seat, I winced when my arm shifted. What I really needed now more than anything was to go for a run. Unfortunately, running was out of the question until I healed more.

So how's everything else going? How's Sophie?

I sensed Sara roll her eyes at my change in subject, but she acquiesced. *She's doing really well. For the first time in years, she's laughed every day.*

A smile spread across my face when I accelerated onto the interstate. Dozens of other cars were also driving along I-29.

Since the state borders had opened several months ago, it seemed every day more and more travelers emerged. *That's great to hear. Do you both plan on staying in South Dakota?*

Yeah, I think so. Since we don't have anywhere to go, it seems like a good place to stay.

And Sharon? How's she?

Worried about you. When did you last speak?

Yesterday but briefly. My mom and I were heading out for my afternoon walk when she called.

Speaking of that, how is your chest and arm?

I put my blinker on before carefully swinging into the left lane to pass a car. *Sore but fine. It'll heal.*

And… Um, Dr. Roberts… Where's he?

Still locked up I'm assuming.

Good. Let's hope he stays there. Her chilled words blew across my mind.

We kept up a steady stream of conversation during my drive. Sara spent most of it filling me in on Compound 26's former Kazzies. Victor and Sage were currently living the bachelor life in Colorado. Dorothy had moved home to be with her son in southern California, and Garrett had returned to his home state of Michigan. She said they all asked about me regularly, especially since I'd been shot. Hearing about all of them helped fill the aching void in my chest.

I pulled into my apartment's parking lot a moment later. A groan of annoyance escaped me when I saw what waited.

Half a dozen reporters were camped around the front door of my apartment building.

What is it? Sara asked.

The reporters. They're still here. I had hoped they'd be gone by now. Since I hadn't been home for over a week, I figured they'd have given up on constantly pressing me for statements.

Unfortunately, they didn't seem to be letting up.

Her breath sucked in. *They're at your parents' house now?*

No, I'm at home. I just pulled into my apartment building's parking lot.

What? You've been driving to Sioux Falls the entire time we've been talking? But I thought you were staying in Vermillion until you got better?

I sank lower in my seat so the reporters wouldn't see me. *I was going to but plans changed.* Sara already knew that Bethany had come to my parents' house yesterday, but Sara didn't know I'd decided to return to work so soon.

Once I finished explaining, her disapproval flashed through our connection. *Bad idea, Meg. You're hardly ready to work. You were just shot!*

I grumbled. *Are you really going to give me a hard time too?*

She sighed. *Sorry. No, I just... Never mind. But anyway, back to these reporters. Have they spotted you?*

Not yet. Otherwise, they'd be swarming my vehicle.

What if you talk to them? Will they go away if you do?

I groaned. *No. I tried that before, but they just keep coming up with more questions and never leave. You'd think one statement would be enough, but as soon as something new happens with the Kazzies, they start harassing me all over again.*

She made a disgusted sound. *Is there a back door, or somewhere else you can sneak in?*

I unclicked my seatbelt and carefully maneuvered my injured arm. *Yes, there's a door on the west side. Hopefully, they won't see me when I get out.* I sighed and grumbled. *Are they ever going to lose interest?*

Sooner or later they will, but since you're the poster child for the movement to free us, you're their favorite target. And since you were also shot by the former Director of Reservation 1, you're the most exciting thing that's happened in this country since the vaccine.

Don't remind me.

We shut down our connection with promises to talk soon.

With a deep breath, I contemplated how to carry my bags while also getting around the reporters. Thankfully, since I'd parked in the far corner of the parking lot, they still hadn't spotted me.

Opening my door as quietly as possible, I snuck around to the trunk and grabbed my purse and laptop only. I'd have to retrieve my larger bags later.

Pulling my hood up, I kept my face down as I walked to the back door. Just as I was about to round the corner of my apartment building, a shout came from behind me.

"There she is!"

My heart raced wildly as I hurried to the door, but given my injury, I didn't stand a chance at beating them. By the time I grasped the door handle, I was surrounded by six reporters. Microphones were shoved in my face as questions were fired at me like bullets from a machine gun.

"Have you heard the stories circulating around the country about those exposed?"

"What made Dr. Roberts shoot you? Did you do something to provoke him?"

"Senator Douglas is claiming that someone's gravely ill after being exposed to *Makanza*. What do you have to say about that?"

Pain burned in my chest when I yanked the door open. Since my apartment building was private property, the reporters couldn't step inside. It didn't stop them from blocking my way. Another twinge of pain traveled down my arm as I pushed past a reporter.

He muttered an angry reply, and I shot him a dirty look.

Of course, the camera swung on me just as I did and caught my glare.

It was only as the door started to close behind me, that I heard what they were saying.

People are sick.

My stomach plummeted as I raced to the stairwell.

By the time I climbed the steps and reached my apartment door, my wound felt on fire. It was only when I locked myself safely inside my tiny apartment that I slumped to the floor. Tears threatened to pour down my cheeks, but I held them back.

It was inevitable that some people would become sick after being exposed to *Makanza*. It didn't mean anything in the long run. So far, nobody had died or Changed after being exposed to the virus, and becoming ill for a short period of time was to be expected in some people.

I'd been gravely sick for five days when I'd been exposed. Still, people were paranoid. And more than a few believed the vaccine didn't work.

In a week, it will be better. They'll have gone through the stages and then they'll know that the vaccine is effective.

I closed my eyes. Shouts from the reporters carried faintly through my living room window. The accusations burned my eardrums. Pulling out my phone, I debated calling the police.

I nibbled my lip. Calling the police could backfire since it could draw more attention to me. I tapped the screen.

My breath sucked in.

A voicemail from Davin waited.

All thoughts of phoning the cops vanished.

My finger hovered above the screen. So far, I'd deleted all of his messages. But that nagging doubt again bit at my conscience like an annoying lap dog that constantly nipped at one's heels.

Maybe Sara's right. Maybe I should hear him out.

What I needed right now more than anything was his calm voice and steady reassurances. Drawing my eyebrows together, I knew what I was about to do wasn't wise, but if I thought too much about it, I'd change my mind.

Tapping my phone with a shaky finger, I brought his voicemail to my ear.

2 – BACK TO WORK

The deep sound of his voice rolled over me. It was such a familiar, comforting sound. *"Meghan, I'm sorry."* He paused, as if trying to find the words. *"Like I've been saying, I didn't know Jenna would show up like that. I can tell her being back in my life upset you—"*

I snatched the phone from my ear and hastily hit the delete button.

Unsteady breaths made my chest rise and fall. The familiar panic tightened like a vise around me.

My hands shook as I stared at my phone. *Jenna's back in his life. It's official. She's back in his life.*

I dropped the phone at my side. It clattered to the floor. The sound filled my quiet apartment as I squeezed my eyes tightly shut.

For months, before the Kazzies were released, I'd been fighting to free Davin and my friends from Reservation 1. I'd given them my heart and soul. I'd dedicated my life to saving and freeing them. And Davin had made me think he'd do the same for me.

Instead, he'd been talking to Jenna the entire time. He'd

been planning to meet her while knowing she had romantic interests in him.

But he thought you were with Mitch when he'd written Jenna letters. He thought you'd moved on and that he'd never see you again.

Logic once again threatened to diminish the aching sense of betrayal that coursed through my veins.

For a moment, I kept my eyes closed and pretended that everything was okay. I pretended that Davin and I loved each other. I pretended that nothing would ever come between us. I pretended that he was sitting right beside me, his comforting presence like a looming weight of loyalty and love.

But then I remembered what pretending had done to me before.

I snapped my eyes open.

For many years, I'd pretended that my dead brother was alive. When times were too tough for me to handle things on my own, I'd pretend that Jeremy was sitting in my apartment. I'd have a conversation with him as if he were actually here— living and breathing. It was how I'd dealt with things since I didn't have anyone to turn to.

But I wasn't going back to that.

I'd worked too hard to overcome it. *You're stronger now, Meghan. You've learned how to stand on your own two feet. Don't let that go.*

Pushing up awkwardly from the floor, I wiped the tears from my cheeks and reached for my purse. My wound throbbed. Pulling pain medicine out, I downed a few pills before padding gingerly to my bedroom to change and get ready for bed. It was already evening, and tomorrow would be a big day.

THE NEXT DAY my alarm went off at five. I'd promised

Bethany that I'd meet her at Compound 26 this morning to begin tests. With any luck, it would help me and my colleagues better understand Bethany's unique physiology and how *Makanza* affected her.

Since Bethany was staying with a friend in Sioux Falls, she wouldn't have to travel far. Whoever accompanied her had to be a good friend. They'd traveled all the way from Minneapolis.

Thirty minutes later, as I was awkwardly brushing my damp hair, my cell phone rang. Knowing it could be Davin, my heart rate picked up. With trepid steps, I walked to my bedroom. My cell phone waited face down on the nightstand.

I turned my phone over and sighed in relief when I saw my co-worker's name on the screen.

Tapping the answer button, I brought the phone to my ear. "Hi, Amy."

"Hey, Meg. I hear you're coming in with a Kazzie today." Her voice sounded scratchy, as if she'd just woken up.

I shook my head. "How is it that news travels so quickly through the Makanza Research Institute?"

Amy cleared her throat. "Oh, you know how it is. It's like we're a bunch of old gossiping ladies. The latest I heard is that a Kazzie with strain 15 turned up on your parents' doorstep asking you for help. Is that true?"

"Yes. It was Bethany, one of the Kazzies from Minnesota. She's hoping we can find a cure."

"A cure? A vaccine isn't enough?"

I sat down on my bed. The mattress sank beneath me. "She doesn't want to be a Kazzie anymore. You should've seen her, Amy. She's devastated. She doesn't want to live with the Changes the virus has made within her."

"Yeah, I guess that makes sense. It probably isn't helping

that they're being harassed. Did you hear that latest news story from Colorado?"

My stomach tightened. "I heard. Some guy with strain 13 had rocks thrown at him while he was walking in his neighborhood, right?"

"That's the one. Too bad there weren't any glass buildings nearby. Then he could have climbed away with his suction-cup hands."

Since strain 13 created suction-like appendages on a Kazzie's hands and feet, he could have easily scampered away in the right setting.

"It makes me sick what those hecklers are doing." Amy muttered a sound of disgust. "But anyway, how's your arm?"

"Getting better." I lifted my shirt and peeked at the wound. I'd just put a fresh bandage on after my shower. Only a little spot of blood oozed through it.

"I can't believe you're already coming back to work."

I rolled my eyes. "You sound like my mother."

"Well, she has a point. You were shot a week ago. Dr. Sadowsky would be more than willing to give you the month off."

"I know, but there's work to do."

Amy clucked her tongue. "I'd argue, but I know better."

"Are Mitch and Charlie working today too?" I asked hopefully.

"As far as I know." Amy yawned. "So I just got out of bed, but I'm guessing you've been up for a few hours by now. Are you about to head into work?"

"How did you guess?"

Amy chuckled. "Oh, I don't know. Just this hunch I had, since you've beaten everybody into the Compound for the last year."

I smiled. "I'll see you in the lab?"

"Yeah, see you in a few hours."

GETTING TO MY car was easy at six in the morning. Apparently, the reporters were still asleep. It helped that it was dark out. Since it was the beginning of January, the long nights allowed me to scurry undetected to my vehicle.

Ten minutes later, I was merging onto the interstate and mulling over how we could develop a cure. There had been progress with other viruses. It was possible we could do something similar. Hepatitis C anti-viral drugs had been developed years ago. Those drugs targeted the proteins that helped the virus grow and spread. Or we could pursue a protease-inhibiting drug, similar to the ones used to control HIV. It was possible a similar strategy would work for *Makanza*. However, those types of anti-viral drugs were notoriously unreliable.

The Compound's exit sign flashed by the window and stopped my brainstorming. The clock on the dash read 6:24 a.m. Bethany was due to arrive at the gates just after eight which gave me plenty of time to get settled in before she arrived.

Compound 26 grew steadily larger as I drove along the access road. It looked like a dark mound on the horizon. The sun still hadn't risen, but the full moon illuminated the grounds. Vast rolling prairie spread out from the giant structure for miles.

A solid walled perimeter, that appeared black at night, stretched around the massive enclosure. The wall was at least twenty feet high, maybe taller. Over a year ago, when I'd first started working for the Compound, that wall had been incredibly intimidating. Now, I didn't look at it twice.

My brakes squeaked when I reached the main gates. Only a few other cars were being admitted.

Twenty minutes later, my car was parked, and I was walking slowly toward north door 64. Winter wind bit into my cheeks, like a thousand frozen needles. I'd left my sling at home. Consequently, my arm dangled freely, but it was better than all of the attention the sling would garner.

As usual, Private Williams was on duty when I finally reached my wing. The young guard's husky frame and thick muscled arms were swallowed in a parka. The bulky coat made him look even bigger than usual while he held his assault rifle.

In a way, it was strange to be entering Compound 26 again. The last time I'd walked through my admittance door was before the Kazzies were freed. Before I'd driven to Reservation 1 with plans to welcome my friends to freedom. Before I'd been shot.

Before I'd left Davin behind.

My breath stopped.

Pulling out my bottle of pain meds, I dry swallowed two pills as I gingerly stepped in to the quiet reception area. It was so early not even, Carol, our wing's secretary was here.

Several times while walking down the vast hallways toward my office, I had to stop when moving hurt too much. It didn't help that I carried my purse and laptop. I hated to think that my mother was right. That I was pushing myself too hard and that I shouldn't be here.

I'll be fine. The pain meds just need to kick in more and then I can get back to work.

But by the time I reached my office and peeked under my shirt again, fresh blood seeped through my bandage. I closed my office door behind me before sitting down on my desk chair. With a grimace, I gently pulled the tape back and inspected the bullet wound.

The tissue was healing, and I didn't see any signs of infection. However, I must have done something too strenuous this morning. The fragile skin had torn. Fresh blood oozed from one corner.

My mother would be irate if she saw this.

Frowning, I counted the additional bandages I'd packed in my purse. Three. Only three. *I should have brought more.* Carefully pulling one out, I applied it after throwing the soiled one away.

Biting my lip, I debated my options. If my wound kept bleeding like this, I'd most likely have to find Dr. Fisher and have him dress it more securely. My brow furrowed at that thought. Thinking of the Compound's lead physician only reminded me of what happened last summer.

Something I still often thought about.

Before I'd been exposed to *Makanza*, Davin had gone into a catatonic state. On that fateful day, he'd been unresponsive for four hours. It was only when I'd ventured into his cell, removed my biohazard suit, and touched his skin, that he'd snapped out of it.

Following that, he'd been put through a plethora of tests. Dr. Fisher had worked with him extensively to try and uncover what had caused that strange medical phenomenon.

To this day, I didn't know. I knew Davin and Dr. Fisher had discovered something since Davin had visited regularly with the Compound's lead physician following that episode. However, Davin would never tell me what they talked about. He'd always been cagey and secretive whenever I'd brought it up.

And now, I may never know.

I checked my phone, almost hopeful that I'd see another message from him. I knew it was silly. Davin had made multiple attempts to contact me since I'd left Reservation 1's hospital. It was me stopping us from talking, so I didn't know why I was checking to see if he'd called.

Old habits die hard, I suppose.

As memories of Davin's betrayal, that strange catatonic state he'd been in last summer, and everything else that had transpired between us during the past few months turned over in my mind, pain once again welled up inside me.

Pain that had nothing to do with my injury.

"Better get to work, Meghan," I whispered. I placed my purse in my desk drawer before turning on my laptop.

My computer had just fired to life when a knock sounded on my door. Startled, I glanced up just as a muffled voice said, "Megs? Is that you in there?"

The deep voice and nickname my co-worker had given me could only come from one person.

"Yeah, Mitch, it's me. Come on in."

Mitch opened my office door and strolled inside. He hadn't changed in the weeks since I'd seen him. At six-four, he towered over most people. His large, intimidating build had made me nervous the first time we'd met, but Mitch was a good guy. Even though he dabbled in the black market, and didn't seem to mind engaging in illegal activities, he wouldn't hurt anybody.

I smiled. "Good morning."

Sitting down on the chair opposite from me, he clasped his hands in his lap. Cornflower blue eyes met mine as shaggy blond hair fell across his forehead. "Morning to you too. How's your injury? I couldn't believe it when Amy told me you were coming into work today."

My hand automatically went to my wound. The bandage felt puffy under my shirt. "I'm fine."

His brow furrowed, and I could tell he was about to say something else regarding my injury, so I quickly changed the subject. "You've shaved."

Mitch rubbed his smooth cheeks. "Yeah, don't remind me. I don't know why I thought it was a good idea to shave in the middle of winter. I obviously didn't think that one through." He winked.

I chuckled and then gazed at his t-shirt. As usual, he wore a typical, comedic tee. *Dear algebra, stop asking me to find your X. She's not coming back.*

"Are you still buying your t-shirts on the black market?"

He leaned back and cradled his head in his clasped hands. "Nope, this one was completely legal. I bought it on a trip to Colorado."

"Colorado? When did you go there?"

"Over the weekend. I've become a weekend warrior."

I settled back on my chair. Thankfully, the pain in my wound was diminishing. I figured the pain meds were starting to kick in. "What did you do there?"

He shrugged. "The usual. Stayed in a cheap motel and took in the surroundings. They have some great restaurants in Boulder. You should check it out sometime."

"You're right, I should."

A curious gleam grew in Mitch's eyes. "So I hear a Kazzie showed up on your doorstep the other day. And she's coming in this morning?"

I rolled my eyes. "I'm assuming Amy told you that?"

"Of course, she knows more about what's happening in the MRI than anybody. So it's true?"

"Yes. Bethany, the Kazzie from Minnesota with strain 15, came to my parents' house the other day. She begged me to help her. She's hoping we can find a cure."

The gleam in Mitch's eyes grew. "So the rumors *are* true. I figured this would happen sooner or later, especially now that they're free."

"Were you in Colorado when that Kazzie was harassed?"

Mitch nodded. "Yeah, but it happened in Denver so I didn't see anything." He sneered. "The damn public is still afraid they're gonna die from *Makanza*. But it's only a matter of time, and they'll see that there's nothing to fear. Things should be all right then."

"I think Bethany's concern isn't the public, but more that she doesn't want to live with her Changes." Given that her bat-like wings were impossible to hide, I understood her desperation.

Mitch raised his eyebrows. "And if we can't find a cure? Then what?"

"I suppose there's always plastic surgery. My plan was to have Dr. Fisher examine her this morning to see if surgical intervention could help her appear normal. Of course, a cure would be ideal, but I also know we may never develop one or it could be years before we do."

"We managed to develop a vaccine in months, why not a cure?"

I smiled. "You're right. Why not in a few months?"

Mitch and I fell into conversation about how we could do that. It was only as we stood to grab a cup of coffee that my office phone rang.

Carol's voice breezed through the connection when I picked up. "Dr. Forester, there's a woman here to see you. I believe you're expecting her?"

My eyes darted to the clock. It was only 7:30. Bethany was early. "Yes, I'll be right down." With a shaky hand, I hung up and met Mitch's gaze. "She's here."

3 – BETHANY

I entered the lobby alone. Given how shy Bethany was around strangers, I'd asked Mitch to wait in the lab.

Carol smiled politely from behind the reception desk when I passed her on my way to our visitors. As usual, Carol's hair was pulled back neatly. Pearl earrings adorned her ears. Everything about her screamed order and efficiency.

My feet tapped on the floor as I approached Bethany. The Kazzie was trembling. As before, a cloak draped over her shoulders, hiding her bat-like wings. From her fearful eyes and folded posture, I felt certain that being within a Compound brought back painful memories.

A woman stood beside her who I assumed was her friend from Minneapolis. She appeared heavily pregnant and clutched Bethany's hand tightly as she gazed around, her eyes wide with awe.

I wondered if she knew that she was the first civilian to be admitted within these walls in ten years.

"Bethany." I called the Kazzie's name as I approached. My pace was fast. Too fast. Pain once again fired through my chest and arm. Forcing myself to keep walking normally, I bit my lip tightly so I wouldn't wince when I reached her side.

"Meghan! I mean, Dr. Forester." Bethany eyed me sheepishly.

"Please, call me Meghan. Did the admittance procedure go okay?" I had to look up at Bethany. She was tall. At least five-ten. Her friend was around my height, though. Five-six.

Bethany nodded tightly. "Yeah. It was fine."

Her wide, doe-like eyes were a dark chocolate brown. It was similar to the shade of her skin. Bethany still gripped her pregnant friend's hand and then nodded in her direction. "This is my sister, Makayla."

So not a friend, but a sister.

"Nice to meet you." I held out my right hand tentatively and had to bite back a grimace when Makayla's strong grip pumped my arm.

"I've heard a lot about you, Dr. Forester," Makayla replied when she let go. Corkscrew curls sprang from Makayla's head in a stylish afro. That coupled with full lips bathed in a deep-red lipstick made her very pretty. "Thank you for helping my sister. She said you're going to find a cure." She rested her hand on top of her protruding belly. Unlike Bethany, Makayla wore a normal winter coat since she was Makanza-free. But her jacket remained open to give her ample stomach room.

"Well, we're certainly going to try."

The guards stationed near the entrance eyed us. It was probably the most interesting interaction they'd seen in years.

"Will you both follow me?" I nodded toward the back hallways.

I led the two women through the maze of corridors into the Compound while explaining what our plans were for the morning. "The first thing we're going to do is obtain fresh samples from you, Bethany. I hope that's all right."

Our shoes tapped along the concrete as we traveled past the blinding white walls.

Bethany nodded, but her mouth tightened.

"We can extract those samples in the lab. There's no need to venture to the Experimental Room," I explained.

Bethany let out a shaky breath and smiled. "Oh, good. Then yeah, that's fine."

Makayla merely raised an eyebrow at her sister. I guessed that Bethany had yet to divulge the more painful experiences she'd been subjected to during the past ten years.

We turned down the next hall. Since it was so wide, all three of us walked alongside one another. Thankfully, neither commented on the slow pace I'd set. I could only hope they thought I walked slowly to accommodate Makayla's waddling.

"After we have fresh samples, I'd like to have our lead physician examine you." I brought my right arm closer to my side so it would stop jostling. "While the MRI endeavors to discover a cure, I think it's prudent that we also consider alternatives. It's possible your wings may be removed surgically. He'll let us know if that's an option."

Bethany balked. "You mean... *cut* them off?"

When we reached our first access door, I scanned my badge and placed my palm against the handprint scanner. After it flashed green, I pulled the door open. Pain again seared through my chest.

I stifled a groan. "Yes, that's what I mean. It's one alternative if a cure isn't possible. It's also something we can consider if developing a cure takes years."

Bethany wrung her hands together as we stepped through the door and approached the lab. "Um... okay. I guess that would work, but I was really hoping for a cure. You know, so I could be normal again."

I stopped outside the lab. Through the long stretch of windows that ran the length of the hallway, I spotted Mitch. He was pipetting a solution at his bench. Amy and Charlie were also at their lab stations. Amy's red hair was like a bright flag drawing attention.

"We'll try really hard to find a cure, but we also need to be realistic. It's possible we'll never find one."

Bethany's face fell.

Makayla put a hand on her shoulder. "It's okay, sis. You can still have surgery."

Bethany nodded mutely just as my cell phone buzzed. Reaching into my back pocket with my good arm, I pulled it out.

A text message from Davin appeared. My breath stopped.

It was only two words.

Meghan. Please.

My throat tightened at his quiet plea. For a moment, all I could do was stare at those words. My lips trembled as the last word leaped out at me. *Please.*

Shoving it back into my pocket, I took an unsteady breath and blinked rapidly. Once again, tears threatened to overwhelm me. *I can't think about him right now. I need to help Bethany.*

Swallowing down the rising emotional tide of betrayal, unrequited love, and that niggling doubt, I opened the lab door.

With a forced smile, I said, "Follow me."

THE MORNING AND afternoon passed in a blur. Bethany complied with all of the tests and procedures that we asked of her. It was only when she removed her cloak during Dr. Fisher's examination that I saw the extent of the Changes *Makanza* had made in her.

Long, thin skin hung from her arms. When she spread her arms wide, that skin stretched taut. She demonstrated how she flew. Leaping gracefully from the metal railing platform above our lab station, she soared around the expansive room. At times, she flapped her arms, causing her to stay aloft.

With the labs twenty-foot high walls, she didn't have much room to show off her skills, but it still made my mouth drop.

A few times, I screeched in concern when I thought she would collide with a wall, but each time she turned effortlessly and continued to fly. Luckily, she appeared fully healed from the wound she'd suffered within Reservation 1—when she'd been shot from the sky.

"Pretty wicked." Charlie shook his head as the six of us stood in the corner. He crossed his thin arms over his chest. With jet black hair, slanted eyes, and a small Asian build, Charlie wasn't much bigger than me. "Flying must come in handy sometimes."

Mitch chuckled. "Are you jealous you're not batman?"

Charlie opened his mouth to respond, but I elbowed him before he could. Makayla watched them from the corner of her eye, and from the discontented frown on her face, my guess was that she didn't enjoy their joking.

Clasping her hands in front of her protruding belly, Makayla turned her attention back to her sister.

Bethany cupped her wings and glided to the floor. She had to hop a few times before she came to a complete stop. From there, she ran to her cloak and quickly donned it. It took a few adjustments before all of her loose skin was tucked under the long material. From there, she hurried to her sister's side.

Makayla put an arm around her and squeezed.

"That was amazing." I stepped closer to Bethany.

Keeping her gaze on the floor, Bethany shrugged. "Sometimes I enjoy it, but it's not worth…" She lifted an arm and her skin peeked out. "This."

Nodding, I smiled sadly. Being different was never easy. "I understand."

Dr. Fisher finished typing something on his tablet before he approached. Pushing his glasses up his nose, he said, "Why don't you all get some lunch and then come to my office. I'm hoping to have the results of your tests by then."

Bethany nodded but kept her eyes downcast.

Flanking Makayla's side, Amy jerked her chin toward the door. "Come on. I'll lead the way."

IT WAS MID-AFTERNOON when we stepped out of the cafeteria. Other MRI employees passed us in the hallway on their way into and out of the cafeteria. I stepped closer to the wall so none of them would brush against me.

The large vent above us hummed. A slight draft ruffled the hair around my shoulders. Peeking under my shirt, I breathed a sigh of relief that my wound wasn't bleeding through again. I'd already changed the bandage twice.

Amy was frowning when I looked back up. "See you back at the lab when you're done?" she asked.

Her gaze was knowing as she watched me. I knew she hadn't missed when I'd slipped away twice during the morning to change my bandage. I also knew she'd seen me discreetly swallow more pain pills during lunch.

I tucked a strand of long, brown hair behind my ear. Her gaze reminded me of the look my mother had given me the other day. "Yeah, see you then."

Mitch and Charlie waved goodbye. As I turned to leave with Bethany and Makayla, Amy grabbed my hand.

"Meghan? Are you sure you should be here?" Amy's voice was low, but I still caught Bethany's frown when she overheard my co-worker.

I carefully pulled my hand away and gave Amy a pointed look. "Yes, I'm *sure* I should be here."

Amy sighed heavily, her brow furrowing. I could tell she wanted to say more, but when I nodded toward Bethany and her sister, Amy straightened.

"Okay, see you back at the lab. We have a lot to *discuss.*" Her eyes glittered.

I sighed and rolled my eyes. Thankfully, my back was to our guests so they couldn't see.

When Amy finally strode after Mitch and Charlie, Bethany's frown grew.

Smiling brightly, I made myself walk at a normal pace even though my wound throbbed. I guessed Bethany would willingly slow her pace to accommodate my injury, but I didn't want her focus shifted to me. She had enough to deal with already so I internally gritted my teeth. "This way."

Ten minutes later, tears threatened to fill my eyes at how bad the pain was. Thankfully, Dr. Fisher's office was within view. It had been a hike to his office since it was in a completely separate wing. *We should have taken the rail system.*

Dr. Fisher's secretary nodded to his door when we approached. "He's expecting you. Please go in."

Inside, Dr. Fisher sat at his desk and waved us forward. Compound 26's lead physician was not the picture of health. He had to be in his fifties, with balding hair and a paunch belly, but his wealth of knowledge about diseases and conditions surpassed that of any medical student graduating these days.

His office was similar to those in upper administration. There was a large desk, chairs in front of it for patients or visitors, a lounging couch along one wall, several full bookshelves, and a small bar in the corner. But best of all was the large window on the far wall. Outside, snowy prairie stretched across the land. From the third floor, it was a pretty view.

I glanced at the couch. It was perfect for someone to sit on while having a long chat with the physician.

Is that where Davin used to sit?

I pushed that thought away.

"Please, have a seat." The doctor waved at the chairs in front of his desk.

The three of us settled onto them. A sigh of relief escaped me. I hated to admit it, but it felt so good to rest.

"Now, I'm sure you're anxious to hear your results." Dr. Fisher leaned forward, his brow furrowing. "But I'm afraid the results aren't good."

Bethany frowned. "Oh?"

Dr. Fisher took off his glasses. Sunlight streamed in through the large window, setting his desktop aglow. "The scans show that various large arteries supply blood to your wings. Of course, we already knew that from what we know of strain 15, however, in your case, the arteries are even larger than normal. Given their size, I'm very hesitant to surgically remove your wings. There's a strong possibility you'd hemorrhage on the operating table."

My shoulders fell.

"Hemorrhage?" Makayla's eyebrows drew together.

"Bleed to death." Dr. Fisher clarified.

"Really? Surgery's not an option at all?" Bethany's voice rose.

Dr. Fisher nodded sadly. "That's correct. It's not an option."

"But surely there must be a way. Can't you just, I don't know, pinch off the vessels so I don't bleed?"

Dr. Fisher shook his head. "I'm afraid it's not that simple. It would be a very risky surgery."

Makayla covered her sister's hand and said, "But surely you could do it. You're the best, aren't you, if you work here?"

The physician sighed heavily. "I'm sorry. I know it's not the news you wanted to hear, but surgery is not an option. There would be a high chance you wouldn't survive it. I won't take that risk."

At least ten seconds of silence followed.

Bethany's lips quivered. "I see." She folded her hands in her lap and looked down. "So the only way for me to ever be normal is a cure."

"At this point, yes," Dr. Fisher replied. "But there's always the possibility that a surgeon who's skilled enough could remove the excess skin under your arms, but given how few skilled surgeons exist today—it's not likely."

Tears filled Bethany's eyes. I placed my hand over hers.

Dr. Fisher's voice softened. "I'm sorry to deliver this news to you, but it's important that you know the truth—as hard as that is."

Bethany nodded. Large tears fell onto her cheeks.

"Can you give us a minute?" Makayla asked. She inched closer to her sister and put her arm around her.

Dr. Fisher and I stood from our chairs and retreated to the hall. Bethany's quiet sobs faded behind us but ignited my desire to try harder. However, I quickly learned that Dr. Fisher's attention had not only been on Bethany.

Once in the privacy of the hallway, the physician crossed

his arms. "Dr. Forester, you don't look well. I question if you're healthy enough to be here." He leaned closer, assessing me with a clinical gaze. "The entire country knows you were shot last week."

I stiffened as his probing eyes wandered over my frame. I knew everyone had good intentions, and their worry came from genuine concern, but I still hated all of the attention my wound had garnered today. Despite pain rolling through me in steady, throbbing waves, I managed a tight smile.

"I'm fine. It's Bethany we need to concentrate on. Is there really nothing you can do for her?"

The physician shook his head. With a sad smile, his next words hit home. "I'm sorry, Dr. Forester, but I'm afraid finding a solution is going to fall upon the MRI's shoulders."

THE REST OF the day I barely kept it together. My wound ached so deeply it felt like my bones were being squeezed. And Bethany and Makayla's tears only added to the pressure that weighed down on me like a heavy, sinking anchor.

I knew finding a cure wasn't entirely up to me. The MRI employed thousands of scientists. Working together, we'd developed the vaccine. And together we could find a cure.

Still...

For so many months the Kazzies had turned to *me* for help. I'd become the beacon of light to so many of them, promising a brighter future full of hope. So when Bethany gripped my hands and pleaded with me to find a cure before she and her sister departed for the day—it felt like if we didn't, *I'd* have failed her. Not my co-workers. Not the Makanza Research Institute.

Me.

Amy seemed to sense how heavy my heart was when I returned to the lab. She didn't press me to discuss anything. Nor did she question when I packed my things to leave. It was only four in the afternoon, yet I couldn't work anymore. Between my throbbing injury and Bethany's solemn eyes—for the first time in my entire career—I just couldn't.

"Rest tomorrow." Amy's quiet words filled my ears as she sidled next to me at our lab station. "I mean it, Meghan. Don't come to work. You're so pale you make chalk look colorful."

I managed a humorless smile at her joke. "We'll see. I may feel better tomorrow."

Amy eyed my shirt and frowned.

I followed her gaze. A fresh spot of blood stained my blouse. It had obviously seeped through my wound since I hadn't changed my bandage since lunch.

"Stay home, Meghan. I mean it. If Dr. Sadowsky saw that, he'd ban you from work." She squeezed my good hand and gave me a reassuring smile before I left.

BACK AT MY apartment building, I again had to fight through a swarm of reporters to reach the main door. By the time I was inside my tiny home, all I wanted was to sink to the floor, close my eyes, and make the world disappear.

Forcing myself into the bathroom, I carefully lifted my shirt before peeling off the saturated bandage.

The ugly, red wound on my chest stared back at me. In the mirror, it looked like a battle wound. As if I'd gone to war and fought in actual combat.

Scrunching my nose up, I washed and redressed it before pulling on a loose sweatshirt and sweatpants. I knew my wound was bleeding too much. I also knew why.

I was overdoing it. Just like my mother feared.

Back in the living room, I gingerly lay down on the couch and closed my eyes, but a sharp knock from my front door had them flashing open.

I tensed.

Images of reporters hovering in the hallway filled my mind. Pushing to a stand, I tiptoed to the door and listened.

Nothing.

If it was reporters, they were breaking the law by coming directly to my door. Looking through the peephole, I cursed that it was too foggy to see who it was. I hadn't cleaned the old lens recently, but from the distorted image it appeared to be a lone person.

Surely, it's not a reporter. They know better.

Pushing aside my worry, I grasped the door handle and pulled it open. The sight that greeted me had my eyes widening and heart pounding.

Bright-blue eyes that glittered like sapphires stared back at me. Midnight hair that curled at the ends looked as if the occupant had run his hands through it for days on end.

My heart caught in my throat as Davin's tall form filled my apartment's doorway. His uniquely alluring scent of soap and aftershave wafted toward me. My head spun.

"Davin," I whispered.

His hands balled tightly as a muscle ticked in his jaw. "Meghan, we need to talk."

4 – UNEXPECTED VISIT

"I…" The words wouldn't come out. Davin stood before me. In my apartment building. Free from Compound 26 and Reservation 1. In the real world.

How long have I dreamed of this moment? To have him here and free? Pain welled up inside me like a geyser that threatened to blow. *But that was before Jenna. When everything was still okay.*

His chest rose and fell quickly. That beautiful, magnificent, chiseled chest that I'd spent so many nights dreaming about was only covered with a thin t-shirt. No jacket. No sweater. He wore just a t-shirt, jeans, and boots.

"Meghan, I'm coming in whether you invite me or not. So you can either step aside, or I will pick you up and carry you in with me."

I opened my mouth and then closed it. Words still stayed trapped in my throat.

The emotions fluttering around inside of me warred for attention. While one side was thrilled to see him, screaming internally like an overexcited teenager, the other side wanted to slam the door on his face as images of Jenna's letters flipped through my mind, like a slideshow that wouldn't stop.

My hand tightened on the door handle.

"Meghan..." His voice grew deeper.

Before I could decide which option to choose, Davin morphed into a blur. A rustle of air caused hair to flow across my cheeks before he reappeared in my entryway, standing right beside me.

I stiffened. His scent fluttered to me again—that achingly familiar scent of aftershave, soap, and something that was all Davin.

Reaching down, he gently pried the door handle from my grasp and closed my apartment door. The sound of the bolt sliding into place came next.

"What... How?" The words finally came out as I gazed up at him.

His eyes softened. "I would have come sooner if it hadn't been for that damn snowstorm outside Rapid City. The interstate was covered with ice for two days straight. There was no getting through."

A storm?

It felt like eternity passed and passed again as we stood there.

When he seemed sure that I wouldn't start screaming and telling him to leave, his balled fists loosened. Putting his hands on his hips, his rounded shoulders stretched against his thin t-shirt as he gazed around.

"So this is where you live. I've always wondered what it looked like." He stepped away to study a photo hanging on my fridge. It was of me and Jeremy when we were kids. We'd gone on a weekend camping trip for school. Someone had snapped the shot as we sat around a campfire roasting marshmallows. Even then, even in school, we'd been inseparable.

"Jeremy?" he asked quietly.

I nodded. It was all I could manage as tears filled my eyes. It was all too much. My throbbing wound. The emotional day with Bethany. Davin showing up unannounced. Memories of Jeremy now filling my mind.

In another blurred move, Davin was at my side again. He placed a finger under my chin, his brow furrowing.

My breath sucked in as nerves alighted in my traitorous body.

"We need to talk. I wish it could wait until a better time if now isn't, but…" He dropped his finger and growled quietly. "I can't give you that. Not now. I need answers. I need to know what the hell is going on."

Aghast, a tear streaked down my cheek. "Shouldn't I be the one asking *you* what's going on? Your ex-girlfriend showed up at the hospital, probably for the date you'd set up."

His mouth dropped. "What the hell are you talking about?"

More tears filled my eyes as the letters spiraled through my mind. Davin still had no idea that I'd seen them. My hands trembled as I finally admitted what I'd done. "I saw them." My voice shook with emotion. "I *saw* the letters she wrote you! That morning when I woke up in your bed on the reservation, while you slept on the couch, I found Jenna's letters that you were hiding. I know you planned to meet her."

His head snapped back, his face going pale.

Another tear rolled down my cheek. "So that's what's going on. That's why I cut you out of my life. If you want her, fine, but don't expect me to watch."

I squeezed my eyes tightly shut. I couldn't look at his stricken expression anymore. It felt like eons passed.

"Jesus." He finally breathed.

I opened my eyes to see him raking a hand through his hair. He did it over and over until his hand turned into a blur. Then, he began pacing.

"I've been trying to figure out what I did." He paced back and forth so quickly that I could barely follow his movements. "I knew Jenna showing up like that upset you, that was pretty obvious, but I didn't know you saw the letters too. So that's why…" He stopped and shook his head. "Fuck me. I wish I knew you'd seen those."

I swallowed tightly. It was taking everything in me to not begin sobbing.

"So you think I'm with her?" he said quietly.

I nodded. "That guilt on your face when she showed up…" I bit my lip painfully. "And how you agreed to meet her in the letters…" I swallowed the thick lump in my throat. "It didn't take a genius to figure it out."

"But you have it all wrong!" His voice rose. "It wasn't a date. She wanted to casually meet, and I agreed to it."

Despite his protest, the tears increased. "Is that why she drove all the way to South Dakota, to the *reservation*, from where… Texas, wasn't it? Just for a casual meeting? That doesn't seem very casual to me."

"I didn't know she was going to do that."

I made a move to cross my arms which got a hiss of pain out of me.

Davin straightened, his gaze darkening. "You're hurting."

I tried to shrug it off but knew there was no point. He could always see through me as if he saw inside me.

"Have you been taking your pain meds and resting like you're supposed to?"

"I've taken my pain meds around the clock."

He stepped closer until our toes brushed. "And the resting

part? Have you been doing that too?"

"I…" I looked away. "Kind of. I spent four days at my parents' house."

"But you haven't been resting today, obviously, since you're here." His tone grew deeper.

I met his gaze again. "Speaking of which, how did you know where I lived?"

"My mom."

Of course. "But how did you know I'd be here and not in Vermillion?"

"Sara."

Double of course. The twin had been strangely quiet all day. Perhaps she was feeling guilty for going behind my back to apparently conspire with Davin.

"So… have you been resting?" A dark lock of hair fell across his forehead. He made no move to brush it back.

"No, not today. I worked today."

"Dammit, Meghan." The words were quiet and soft. Frustration lined them. "Are you *ever* going to take care of yourself?"

"I'm home, aren't I? And it's not even five o'clock." My voice rose with each word. "Besides, Bethany needed me."

His head snapped back. "The Kazzie from Minnesota?"

"Yeah." I brushed away the tears on my cheeks that had settled like raindrops on a leaf. "She showed up at my parent's house the other day, but all of that is beside the point. I believe we were talking about your relationship with Jenna."

He rolled his eyes. "There is no relationship with Jenna, which you would already know if you'd talked to me. Or called me back. Or read any of my damned text messages, which I'm guessing you never did since you think I'm with her." He grumbled again before kicking his shoes off and placing his hands on his hips. "Have you eaten today? Drank enough?"

I shuffled uncertainly. *There isn't a relationship?* "Yes and yes."

"In that case, we're moving into the living room so you can sit down. You look as pale as a ghost."

Probably from all the blood I've lost. I kept that sarcastic comment to myself.

Hovering at my side, Davin took my good arm and steadied me. It was silly. Fifteen feet was all that stood between me and the couch, yet Davin acted like it was a twenty-mile hike. It didn't help that my body betrayed me. The feel of his warm, large hands closing gently around my arm made me want to lean into him.

It also didn't help that I now seriously doubted my reaction when Jenna showed up at the reservation's hospital. *Yet she visited him at least twice over the weekend. Why would she do that if there's no relationship?*

I stiffened and pulled my arm away.

Davin's nostrils flared, but he didn't reach for me again.

Once on the couch, I settled back as best I could. When Davin made a move to sit beside me, I placed my hand over the cushion to block him. "How about you sit on the chair?"

Muttering under his breath, he stalked to the lone chair. But he didn't sit. Instead, in another blurred move, he hauled the chair closer to me before plopping down.

"Happy?" Frustration again filled his words.

"Hardly." I folded my hands in my lap since I couldn't cross my arms. "I'm not sure how to feel right now."

He sighed heavily before gazing at the ceiling. If I didn't know better, I'd say he was softly counting to ten.

I froze when our gazes connected again.

Those electric blue irises would be the death of me. When

he looked at me as he was right now, I wanted to forget all about Jenna, the letters, and him agreeing to meet her.

"What can I say that will reassure you that I never wanted Jenna?" His tone while frustrated was soft. "I've only wanted you since we met."

I frowned. "Then why was she at your house over the weekend?"

His head cocked. "How did you know about that?"

"Sara."

He grumbled under his breath. "Did she tell you anything other than Jenna stopped by?"

"No."

"That's probably because she doesn't actually know anything about me and Jenna. She should mind her own damned business."

I tucked a strand of hair behind my ear. "She *did* try to tell me that I had it wrong. She told me she didn't think you wanted Jenna."

He rested his elbows on his knees. "Yet you didn't believe her." His voice sounded hurt.

An image of the letters, once again, filled my mind.

"I can't wait for us to meet again. And I agree, meeting in Rapid would definitely be nostalgic. If you're ever free, that's where we should meet."

Those words had haunted me for weeks. Scrunching my eyebrows together, I asked, "Why would you agree to meet with her, when you knew she wanted you, if you didn't have feelings for her?"

A muscle ticked in his jaw. "Because I was angry. Really angry. When I wrote those letters to her, I thought you had moved on and were with Mitch. Every day, I had visions of you with him. You in his bed. Him touching you. His hands everywhere." His nostrils flared. "It drove me crazy."

Taking a deep breath, his gaze dropped to the floor. "I know it was stupid, to try and forget about you by talking to Jenna, but at the time, I honestly never thought I'd be free from Reservation 1. I thought she and I would be old-fashioned pen pals and nothing would ever come of it. And writing letters back and forth with her helped keep me from thinking of you with Mitch."

I arched an eyebrow. "That seems rather immature."

He snorted. "Tell me about it. My mom's pretty upset with me. I thought my homecoming was going to be filled with fun and some relaxation. Instead, she's been pestering me for the past five days about you and what the heck Jenna's doing back in my life."

My mouth dropped. "Sharon? *Pestering?*"

He smiled wryly. "I know. It's not a trait I've seen in her before either, but she's pretty unhappy. She saw how upset you were when you left the hospital."

I took a deep breath. The entire past week had been full of ups and downs. It was hard to believe a week ago I'd still been in the hospital, getting ready to be discharged.

"So…" I said tentatively. "What's going on with you and Jenna right now?"

"Nothing. I swear. She stopped by a few times to try and convince me to give us another chance, but each time, I told her that I couldn't."

So those were the two visits that Sara was talking about. "And where is she now?"

He shrugged. "I don't know, but I imagine she's either visiting her old friends in Rapid, the ones that made it through the First and Second Wave, or she's on her way back to Texas."

Despite feeling a sense of relief at hearing that Davin *wasn't* with Jenna, I couldn't help a flare of irritation. "So you wrote letters back and forth with her for weeks, gave her the impression you were interested in her, and then when she drove across the country to surprise you—you sent her on her way? That's hardly a nice way to treat someone."

He hung his head while flicking his fingers back and forth. The movement turned into a blur. "I know. Trust me—I'm not proud of myself. I've already told her a hundred times how sorry I am."

My brow furrowed. "But how did she know you'd be at the hospital if you'd never arranged to meet?"

I tensed, waiting for his response. While I wanted to believe him, that guarded feeling remained. It had been uncanny how she'd shown up just as I was discharging.

"The guards told her."

My eyebrows rose. "You mean… Reservation 1's guards?"

He nodded. "She said she drove to our home in Rapid first, thinking we'd be there, but when the neighbors told her we'd never arrived back from the reservation, she took a chance and drove to Mobridge. When she reached the gates, the guards told her about you and that I'd been at your side in the hospital."

I sank further back into the couch cushions. "So that's how she ended up there."

"Yeah, that's how." His brow furrowed. "Did you really think I'd agreed to meet her at the same time you were being discharged with a gunshot wound? A shot that should have hit me?"

The hurt in his words needled my heart. I shrugged helplessly. "I honestly didn't know what to think. But when I saw that guilty look on your face after she arrived—I assumed the worst."

In another blurred move, he was off the chair and kneeling in front of me. My breath hitched. He'd move so fast!

Taking both of my hands in his, his cobalt gaze swam with so much emotion, I thought I'd drown in it.

Squeezing my hands tighter, his words came out in a low whisper. "I love you, Meghan. I have for the past year, ever since you brought me that photo from my Mom. And the thought of what I'd done—talking to Jenna, giving her the impression I'd be with her, after you'd risked everything to save me—it felt like a punch to my gut. In that moment, it finally hit me how much that would hurt you. *That's* why I felt guilty. *That's* the reason I had whatever look you saw on my face. It wasn't guilt because I wanted her and didn't tell you." He squeezed my hands more. "It was guilt because I felt like I betrayed you. And that's something I never want to do."

My mouth parted as more tears filled my eyes. His hands felt so warm and solid around mine.

He loves me? Did he really just say that he loves me?

In the few times we'd hinted at our feelings for each other, neither of us had ever been so open or honest about how we felt. It had always been like each of us was too afraid to take that final step. Some barrier that seemed impossible to cross had always kept us from one another.

But now, those barriers were gone.

And Davin had just said he loved me.

A smile pulled my lips up. "I love you too."

He grinned in return. "So you forgive me? For acting like an immature idiot with Jenna? I swear to you, Meghan, *nothing* happened with her. Just like nothing ever happened with you and Mitch."

His reminder about Mitch solidified that it wasn't fair for

me to hold this against him. When Davin and I had spoken for the first time, after I'd finally re-established my link with Sara while they'd been captive on Reservation 1, he'd listened to why I'd lied about saying I was dating Mitch. I'd done it to protect him. But it had been a lie. A betrayal in a way.

Yet he'd readily forgiven me.

And right now, he was trying to help me see that he'd never betrayed me either. But more than that, he was asking me to forgive him too.

I squeezed his hands back, my fingertips relishing his hard callouses. "You're right. We've both made mistakes." So many tears filled my eyes, they threatened to spill onto my cheeks. "And, of course, I forgive you. I should have listened to you sooner. I shouldn't have jumped to conclusions."

"We can talk more about that later, but right now, I need you to say that you're with me. I need to know that you're my girlfriend and that I finally have you."

My heart pounded. "That sounds rather possessive."

He moved to sit beside me. "Is it a problem if I am? I want you to be mine."

My gaze fell to his lips. His perfectly shaped lips looked so warm and inviting. "No. That's not a problem." My voice came out breathy and constricted. With every second, he was leaning closer. "As long as it's two ways. You're mine too."

The corner of his mouth tugged up. "I'm more than okay with that. So does that mean you're officially my girlfriend? And I'm officially your boyfriend?"

His mouth was only inches away now. My gaze kept drifting between his incredible bright blue eyes to his firm lips. "Yes. I'm yours and you're mine."

He growled in satisfaction. "Good."

And then he kissed me.

5 - NEWS SEGMENT

Minutes or hours passed. I didn't know. As Davin's lips moved over mine, I lost all sense of time.

In a blur, Davin hauled me into his lap. He did it so fast, only the slightest hitch of pain followed. Regardless, I didn't care. All I wanted was to feel him. To taste him.

His hard thighs felt like steel beneath me while his hands roamed over my body. Instinctively, he seemed to know what areas to avoid and what areas to attend. His large palm settled onto my back, behind my sore shoulder. Strong fingers gently kneaded the muscles while he continued to plunder my mouth with his tongue.

It was heaven and bliss wrapped into one.

I moaned against him. The feel of his fingers working the sore knots from my muscles felt wonderfully relaxing, while the taste of his mouth and heat from his body felt deliciously thrilling. I became a puddle in his arms.

He chuckled into my mouth and pulled back.

A soft protest escaped me.

He moved to my jaw and then my neck, trailing little kisses

down my jugular. I tilted my head to give him better access.

Another growl emitted from his throat.

Squirming against him, my eyes flashed open when the hard bulge in his pants became evident.

He paused only long enough to whisper, "When you're healed, I'll make you completely mine."

That promise sent another thrill down my spine, yet I didn't want to wait. Putting both hands on his shoulders, I pulled him closer. That was a mistake. White-hot pain shot down my arm at the abrupt movement.

"Ahh!"

Davin jerked back. "Meghan? Are you okay?" Concern filled his gaze as he looked me over. Understanding dawned. In another blurred move, he was across the room.

Miraculously, it didn't hurt. Somehow, he'd managed to extract me from his lap, while moving the fifteen feet across the room, all without jarring my injury or causing me additional pain. Strain 11's effects on him were mind-boggling. *Makanza* gave him the strength and grace that a normal human couldn't rival.

Yet, it wasn't that realization that had me gazing at him with wonder. Instead, it was all that had transpired between us in such a short amount of time.

Davin loved me.

He'd never been with Jenna and had never intended to.

I loved him.

We were officially, *finally*, together.

I giggled.

Davin stopped pacing and grinned. "Stop looking like that or I'm going to forget my noble intentions and pounce on you."

I lifted an arm to casually drape it across the couch-back

while crossing my legs. Only thing, that didn't go as intended. The second I lifted my bad arm, like a complete idiot, a hiss of pain shot out of me reminding me I had *zero* experience in the art of seduction. It was hard to believe I'd only kissed Davin a couple of times, the last time being on the night the Post Wave Rehabilitation Act was announced.

All smiles and joking left him. In a whizzed move, he was at my side again. His eyebrows drew darkly together. "Dammit, Meghan."

He moved me gently and tugged on the neck of my shirt to see my wound. "You're bleeding."

I made a face. "I've been bleeding all day."

"You have? Have you told your doctor?"

"No. It only bleeds if I move around a lot."

"You're doing too much. Come with me. I'll redress it."

Considering Davin had been at my side during the entire hospital stay, he'd also heard all of the instructions on how to care for my wound. Once in my bathroom, he lifted me onto the counter and told me to scoot back. My legs dangled over the edge as he tugged at my shirt.

"Take your shirt off."

My eyes bulged.

He chuckled. "I know. It's not exactly how I imagined undressing you for the first time either, but I need to see your wound and your shirt's in the way."

With scarlet cheeks, I began to lift it with my good arm.

He watched my every move, his pupils dilating. When my shirt was over my head, I struggled to get my arms out.

Reaching gently for the sleeve, he slipped it off.

When I sat before him in nothing but my sweatpants and bra, I had the most ridiculous urge to cover myself. The white bandage taped to my upper chest and the old bra I wore were hardly attractive. If I had known an hour ago that I would be in this position, I would have worn my new yoga pants and lacy red bra. I'd found them on special last year during one of the government's double quantity apparel releases. They were infinitely better than the old gray sweats and plain white bra I currently wore.

He tilted my chin toward him. "You're beautiful."

That admission stopped my fidgeting.

"Now, I just need to stop looking at you like your boyfriend and more like your doctor."

The way he said *boyfriend* made goosebumps rise along my arms.

With gentle fingers, he pried the tape off. A few times, his hands brushed the tops of my breasts. Each time, his breath stopped but then he resumed removing the bandage, that serious expression back in place.

When the bandage finally came free, his lips turned into a tight line.

I forgot how horrible the wound looked.

A perfect red circle with jagged edges made a hole in my chest. Since the bullet had hit bone in my upper ribcage, there wasn't an exit point. However, that also meant I'd had to undergo surgery immediately following the gunshot to repair my bone and remove shattered bullet fragments. That resulted in an incision sutured together—an incision that was currently oozing. I didn't remember any of it, though. The three days after I'd been shot were a blank void.

But while having a fractured bone meant a longer recovery for me, that was better than having the bullet hit my subclavian artery. If it had, I would have died.

I shuddered.

Davin's hands stilled. "Are you okay? Am I hurting you?"

"No, it's not that. It's…" I shook my head. "Nothing."

He set aside the bloody bandage. All of a sudden, the open hole in my chest made me nauseous. I began to tremble.

"Babe, what's wrong?" Davin gently held my shoulders.

I sniffed. Davin had just called me *babe* for the first time, and all I could think about was my wound. It was so stupid. Even though I'd been shot, I'd done really well at not thinking about it. The doctors and nurses at the hospital had said it was normal to have anxiety and nightmares when something traumatic like that happened, but I'd brushed all of that off.

I was no stranger to anxiety, and considering what the Kazzies had gone through, a gunshot wound was nothing. Yet, there had been times during the past few days, when out of the blue, an image of Dr. Roberts raising his gun would rise up in my mind. Like a tidal wave that came out of nowhere.

Each time, I'd pushed it back, burying it, denying it—yet now that I was here with Davin, it wouldn't subside. It was like my body knew I was safe with him. That with him I could let my walls down and feel the anxiety and fear that wanted to claw through me.

"Shh, it's okay." He pulled me to him, his warm chest pressing against my bare one. He was careful to not touch my injured shoulder.

I inhaled deeply. His scent was everywhere. Amazingly, it was like he knew what to do. He didn't ask further questions. He didn't try to force anything out of me.

He just held me.

Closing my eyes, I savored the feel of his arms. My head spun. Davin was in my apartment, in my bathroom, holding me while the fear slowly subsided. For months, I'd dreamed of this.

And now, it was coming true.

"I'm okay, really, I am. Thank you." I wiped the moisture from my eyes. It was crazy how easily emotions surfaced around him.

His gaze searched mine. Flecks of dark blue smattered throughout his electric-blue irises. Once again, I wanted to stare at how beautiful he was.

He traced a finger across my cheek. "Do you want to talk about it?"

I shook my head. "Not really. I'm just trying to forget it. I got shot, but I'm still alive, and you're free and safe so it turned out okay. I keep reminding myself of that."

His jaw clenched and unclenched. Warring emotions oscillated across his face. One moment it was pain, the next anger. They came and went like undulating waves in the ocean.

"It still haunts me too," he said quietly. "I have this vivid picture of you throwing yourself in front of me. It's frozen in my mind, as clear as day."

Stepping closer, he put his hands around my waist.

I parted my legs so he could step between them.

Resting his forehead against mine, his lips were only inches away, and his sweet minty breath puffed toward me. "Promise me you'll never jeopardize your safety for me again. That bullet was meant for me. Not you."

I laid a hand across his cheek. Rough stubble grazed my palm. "Promising that is like asking you to never protect me if someone tries to hurt me. It's pointless. You know I'd do it again, just like I know you'd defend me."

His grip tightened on my waist. "But you could have died."

I moved my palm to his chest. Hard muscles jumped beneath my touch. "Well... I have a sneaking suspicion it's not something we'll have to deal with often. After all, I doubt people will try to shoot me every day."

His lips tugged up.

I smiled as the mood around us began to lift.

Chuckling, he gently pushed a lock of hair behind my ear before pulling his head back. "Are you hungry?"

"A little."

His stomach growled.

My smile widened. "I take it, you are?"

He shrugged. "I didn't stop for lunch when I drove here. I'm sure you can understand why."

Hearing that made my smile disappear. He'd hurried as quickly as he could to Sioux Falls. All because I refused to speak to him.

"I'm sorry that I didn't listen to you, and I'm sorry again that I jumped to conclusions."

He put his fingers to my lips. "It's fine. I don't hold it against you, really, I don't. But promise me you'll talk to me in the future. Next time something happens, because it's inevitable that something *will* happen, promise me that you'll come to me first. Don't run away. Stay with me and we'll talk through it."

I swallowed tightly. Love beat so strongly in my chest. "Yeah, I promise."

Davin redressed my wound and then helped me pull my sweatshirt back on. He also made sure I took another dose of pain meds as well as my antibiotic. His attentive and caring behavior brought back memories of my time in the Inner Sanctum, after I'd been exposed to *Makanza*.

Thirty minutes later, we were leaving my apartment to venture to the South Dakota Food Distribution Center. I had zero fresh groceries. Thankfully, we were able to sneak out the back door of my apartment building without drawing attention to ourselves.

Only a few reporters remained at the front. In the ten degree weather, they didn't seem very alert. Most huddled together trying to keep warm. The rest had apparently either returned to their stations, or had stayed in whatever hotel was their temporary home.

"How did you get past them?" I whispered as we skidded down the slippery sidewalk.

Davin pulled me closer to his side. "I moved at my speed." He chuckled at my wide eyes.

Pulling my scarf up higher as a gust of cold wind hit us, I asked in a muffled voice, "So, they didn't see you?"

He shook his head as we reached his car. "They would have noticed the door opening and closing behind me, but I moved at my top speed so there was no way they could have seen me."

"I wonder what they thought."

Opening the car door for me, he winked. "Considering how windy it is, they probably thought a wind gust pulled the door open."

Once inside Davin's car, we hightailed it out of the parking lot before the reporters could notice. The streets weren't as slippery as the sidewalk, so Davin sped down the road.

Streetlights clicked on as we passed beneath them. Even though it was only early evening, the sun had disappeared, bringing with it another long winter night.

Flipping the heater on, I eyed him curiously. "How did the drive go from Rapid? It's been awhile since you've been behind the wheel, right?"

He raised an eyebrow. In the dark cab, shadows fell across his high cheekbones. "What are you saying? That I'm a hazard on the road?"

I laughed. "Were you?"

"I didn't hit anybody and managed to stay between the lines if that's what you mean."

Another laugh bubbled up in me as happiness swam through my veins. *How is it possible that only a day ago I was miserable at the thought of my life without Davin, and now, the future suddenly seems so bright?*

WHEN WE PULLED into the South Dakota Food Distribution Center's parking lot, there were dozens of other cars. It was a busy time of day to shop. Most people had recently left work and were picking up last minute items before venturing home.

I watched Davin as he perused the aisles. I couldn't help it. He'd often stop with wide eyes to pick up a food item, smell a piece of fresh produce, or lift a loaf of bread to feel its spongy exterior. It was like watching a blind man see for the first time.

While Davin had no doubt gone grocery shopping before becoming infected, I also knew it had been years since he'd done such a normal, mundane task. That realization brought tears to my eyes. This was all I'd ever wanted for him. To be free. To be happy.

I hastily blinked back the tears when he looked my way.

He merely smiled before moving onto the next item, oblivious to the inner emotions that swirled inside me like a tornado.

I trailed behind him, watching his broad shoulders through his thin shirt. Even in the dead of winter he only wore a t-shirt thanks to his enhanced metabolism, another Change made in him by *Makanza*. That thin material hugged his body, his muscles visible beneath. And with his worn jeans, boots, large hands, and drop-dead gorgeous face—it was hard not to stare.

I wasn't the only one noticing his devilishly handsome

good looks.

Several women stopped to watch him, even the middle-aged ones who had teenage kids following behind them. They all did a double-take when Davin strolled by. Some even blushed when he glanced their way.

I wondered if they knew Davin was a Kazzie. Probably not. Since he outwardly appeared normal, the general public would have no idea he was infected. They'd also be completely unaware that being so close to him, and touching things he'd just brushed against, would also infect *them*.

Since the three-week quarantine law had died with the Post Wave Rehabilitation Act, it was inevitable that in the next few days, most people in this store would feel some type of symptom. Those symptoms could feel like the common cold, or the achiness from an impending flu, or a more severe reaction like I'd had, but many of them would have *some* reaction.

But they'd all been vaccinated.

So after a few days of feeling unwell, they'd be fine, most likely none the wiser that they'd just been exposed.

At the checkout, Davin kept his lightning-fast speed in check. I had a feeling he was more conscientious about his inhuman abilities now more than ever. He seemed to be slowing his movements as if trying to not draw attention to himself. Despite this being my home turf, hecklers were everywhere.

But his tamed actions didn't stop the *other* type of attention he was attracting.

The checkout girl kept stumbling and dropping things as she batted her eyelashes at him. She barely glanced my way even though I'd been shopping at this store for years.

A dozen shoppers waited in the other checkout lines.

Some eyed me and whispered to their family or friends.

As always, my face attracted attention. I'd spent the past six months in the public spotlight. That was the one part I'd hated about the political endeavors I'd pursued to free the Kazzies. But it had been necessary to free them.

A slight thrum of anxiety rose inside me as the attention on me grew.

Making myself take deep breaths, I continued to let Davin place the grocery items on the conveyer belt. I didn't try to help. While the pain meds were kicking in, and my injury wasn't quite as sore, Davin was right.

I'd overdone it today.

The last thing I needed was my wound bursting open as blood seeped through my top. If my face didn't draw attention, *that* certainly would.

"That will be three hundred and ninety-eight dollars." The checkout clerk held out her hand to Davin, her cheeks a rosy pink.

I fumbled for my Sioux Falls SDFDC card and handed it to her. Since food was still rationed, each citizen was only allowed a specific number of food items per week. "It's on my card. He's not a resident here."

"Oh, that's too bad." Her cheeks grew pinker as she gazed up at Davin.

Davin seemed oblivious to her flirtations. Either that or he ignored them. He turned his attention to the TV on the wall as he absentmindedly rubbed my back while I paid.

Humming from the show droned on behind me as the checkout girl counted my change. The national America News Network evening program had just started.

Other shoppers turned idle glances to it when a grisly picture of a sick, young girl flashed on the screen.

The reporter's voice came next. "Another family is claiming their child is gravely ill after being exposed to *Makanza*. Zoe Mathison, an eight-year-old girl, was admitted to Chicago Children's Hospital this afternoon after coming down with mysterious symptoms. Doctors have neither confirmed nor denied if her illness is caused by *Makanza*, but the family is insistent it is."

Davin's hand fell to his side as I dropped the coins I'd been stuffing into my wallet. They clattered to the floor, clinking and clanging on the linoleum.

Davin stiffened, his brow furrowing as he turned his full attention to the screen.

The scene shifted to a new segment, showing Senator Douglas outside of the Chicago hospital. His chest puffed up when the camera swung his way, his beady eyes exuding arrogance.

I snorted in disgust and stuffed the coins into my wallet.

"Is it true that Zoe Mathison was exposed to *Makanza* and may now die?" The reporter thrust her microphone under the senator's chin.

The senator's expression turned grim. "The family reports that she was sledding in a park two days ago when a male Kazzie entered it."

"How did they know he was a Kazzie?" the reporter asked.

With a curled lip, the senator replied, "He didn't look like you and me. He had one of the strains, obviously, from his strangely long arms. The family tried to vacate the area, but the Kazzie brushed against Zoe when they passed. So now, their daughter's been exposed and may die." His gaze turned to the camera. "Let this be a warning to the American public as we fight to overturn the new law. If you see a Kazzie, run the other way. The MRI's lies won't protect you. Only quarantine will."

A murmur erupted in the crowd of shoppers. Everyone watched the screen. The sound of splintering plastic came next, making me jump.

Davin's face was contorted in rage as the plastic counter he'd been gripping exploded under his palm.

The checkout clerk's wide eyes swept from Davin to me as she jumped back.

I hurriedly reached for our bags.

Pain shot through me at the sudden movement. My wound opened. Again. I could feel hot, thick blood trickle onto my skin.

"Davin. Let's go." My voice shook.

Hearing my trembling words kicked Davin into action. He grabbed all of the bags from me, his movements an impossible blur.

The checkout girl gasped.

"You've been vaccinated. You'll be fine." I tried to reassure her, but her gaze swung between Davin and the news segment. Understanding at what Davin was filled her eyes. Terror came next.

Other shoppers seemed to be connecting the dots together as their gazes followed me and Davin. Whispers erupted in the crowd as flashes of fear crossed some people's faces.

Davin reached for me with his free hand and pulled me gently toward the door.

I seethed quietly as pain throbbed in my chest. *Damn Senator Douglas and his lies!*

It was possible Zoe Mathison was gravely ill from being exposed, as I had been, but I still knew she'd be okay. The vaccine was 100% effective. The senator was again stirring fears to fuel his own agenda. Whatever that agenda was.

Still, from the terrified whispers that followed us out of the store, I couldn't help but wonder if the war was not yet won.

6 – CONFESSION

Back at my apartment, I had hoped for a quiet, romantic dinner with Davin. It didn't seem that was going to happen. He paced back and forth in the kitchen. The groceries sat forgotten on the counter.

I stood by the stove, watching him. "Zoe will be fine, Davin. *Makanza* won't kill her—if she even contracted it."

His movements grew faster. A few times he turned into a blur before slowing so I could see him. "How do you know that? What if she *does* die? Then they'll lock us up again! And a child would have died... because of us!"

My heart stopped.

A dead child. Davin locked up. My friends back on Reservation 1.

No. Stay calm. Remember the science.

Trembling, I gripped the edge of the kitchen counter tighter. My injury throbbed, yet I bit back my grimace. "No. That won't happen. She'll recover, as will everyone else who's been exposed. In a week, this will all blow over."

He stopped and faced me. His anguished expression made

my stomach plummet.

"You don't know that, Meghan. What if all of this…" He waved at my apartment. At me. At freedom. "What if all of *this* is just a dream? A dream that they snatch away from us after they realize they can't control *Makanza?*"

His chest rose and fell. Panic emanated outward from him, like solar flares bursting from the sun.

I padded toward him unsteadily.

Concern flashed across his eyes when I gripped the counter by the sink to steady myself.

"Those people you speak of?" With my free hand, I grabbed his palm and squeezed tightly. "The ones you're afraid will snatch your dream away? Those people are me and my co-workers. The Makanza Research Institute. It's *our* research that deemed you safe to walk among the public. It's *our* perseverance that made it safe for you to leave the reservation. Have faith in us. Have faith in *me*. Our research is solid. The vaccine works. The government would have never let you out otherwise."

His eyes dimmed. "But what if there's an exception? What if… your research is wrong?"

Try as I might, I couldn't help the small smile that tugged at my lips. "You remind me of the terrified public that I spent weeks speaking to. Trust me. The research isn't wrong. You'll see."

Some of the tension in his shoulders abated. He hung his head before muttering in disgust, "I'm sorry. Look at me. I'm no better than the ones who think we should be locked up. Throw a grandiose news story in my face, and I panic."

I squeezed his hand again. "It's okay. You're not the only one feeling this way." My tone darkened. "I'm sure that's exactly what Senator Douglas wants. He's still preying on people's fears, and that poor girl, Zoe Mathison... she's probably lying in a hospital bed right now while reporters hound her parents. All because fear still rules this country."

He pulled me closer until we were only inches from touching. "I wish it would all go away. I wish it was years in the future, and you and I were sitting on our porch watching the sun go down."

My breath caught in my throat. Before today, we'd never spoken of the future. Not really. At times, we'd hinted at the coming weeks or months. But never years. Years were too definite. Too solid. They'd always been something that could disappear at any second.

Swallowing the tightness in my throat, I gazed up at him. "I'd like that."

He pulled me closer and wrapped his arms around me.

With my good arm, I hugged him back. The feel of his solid chest and the smell of his intoxicating scent made me melt against him and close my eyes. But the other side of me, the side that shot my hormones into overdrive, wanted to squirm as an aching need to *be* with him coiled in my belly.

His heartbeat increased against my ear as his hands roamed up and down my back.

Shivers struck me as I pressed myself closer to him.

Cursing under his breath, he stepped back and put a solid foot of distance between us. "How is it that you continually make me forget that you're injured?"

I giggled which got a smile out of him.

He lifted me into his arms and cradled me against his chest.

My breath stopped. Once again, he'd moved so fast that it didn't hurt.

Gliding to the table, he sat me down and then rearranged

the other chair so I could prop my feet on it. "I'll make dinner. You sit and watch. You're still looking pale."

"Sounds fine to me. You haven't seen me cook." I settled back against the hard chair, but no matter how many times I shifted, the chair's firm back jarred my shoulder.

He frowned while watching my movements. "Hold on."

He turned into a blur.

In less than a blink, the lounge chair from my living room appeared beside me. Another blink, and the kitchen table was against the front door, creating more room in the tiny area. A third blink and the lounge chair was positioned where the table had been, allowing one sitting in it the best view of the kitchen.

Gently molding his arms under my knees and around my back, he lifted me before I could protest.

I was already seated in the lounge chair before I said, "I'm perfectly capable of walking."

He grinned devilishly. "I know, but what fun would it be if I couldn't show off my skills?"

I laughed as he made a few more arrangements with the furniture.

When I was seated with my feet reclined, Davin placed a blanket over me, and then handed me two pain meds and a glass of water.

"It's been a few hours since your last dose. You better take these."

Biting back a smile, I downed the pills. "My mother would approve of your hovering."

He cocked his head. "How was it with your parents over the weekend? You haven't said much about them."

After another swallow of water, I shrugged. "It was surprisingly... good."

Grunting, he moved back to the stove. "I'm glad to hear

it."

He pulled out the chicken and fresh veggies we'd purchased. In my small kitchen, he seemed larger than life. Between his broad shoulders that bunched and moved under his thin t-shirt, to his large hands that swallowed the whole chicken in his palm, or the brightness of his eyes every time they flashed my way... I'd never seen a more delectable scene in my apartment.

Squirming that had nothing to do with my injury made my cheeks flush. Trying to cover it up, I asked, "Do you know how to cook now?"

The one time we'd made dinner together had been on Reservation 1, right after the gates had finally opened to family members and friends. That night, both of us had been like fish out of water until Sharon showed up. Thankfully, she'd made dinner.

Davin shrugged as he hunted for a knife. Squeaking from the kitchen drawers being pulled open followed. "I'm no expert, but my mother has helped me remember the basics over the past week. Besides, she warned me to never let you loose in the kitchen."

My mouth dropped which got a deep laugh from him.

"She said you're good at stirring things, though."

This time, *I* laughed. "She's right. Trust me. It's much safer if I stay over here."

Of course, Davin didn't make dinner like a normal human. After he found the culinary equipment he needed, he did everything at his speed, which basically meant it looked like a tornado whipped around the room.

Delectable scents soon filled the kitchen. With the chicken seasoned and roasting in the oven, potatoes peeled, cubed and ready to be boiled, and a fresh salad with homemade french dressing sitting beside it—he'd effectively completed something I'd never managed—a homemade, delicious supper just waiting to be eaten.

"Sharon's done well. I had no idea you could do all of that."

He wiped his hands on a dish towel. "Yeah, it's been awhile since I've cooked, but it's coming back."

I sighed in bliss. "Good. I hate cooking. How about you always do it?"

A dark lock of hair fell across his face as he set the timer on the stove. "Fine with me, but that means you're doing the dishes."

BY THE TIME we finished supper and cleaned the kitchen, it was nine at night. Embarrassingly, I had a hard time keeping my eyes open and despite Davin's arrival, I still had to work tomorrow. A cure was needed.

Yawning, I covered my mouth. "I'm sorry. I'm just… tired."

Davin's brow furrowed. "It's because you're doing too much. You shouldn't have gone into work today."

"But Bethany—"

In a flash, he was at my side and putting a finger to my lips. "Thousands of people work at the Compounds. They can help Bethany. Right now, you have a fractured rib and a still healing bullet hole in your chest. You shouldn't be working. At all."

As much as I wanted to argue, I knew he was right. So when he insisted that I go to bed, I didn't object. I also let him lift me from the chair and carry me to the bathroom since he seemed to enjoy it so much.

Once in my bedroom, I quickly changed before slipping

under the covers. Outside my bedroom window, the wind howled as glimpses of the moon appeared through wispy clouds.

It was only when I pulled the covers up that I remembered there was only one bed in my apartment. And unlike Ian, I didn't want Davin to sleep on the couch.

I scooted to the far side of my bed and said haltingly, "Are you… um, you know… going to sleep in here?"

In the dim room, his eyes grew hooded as he stepped closer. "Is that an invitation?"

My cheeks flushed. *At least it's dark in here so he can't see.* "Yes."

The mattress sagged when his heavy weight pushed onto it. "In that case, yeah."

"Um, you still have your clothes on."

He chuckled. "Oh, right."

In a flash, he was out of the room. Rustling sounded from the entryway before my apartment door opened and closed. A few seconds later, the sound of the door opening again filtered into my room. Not even thirty seconds had passed from when Davin left to when he strolled back in… wearing only pajama pants.

My breath stopped. His chest was visible in the moonlight. Strong pectorals and a flat abdomen littered with scars made my mouth go dry.

"What… How?" I sat up straighter. "Did you just go outside?"

He inched closer. "My bag was still in the car. I had to get it."

Eyeing his pajamas again, I raised an eyebrow. "You must have been optimistic you'd be spending the night."

Chuckling, he reached the edge of my bed and pulled the

covers back before slipping under them. "I may have hoped for this."

My heart felt like it would beat right out of my chest. *Davin's in my apartment. In my bed. And the only thing he's wearing is thin pants.*

"Are you okay?" His voice grew husky.

"Yeah," I squeaked.

Inching closer, his hand brushed my abdomen.

My heart beat so wildly I thought I'd faint.

"Is this okay?" He scooted against my side. Heat from his body pressed against me like a hard, hot blanket.

"Yes," I breathed.

Grunting, he settled against me until he spooned my length, his arm possessively locked around my waist.

I closed my eyes, savoring the feel of him even though tension strummed along my limbs. I felt as tight as a guitar string, but I'd dreamed for so long of experiencing this. It seemed too good to be true. *Davin's mine. He's finally all mine.*

His lips brushed my ear, causing my eyes to flash wide open. "You seem rather tense."

"I…" I cleared my throat. "To be honest, I am. I've never… Well, you're the first to…"

He pushed up on an elbow to gaze down at me. A smile tugged at his lips. "Are you saying I'm the first guy to sleep over?"

"In my bed, yes."

A perfect, midnight eyebrow raised. *"In your bed?* Do you care to explain?"

"Ian slept on the couch when he was here."

He grunted again. "That's good. Can't say I'd be too fond of Ian if he'd slept anywhere else."

I laughed.

"But that still doesn't answer my question. Am I the first to... you know... be with you?"

"We haven't been together yet."

He sagged more into his hand. "Why do I get the feeling you're avoiding the question?"

My cheeks had to be bright red by now. *Thank God it's dark in here!* "I'm... you know... I've had dates before."

"But have you *been* with anyone?"

I held my breath as the silence stretched between us. I finally squeaked, "No."

It was silly, but I wanted to bury my head in my hands. I was a twenty-four-year-old virgin. Granted, my social anxiety and long hours in the lab were mostly to blame for my inexperience, but *Makanza* was partly to blame too. For so many years, the public had been isolated from one another which hardly allowed one to date. Anxiety or not. Still... It was embarrassing.

Davin brushed the covers away from my face. His head dipped lower until he whispered in my ear, "I'm glad. I hate the thought of another guy touching you."

I turned more to face him. In the dark, his eyes were like a storm at sea. "You mean, you don't think it's weird that I haven't been with anyone before?"

"No. Why would it be weird?"

Shrugging awkwardly, I replied, "Most people my age aren't virgins."

"Ten years ago, that would probably be true, but now, I imagine you'd be surprised. For so many years, everyone was cut off from one another. This country is probably crawling with virgins."

I laughed again as some of my tension eased. "What about you? Are you a virgin?"

"No."

"I didn't think so." I bit my lip. From what Sharon had told me, Davin had dated regularly before becoming infected. And given how attractive he was, women had probably flocked to him like moths to a flame. I bit my lip harder.

He tilted my chin up. "But there's only you now. There will only ever be you now."

Shivers ran down my spine at his words. His absolute conviction. *I can't believe I ever doubted him.*

Leaning closer, his lips brushed mine.

I wrapped my left arm around his neck and deepened the kiss, but when he shifted closer it jarred my right arm. I hissed when pain coursed through me.

In a flash, two feet separated us as he hovered just on the edge of the bed.

"Dammit." He swore quietly under his breath. "I keep forgetting that we need to go slow."

I groaned as my wound throbbed. "But I don't want to go slow."

He chuckled and inched closer again. "Trust me, neither do I. I've been wanting you for a year. Waiting isn't easy for me."

My heart strummed steadily in my chest as his heat once again enveloped me. *He's so warm.* I loved the feel of him, and his scent kept fluttering to my senses. His tantalizing smell made me want to bury my face in his neck.

"I'll do my best to keep my hands to myself." But just after he made that admission, his palm settled on my hip. He kneaded the muscles there and then inched lower to massage my thigh.

I closed my eyes. "I could get used to this." *Especially considering I'm weeks away from being fully healed.*

The mattress sagged again when he shifted closer. "Please do, because I'm not going anywhere."

As I snuggled into him, his hands did delicious things to my muscles. I idly ran a finger along his chest. His skin was so smooth, yet beneath it, hard muscles bunched. He was granite wrapped in silk.

"Davin? Can I ask you something?"

"You can ask me anything."

My finger continued to trail along his chest, his muscles jumping at times from my light touch. "What happened last summer? When you were catatonic for those four hours? Will you tell me?"

He stiffened. "What made you think of that?"

"I saw Dr. Fisher today. He's helping with Bethany and seeing him reminded me of it."

I held my breath. Every other time I'd brought up this subject, Davin closed it down like the lid on a coffin—definite and absolute.

But this time, he merely sighed. "It was because of you."

My head snapped back. "Because of *me*? What do you mean?"

"Remember how we hadn't been speaking for a few weeks when that happened? How I'd been pushing you away?"

I curled my fingers through the hairs on his chest. "Yes. I remember."

"At that time, I truly believed any chance of being with you would never happen, and I thought that something was going on between you and Mitch. Worst of all, there was nothing I could do about it. I was in love with a woman I could never be with. Every day I was trapped in those damned concrete walls. And my future wasn't looking any better. I'd be moved to a reservation to live behind a fence, like a herded cow. And… I don't know. Something snapped that afternoon. It was like I disconnected." His hand continued to massage the muscles in my thigh, but his voice grew quieter. "Dr. Fisher thinks it was the trauma of all of that which caused the catatonia."

"So when you say it was because of me, you're saying it's because we couldn't be together?"

Davin nodded. "Yeah, but things got better after I started meeting with Dr. Fisher. He spent a lot of time discussing my situation with me. It was kind of like…" He shrugged. "I dunno, therapy in a way, I guess."

"And that's why you wouldn't tell me about it? You were embarrassed that you were in therapy?"

"Partly, but it was more than that. I couldn't tell you how I really felt. If I did, I knew you'd never move on, and I couldn't let that happen. So that's why I never told you. I was afraid of telling you how deeply I felt."

Silence followed as I recalled all of the times Davin had turned cagey and jittery every time I'd brought up that fateful afternoon. *It was because of me that he fell into that state. Because he wanted to be with me as badly as I wanted to be with him, but the Compound would never allow it.*

"Are you glad I didn't give up on you now?" I resumed trailing a finger along his chest.

"More than you could ever know."

7 – DIVISION 5

I woke the next morning to a soft snore in my ear and the feel of a rock-hard body as hot as fire pressed against me. Everything about it felt so good and right. I snuggled closer to Davin, relishing the moment.

I debated going back to sleep when a *buzz* reached my ear. Another *buzz* quickly followed.

My eyes flashed open. *My phone.*

Davin's arm refused to budge from around my waist when I tried to reach my phone on the bedside table. If anything, it tightened more.

Somehow, I managed to extract myself from his heavy limbs. Inching to the edge of the bed, I fell rather unceremoniously onto the floor. I stifled a groan and grabbed my phone just before it went to voicemail.

"Hello?" I whispered while eyeing the clock. 6:43 a.m. *I slept late!*

"You better still be at home." Amy's voice sounded loud and clear from the other end. She was up early.

Glancing at Davin's still sleeping form, I smiled and made

myself stop from smoothing the hair across his forehead. Relaxed like this, he looked so peaceful.

Forcing myself to move, I tiptoed out of the room. Once in the hall, I closed the door behind me.

"Meghan? Hello? Are you still there?"

I hurried to the bathroom. My shoulder throbbed from the fall. *Better get the pain meds.*

"I'm still here, Amy. I just had to…" I closed the bathroom door behind me and spoke louder. "Um, nothing. So what's up? And what do you mean, that I better still be at home?"

"Because yesterday Dr. Fisher mentioned to Dr. Sadowsky that you didn't look well. *And* he told our boss that it wasn't a good idea for you to return to work so soon. Anyway, I just got here, and Dr. Sadowsky was waiting in the lab. He said if you try to work during the next two weeks, he'll personally escort you home."

"But what about Bethany?" I slid two pills from the bottle and downed them with a quick drink from the faucet. In the mirror, my dark hair looked wild, but since my good hand held my phone, I didn't try to straighten it.

"Dr. Sadowsky encouraged her to return to Minnesota for the time being. And he said something else that I thought might interest you, but you have to promise me you won't come into work."

My brow furrowed as I cocked my head. "What?"

"It's about a secret group. They've been working on a cure ever since you discovered how to map out the genome. Apparently, they're called Division 5."

I PACED MY apartment after Amy and I hung up. For once, my arm rested in the sling the doctor insisted I wear. It allowed my frantic walking without creating more pain.

The carpet squished beneath my feet. Its thick fibers threaded through my toes.

It was impossible to go back to bed. My thoughts zeroed in on one thing and one thing only.

Division 5.

The group, that Amy believed consisted of MRI scientists, had been working on a cure for the past year.

So far, they hadn't found one.

A grin still spread across my face. While a part of me was annoyed that I was kept in the dark about this development, it didn't stop my excitement. *That's a year's worth of research that's already been underway. A year of results we wouldn't have otherwise.*

I was so engrossed in my thoughts that I shrieked when two large hands settled on my shoulders.

Davin pulled back. "Sorry, didn't mean to scare you."

He was still shirtless. Tousled hair covered his head, and his electric blue eyes appeared foggy from sleep.

I smiled sheepishly and stepped closer. "Did I wake you?"

With a loud yawn, he stretched. "No, but when I woke up to find you missing, my first thought was that you left for work. I'm happy to see you didn't."

"Amy called and woke me. Apparently, Dr. Sadowsky heard I didn't look well. He's banned me from the Compound for the next two weeks." I nibbled my lip. Despite knowing that, I was itching to learn more about Division 5.

Davin grinned. "Good. That means I have you to myself for the day."

His infectious mood was impossible to ignore. Even though my gaze wandered to the door, I knew there would be hell to pay if I showed up at the Compound.

Davin eyed me curiously. "Everything okay?"

I twisted my hands. "Yeah. Kind of. Amy also told me something else." I summed up what I knew of Division 5.

His eyes widened. "So some group of MRI scientists have already been working on a cure? How come you didn't know about it?"

"She said it's been kept pretty quiet, and I'm not surprised. We had our hands full when we developed the vaccine and then convincing the country that it works has been hard enough. There would be no point in getting everyone's hopes up about a cure if we could never develop one."

"But why didn't they tell you? You're the founder of the vaccine."

I shrugged. "Why does the MRI do anything they do? Your guess is as good as mine."

He cocked his head. "It's killing you, isn't it, that you can't go in?"

I threaded a hand through my hair. "Is it that obvious?"

"Considering you went to work with a broken rib and bullet hole in your chest, and have been a workaholic for as long as I've known you... yeah, it's kind of obvious."

I laughed.

He kissed me softly on the mouth before dropping to the couch. The intimate, easy gesture made my stomach flutter as he reached for the remote.

"Want to join me?" he asked.

Standing over him, I gazed down at his long, lean form.

It suddenly occurred to me that he and I were enjoying our first normal morning together. A morning most couples took for granted.

I settled beside him. The muscles in his abdomen bunched and moved as he shifted to make room. Sounds from the TV filled the background.

Inching closer to him, I forced thoughts of Division 5 aside.

"So… are you hungry?" I asked.

He smiled just as the America News Network morning show started. Leaning closer to kiss my neck, he whispered, "Hungry for you?"

I held my injured arm closer to my side. Despite the sling, snuggling beside him still jarred my wound.

Batting my eyelashes playfully, I replied, "I thought you said we had to wait for my injury to heal?"

His gaze darkened. "There are other things we could do."

My breath caught in my chest at what those *other things* could be, but all wayward thoughts stopped short when the newscaster's words reached my ears.

"We turn to our local Illinois reporter outside Chicago Children's where Zoe Mathison's condition is now critical. Bob?"

The teasing smile on my lips vanished as Davin frowned.

A middle-aged reporter stood outside the hospital. He wore a thick jacket as snow flew around him. Behind him, Chicago Children's loomed. Several windows in the large building were broken, and the sign over the main entrance hung unevenly.

It was such a common sight. Most buildings and businesses had fallen into disrepair since the First Wave. Hospitals were no exception.

The reporter held his hood in place as cold gusts tried to blow it off.

"Thank you, Lily. Behind me is the hospital where young, Zoe Mathison is currently fighting for her life as doctors and nurses work around the clock to try to save her. The latest reports indicate an unknown infection is spreading throughout her body."

The scene cut back to the main desk. The Des Moines anchorwoman shuffled her papers. "And what do you know about Senator Douglas' claims that Zoe was exposed to *Makanza* and that's why she's sick?"

Bob's face turned grim. "Doctors have confirmed that Zoe was indeed exposed to *Makanza.*"

The blood drained from my face as Davin's entire body tensed.

"Is it fair to say, Bob, that Zoe's condition is directly related to *Makanza?*"

Bob sighed heavily. "Doctors have neither confirmed nor denied that. The exact cause of her illness remains unknown."

The scene shifted again to the anchorwoman after Bob promised to continue monitoring the situation. Her words washed over me like a slight breeze—there and then gone.

I vigorously shook my head. "But that doesn't make sense…"

Davin's expression turned dark. "They won't let us stay free if she dies from *Makanza* no matter what protection the Post Wave Rehabilitation Act grants us."

I gripped his hand tightly, ignoring the painful jostle of my injury. "It's not *Makanza* that's doing this to her. I'm sure of it!"

A soft scratch filled the back of my mind. *Sara.* I hadn't heard from her in two days.

"Hold on," I told Davin. "Sara's trying to get in touch."

Closing my eyes, I opened the telepathic link with the twin. *Hi, are you there?*

Sara's anxiety strummed along our bond before her words reached me. *Did you see it? They're saying a young girl is going to die from* Makanza.

I nodded internally. *Yeah, I saw it, but it's not true. Even though she's been exposed, it's not* Makanza *that has made her this ill. I'm sure of it. She's been vaccinated, so there's no way the virus could be the cause.*

But they're saying on the news that she only became ill after encountering a Kazzie. If the twin had been sitting beside me, I felt certain she'd be wringing her hands.

That may be true, but the extent of her illness can't be explained by just that.

How can you be so sure?

Pinching the bridge of my nose, I recounted the numerous trials and studies we'd done with the vaccination. Not one stone had been left unturned with our research. *The vaccine's 100% effective. She'll be fine.*

But a niggling doubt still gnawed at my conscience. I did my best to hide it from Sara. *I should go. Davin's here.*

Oh, yeah, I almost forgot. Sara's feelings shifted, as if she pushed her worry aside. *How are things going? Since you didn't get in touch to yell at me, I'm assuming things are better now?*

I chuckled at her teasing words. *Yeah, things are good. We're… uh… together now.*

Her smile felt like it was a mile wide. *I figured as much. I kept telling him that you two just needed to talk. If it wasn't for that storm, I'm certain he would have come to you sooner.*

That's what he said.

So, can we officially put the Jenna drama behind us?

I sighed. *Yes, we can. I should have listened to you. You were right about her.*

A smug feeling came from her end. *You know I may never be as smart as you, but when it comes to some things, I know a lot. And if there's one thing I know, it's that Davin cares for you more than anyone.*

Don't sell yourself short. You're very smart!

She seemed to find my gentle scolding funny because she

laughed.

The sound helped alleviate my concerns about Zoe. *So when will I see you again?*

Soon hopefully?

Okay, I'll talk to you later. A certain someone seems to be getting a little impatient.

Davin? Impatient? Who would have thought.

When I was alone in my head, I returned my attention to the large Kazzie beside me.

"Is Sara doing okay?" His deep voice filled the room. He'd turned off the TV while I'd been talking with the twin. I knew he was trying to distance me from the news story.

"More or less. She's worried about what the news said, but then we started talking about other things which seemed to take her mind off it."

He raised an eyebrow. "Other things? Such as?"

I gave him side-eyes as I awkwardly pushed to a stand. "Wouldn't you like to know."

In a flash, he stood before me. The air rustled the long locks hanging around my shoulders. I once again felt incredibly aware of how large and powerful he was.

Smiling, he inched closer.

My breath stopped.

Before I knew what he was doing, his arms were around me and he was pulling me closer.

I placed a hand on his chest and trailed my fingers across the strong muscles.

His pectorals tightened.

Emboldened, my fingers trailed lower. Ridges from his multiple scars dipped and weaved under my fingertips. I knew his legs held just as many. My gaze hardened as I stared at the plethora of healed incisions. The joking and carefree moment vanished.

The anchorman's words haunted me. *Doctors have confirmed that Zoe has indeed been exposed to* Makanza.

I settled my palm against his flat abdomen as tears filled my eyes. I knew better. It was silly that I was letting everyone's concerns get to me. Of all people, I *knew* that Zoe would be fine, but I also knew how powerful fear was.

I'd been battling it for a year.

My voice was barely a whisper when I said, "I'll never let them take you back there."

Davin locked his arms around me. "It'll be fine. Like you said, the vaccine is 100% effective. I'm free now because of you, and I intend to stay that way."

With one hand, he tilted my chin up. Deep emotion swam in his cobalt irises. At times, the emotions that ran between us were so deep it felt like a bottomless chasm that would suck me into its grasp and never let go. It was scary how much he meant to me, but I knew I meant just as much to him. He'd experienced traumatic catatonia at the thought of a life locked away, in which we could never be together.

A single tear rolled down my cheek.

"Shh…" Leaning down, he placed his lips on mine.

I closed my eyes and, for a moment, let myself become lost in his kiss. *I've waited for this for so long. I can't let him be taken away again.*

As if sensing my fears, he shifted until his large hands settled on my hips, holding me close.

Deepening the kiss, he seemed intent on making me forget the world. When the kiss finally ended, I was breathless.

Davin threaded his fingers through my hair. Several long locks twisted through his hand. "Should we make breakfast?"

I nodded.

He tugged me away from the couch. In the kitchen, Davin pulled out ingredients for what I could only assume were omelets.

I stared in wonder as he mixed together eggs, chopped vegetables, and slid butter into a pan. I settled onto a kitchen chair to watch him. "You really don't mind doing all of the work?"

"Well, if you're cooking is as bad as you say it is, it's probably for the best."

I laughed despite all of the worry still swirling inside of me.

"So what do you want to do today?" His deep voice sounded over the sizzling veggies in the pan, but despite him trying to act like everything was fine, I still noticed his death-grip on the spatula.

"There's not much to do in the winter, but we could go to a movie, or maybe go out to a restaurant for lunch or dinner, or we could go down to the falls. They're pretty in winter since they're frozen." *Yet, none of that will help Zoe or stop the escalating problems in our country.*

"What could we do that's not local?"

"Not local?" I cocked my head.

"We have a car that's fully charged. You're banned from work for two weeks. And right now, you're in no shape to take on the world." He turned to fully face me, the spatula squeaking in his grip. "Not to mention, last time I checked there were still a few reporters sitting outside the doors to your apartment building. There are no guarantees those reporters won't follow us around the city if they see us together. It won't take long before they put two and two together and realize I'm a Kazzie and you're the MRI's darling girl. If they're looking for a new story, they'll have one right there."

My stomach dropped. "I hadn't thought of that."

So far, nobody really knew about Davin and me. My coworkers, of course, knew that I was very close to the Kazzies, but they had no idea that Davin and I had romantic interests in one another.

It was probably best that we had kept our relationship a secret. Our relationship had the potential to be a public relations nightmare—after all, up until now, the entire country thought I was simply an advocate for the Kazzies.

Not in love with one.

I stood up straighter. "In that case, let's go somewhere."

Davin slid the steaming omelets onto two plates. "Sounds like a good idea to me."

AN HOUR LATER, we were sneaking out my building's back door. Davin was right, only a few reporters remained at the front, but that was a few too many.

Relief filled me that most of them had left. Although, *why* they had left was the bigger question. *It's possible those reporters went to Chicago to follow Zoe's condition.*

That thought chilled me more than the bitter wind.

We were about halfway to the car, slinking along the sidewalk, when I glanced over my shoulder. At just that moment, one of the reporters looked our way.

"She's leaving!" His distant yell carried in the air. The reporter nudged his cameraman. Both took off at a sprint toward us, arms flailing when they hit an icy spot on the sidewalk.

"Davin, they've spotted us!"

Davin grabbed my good arm and half carried me down the sidewalk. He didn't turn into a blur, but he moved fast. Really fast.

My stomach lurched when we reached his car.

"Meghan!" the reporter yelled. They were halfway to us now. "What do you have to say about Zoe Mathison's illness?" he called.

"Davin, hurry!"

Gritting his teeth, Davin hit the unlock button on his key fab. I yelped in pain when I wrenched the door open, but I didn't stop. When we slid into Davin's car, cold and stiff seats greeted us. I clicked my seatbelt on as Davin started the motor.

A bang made me look up.

The cameraman had fallen a dozen feet away, no doubt hitting another patch of ice. It didn't stop his partner.

"Meghan!" He still ran toward us.

With a spin of tires, Davin kicked the car into gear. We backed out at an alarming pace before accelerating down the snowy parking lot onto the road.

"They're jumping into vehicles!" My voice rose with each word.

Davin gripped the steering wheel tightly. "I'll lose them."

I closed my eyes when Davin flew around the corner onto a street, but he expertly handled the vehicle before taking another turn at the intersection. After weaving several times in and out of neighborhood streets, I breathed a sigh of relief. The road was empty behind us.

"I think we lost them." My heart pounded as I nervously eyed the side mirror. "But we better get out of here."

Davin slipped on a pair of sunglasses as we sped toward the interstate. A lock of dark hair brushed the tops of the aviator style. He looked so sexy, that my breath stopped.

Forcing myself to breathe, I asked, "Where are we going?"

"South?" Davin's eyebrows rose. "It's warmer down there, right?"

"How far south do you want to go?"

"How about we keep going until there's no snow."

My mouth dropped. "No snow? That could take an entire day of driving."

"Last I heard you were banned from work and needed to heal."

I nibbled my lip. "Good thing we packed enough clothes for a week."

"Ready?" The eastern sun blazed through the car.

I leaned farther back in my seat. "Yeah, let's go."

8 – ROAD TRIP

We spent the entire day traveling to the southern portion of the country. After alerting my parents, Sharon, and Sara to our plans, Davin insisted we shut our phones off. I think part of that was due to my parents' shocked reaction at my impulsive trip with a Kazzie. They'd had no idea I was romantically involved with Davin. Until now. It didn't help that the last time they'd seen him had been the day I fled Reservation 1's hospital. All they knew was that Davin had upset me, but I'd never told them why.

Despite my parents' worry, Davin seemed bound and determined to have me rest without concerns of well... anything. During the drive, he tried to keep me distracted, but try as he might, I couldn't help it when my thoughts inevitably drifted to Zoe Mathison, Division 5, Bethany, or Senator Douglas. Each and every one of those topics was enough to make me fidget and curse Dr. Roberts for putting me in my current state.

But every time I reached for my phone, Davin gently pushed my hand away and pulled me back to the present.

"You can't work right now. Enjoy this."

Following statements like that, he'd run a finger across my cheek or squeeze my hand. Those small gestures grounded me and reminded me that this trip wasn't just about being together, it was about healing and preparing for what was to come.

HOURS LATER, WE were hundreds of miles from Sioux Falls. Watching the landscape drift by reminded me of long-ago times, before the world shifted into chaos and death—before the First Wave. Even though I'd traveled out of state for work, it still hadn't sunk in that we were truly free to roam this country as we pleased. With no border patrols and no curfew—everything had changed.

"Is it like you remember?" I tilted my head toward Davin in my reclined seat. The sun had just set as Oklahoma sailed past my window.

He shrugged. "In some ways. There are more rundown buildings and abandoned towns now—it's surprising how much fell apart after the Second Wave—but other than that, it's not too different."

As Texas loomed, we stopped again to charge the car's battery. Luckily, we found a high-power charging station so we weren't delayed long. Stars filled the sky by the time we slid back into the car.

As Davin pulled out of the charging station, I settled back in my seat again. "The snow's fully gone. Does that mean we're staying here?" I waved at Oklahoma's never-ending plains. At night, it looked barren and bleak.

"I say we go all the way to the Gulf. Why stop now?" His white teeth flashed in a grin.

A surprised laugh bubbled out of me. "All the way?"

"As long as you're still doing okay?" Davin glanced over from the wheel. In the dark cab, his midnight hair looked as black as oil. Ahead of us, all we could see was the road illuminated by the headlights. "Is the driving getting to you?"

I shifted in my seat. "I'm a bit sore, but I'm okay."

My last dose of pain meds and antibiotics had been two hours ago, and my dressing was still clean. Davin was right. Resting was what I needed.

"Are you sure the jostling from the road isn't hurting too much?"

I smiled tenderly. It wasn't the first time he'd been overly concerned during the drive. His initial excitement over getting away had dimmed when we hit a huge rut in the road in Nebraska causing me to shriek in pain.

"I'm fine, really. I think just sitting here all day while you drive has been good for me."

He grunted. "It's about time you rested."

An hour later, we found a motel along the interstate in northern Texas. Since the rates were decent and they had plenty of empty rooms, we booked one for the night.

"How much farther to the ocean?" Davin asked the check-in clerk as he shelled out payment in cash.

"The Gulf is another six hours. It'll be cold, though, this time of year." The clerk stuffed the money in the cash register. His finger pads were stained black, as if he worked with oil-based machinery in his spare time.

Behind him, a TV hung from the wall. Scenes from protests in South Carolina filled it. My breath stopped. It showed protestors carrying signs, demanding the Kazzies be returned to Reservation 1. Some of the signs said their friends and family had become sick since the Kazzies' release.

I knew Davin saw it to. His hand tightened alarmingly

around his wallet. I waited for the leather to crack under his grip, but he regained control before sliding it into his back pocket.

Careful to keep my face averted, I picked at my fingernails as my heart beat erratically.

The clerk's gaze shifted to me, his head cocking as he got a better look at my face. Quickly turning away, I pretended to study the cheap artwork adorning the wall.

So far, nobody had recognized me during our stops. Luckily. Not only had we managed to avoid detection in public, but we were fully off the grid with our phones off. Hopefully, nobody would find us.

Regardless, my hand drifted to my phone in my pocket again. The news story only emphasized that there was still so much to be done.

As if sensing where my mind was drifting, Davin grabbed our key and threaded his fingers through mine. Heat from his hand sent tingles up my arm.

He tugged me. "Come on. Let's find our room."

Once the lobby was behind us, he relaxed his grip.

Our feet shuffled along the carpet. It was the only sound in the large building.

Davin's face was grim, but when he caught me watching him, he forced a smile. "After we find our room, I'll grab our bags and then we can go to bed. I'm sure you're tired."

His broad shoulders bunched and stretched in his t-shirt. Watching him, I completely forgot the news story, and it took at least thirty seconds before his words sank in.

Go to bed.

I swallowed as butterflies danced in my stomach. Even though we'd slept side-by-side last night, this felt different. More intimate. We were traveling together. Spending every waking moment together. We'd cut ourselves off from everything around us so we could focus on each other.

Other than the problems waiting for us at home, it was all so...

Perfect.

"Ah, here we are." He stopped at our room and inserted the key. I stepped inside just as he turned into a blur. He was back less than a minute later with our bags.

I raised an eyebrow. "Did anybody see you move that fast?"

He shook his head, his breathing even despite his speedy run. "Not a soul. This place is deserted."

Sitting down on the bed, I inched back until I was propped against the headboard. Davin turned into a blur again and pillows suddenly appeared fluffed all around me.

He reappeared just as he finished pushing the last pillow under my arm to support my injured limb. "Is that better?"

I placed my palm on his cheek. "Thank you. For this. It's exactly what I needed."

He moved closer until he leaned over me. "Is your phone still off?"

"Yes."

"Good. Cause the next few days, it's just you and me."

DAVIN WASN'T KIDDING when he said the next few days would only be about us. We drove to the ocean the next morning and found a small motel that was open. Only one other couple had a room, and they seemed to want privacy as much as we did.

The week passed quickly despite my worries over what waited for us at home. For the most part, I was able to disconnect. Thankfully.

The few times I mentioned the Compound, Bethany, Division 5, Zoe Mathison, Senator Douglas, or any of the other real-life problems that waited for us at home, Davin brought a finger to my lips and pulled me closer to his side. Whether that be as we lay on our bed while watching a movie. Or as we lounged on a blanket on the beach as the waves crashed to the shore, it didn't matter.

Davin always brought me back to the present. Grounding me. Reminding me that right now I needed to heal, get better, and take care of myself.

When the end of the week finally arrived, I was sorry to pack and return to Sioux Falls.

"Thank you for this week," I whispered. "Somehow you knew exactly what I needed." I laid my palm on his chest as our packed bags waited at our feet.

His eyes softened as he tenderly brushed his finger across my cheek. "I'll never forget this time with you. I feel like I've fallen in love with you all over again."

Even though we still hadn't done anything other than kiss, his body now felt like a roadmap I'd traveled and studied for years on end. I knew exactly where his ticklish spots were. Where every scar Dr. Roberts had inflicted lay on his body. What he smelled like after a quick run on the beach. Or how his rock hard muscles rippled and moved when he shifted above me.

If we hadn't spent the week together as we had, those things would still be a mystery.

He leaned down, his eyes darkening just before his lips pressed to mine.

Kissing Davin had begun to feel like breathing. We'd spent enough of the week doing it, but each time, when our need for one another became too frantic, he'd pull away and break the contact, putting distance between us.

I was healing quickly, now that I was taking proper care of myself, but I still wasn't 100%. And if Davin was anything, he was stubborn. He'd made up his mind that nothing would happen until I was better.

"Shall we go?" Davin picked up our bags as he held his hand out to me.

I threaded my fingers through his. "I suppose so. The real world is waiting."

WE DIDN'T REACH Sioux Falls until the next afternoon. Neither of us turned our phones back on until we'd almost reached my apartment. When I finally did, my phone dinged to life, and I immediately wished I'd kept it off.

It kept dinging as message after message rolled in.

Davin raised his eyebrows when he swung into a parking spot outside of my apartment building. "You've turned into the popular girl."

I bit my lip. "That's what I'm afraid of."

Outside, even more snow covered the ground. It looked like we'd avoided a heavy snowfall in our absence.

"Who are the messages from?" Davin asked as he cut the motor.

I opened my voicemail. My eyes widened when I saw the list of names. *Amy. Cate. Dr. Sadowsky. Sharon. My parents.* A few more numbers I didn't recognize.

My hands began to shake. "Um… everybody. Crap. We should have left an emergency number with someone."

Davin's hand closed over mine before I could listen to the first voicemail. "Let's get inside first."

Amazingly, not one reporter waited outside the door to my building's entrance. Not even the back door. I glanced around as I shouldered my purse. For the first time since being shot, the movement didn't hurt. I'd also been able to cut down on my pain meds, and I didn't need to wear my sling around the clock. I was definitely making progress.

"Where do you suppose they went?" Worry laced my tone.

Davin shrugged and opened the door. "Who knows. Let's just be glad they're not here anymore."

But as we climbed the stairs to my second-floor apartment, I couldn't stop the sense of foreboding as the distance passed beneath us.

When we finally entered my tiny home, I couldn't take it anymore. I turned on the TV just as I tapped the first button on my voicemail.

It was from Cate, or Dr. Hutchinson as the rest of the MRI called her. As the former Director of Compounds 10 and 11 in Washington, she'd recently pursued a new political position in D.C. However, she was still employed by the MRI.

Her message was from yesterday, and her voice sounded shaky, not as confident as it usually did. "Meghan, call me. I'm sure you've seen the news by now, but don't worry. We'll handle it."

My eyes widened as ANN came to life on the TV. Even though I'd meant to listen to the next voicemail on the long list that filled my inbox, I couldn't.

My phone fell to the floor and landed with a soft thud when I saw the banner filling the bottom of the news screen. It scrolled along, its bright red color drawing attention.

And it only said one thing over and over again.

Zoe Mathison had *Makanza*. Zoe Mathison's parents were seeking legal counsel. Chicago Children's was scrambling as other children showed symptoms.

Because Zoe Mathison was dead.

9 – PANIC ATTACK

I sank to my knees as Davin rushed to my side. "She's dead, Davin. She's really dead."

My hands shook as I stared at my phone. Its bright screen shone back at me from where it lay on the floor. The multiple apps waited patiently, as if beckoning me to tap them.

But I didn't know who to call. Who to turn to.

"She's dead." My words felt hollow. Wooden. Like they'd come from someone else.

Davin gripped my hands, his face ashen. His scent filtered through the pressure that seemed to be holding me down.

Soap and aftershave swirled around me. His palms felt hot, like fire, but my hands had turned to ice as a surge of anxiety burst along my limbs. It felt like the room was closing in. That everything was narrowing into a tunnel in front of me.

They'll blame Makanza. They'll say that's why she died. And then they'll take Davin. They'll take Sara. They'll take all of them and lock them up again even though they did nothing wrong. Even though that poor little girl couldn't have died from the virus.

Or could she have?

My body jolted at the thought.

"Meghan?"

The voice sounded distant and foggy, like someone was trying to reach me from the dark side of the moon. I couldn't concentrate. My breath felt too fast. Too shallow. Icy sweat lined my palms. Blackness filled my peripheral vision.

"Meghan, it's okay. Look at me."

Searing hot hands covered my cheeks and gently turned my head. A noise filled the room. It sounded like gasps, as if someone was drowning.

That's me. It's me making those sounds.

"Meghan, deep breaths. Do it with me. Inhale... one... two... three..."

His voice took over. I closed my eyes. *Davin.*

Somehow, I managed to follow his instructions. I slowed my breathing to match his. The sounds of his voice and cadence of his words calmed me like a quiet symphony.

Breathe, Meghan. Just breathe.

By the time the suffocating panic attack abated, I'd completely lost track of time. Opening my eyes, I was relieved the tunnel vision had disappeared. So had the feeling of being swallowed whole by an unforeseen force.

Soft, yet scratchy carpet shifted underneath the tops of my bare feet. The subtle sounds of my apartment building filtered through my senses—the hum of the HVAC, a muffled voice of a neighbor as they passed by in the hallway.

Davin's scent came next. I was pressed against his chest, his intoxicating smell everywhere. It took a moment before I realized that Davin's arms were around me. He held me in his lap. I was cradled against his chest as my legs rested limply on the floor.

"Oh, wow..." I sat up straighter and hung my head. It had

been weeks since my last panic attack. "That was a bad one."

He tilted my chin up. "Are you okay?"

I tried to smile, but my cheeks reddened. "I thought I was over those."

"You have been for the most part." His gaze darkened. "Except for any time you get sucked back into my world, when you worry the media will turn the public on us or the government will lock us up again. Those seem to be your only triggers."

Davin pushed a long strand of brown hair over my shoulder. "That's why I tried so hard to keep you from me. The fears of my world are the only things that paralyze you."

My brow furrowed as I perched on his long, hard legs.

He was right. I knew it. He knew it. For months, my worsening anxiety, poor sleep and diet, and shrinking weight had been a major contention in our relationship. It was why he'd kept me at arm's length for almost the entirety of my knowing him. He'd been trying to protect me in the only way he could—by distancing me from the dangers of his world.

"Are we going to argue about that again?" I said the words quietly but met his gaze and held it.

His eyes softened as he pulled me closer to him. "No. Never again. We're together from here on out, come what may, but I won't lie. It's hard for me to see you like that."

A scratching feeling entered the back of my mind. "Hold on. Sara's trying to get in touch."

I opened my connection with the twin and told her I was fine. *I just found out Zoe died. And I… uh, panicked.*

Sara's worry pushed through our bond. *I wondered if that's what I felt from you. So you're back in civilization then if you know?*

Yes. We got back less than an hour ago. I sat up straighter on Davin's lap. *Speaking of that, why didn't you tell me when Zoe died?*

You're the only person who could have contacted us.

I sensed worry from her end, as if she were wringing her hands. *I wanted to. Believe me, I did, but I also promised Davin I wouldn't bother you guys.*

I shot Davin a surprised look.

He merely raised his eyebrows, obviously oblivious to what Sara just revealed.

I sighed. I wasn't surprised Davin had asked Sara to not disturb us, but I was surprised that she actually listened to him. Turning my attention back to the twin, I asked, *Was it hard to stay quiet?*

Sooooo hard. I'm so glad you're back.

Sara and I spoke for a few more minutes. I could tell she was as worried as me about what Zoe's death meant for our country. After promising I'd be in touch soon, we shut down our connection.

Davin's hands roamed up and down my back, soothing away the remaining residue of panic that had wrapped its suffocating tentacles around me. "How is she?"

"As worried as me." I leaned against him. "I can't believe Zoe's really dead. And you know this won't end quietly. Someone will pay for her exposure. We both know that. And most likely, the public and government will blame you and every other Kazzie."

His hands stilled for the briefest second before resuming. Taking a deep breath, his voice caught. "I know."

I shook my head. "But it can't be *Makanza* that killed her. It just… can't be!"

I couldn't bear the thought of that idea. That the research my colleagues and I had conducted wasn't sound. That we were to blame for Zoe Mathison's death. Because even though the Kazzies had been the scapegoats for so many perils in this country, they weren't to blame for Zoe's death if it truly *was* related to the virus.

I was to blame.

The MRI was.

The government was.

All of us had convinced the public to release the Kazzies, telling the American people that they were safe to live among us.

I pushed up from Davin and began pacing my living room. Surprisingly, my shoulder and wound didn't ache despite the quick movements.

"Obviously, people are fearful that *Makanza* killed Zoe, but I know that's not the case. I'm 100% certain the vaccine is as effective as we say it is. Something else killed that poor girl. Now, we need to figure out what."

Davin still sat on the floor. He drew his knees up and clasped his arms casually around them. Strong, sinewy muscles rippled in his forearms.

I averted my gaze. The sight was incredibly distracting.

"And how do you propose to do that?" he asked.

"We'll need an autopsy at the very minimum. I'm assuming the MRI has already dispatched a team to Chicago Children's. Most likely, they've been there this entire time." I groaned. "Of course, since I've been banned from work due to my injury, I wouldn't know."

I paused. The swishing movements that my feet had made on the carpet stopped with me. Quiet surrounded us. Biting my lip, a plan started to form in my mind.

"Meghan..." Davin's tone was low and warning. "I've seen that look before, and I'm not sure I like it. What are you up to?"

I sank onto the floor beside him and placed a hand on his

arm. Rock hard muscles flexed beneath my grasp.

"I know you're not going to like this, neither is Dr. Sadowsky for that matter, but I have to return to work. I've healed substantially in the past week, thanks to you, but now..." I shook my head. "With Zoe dying, I can't sit at home. Even though I love being with you, I *have* to help find a cure and figure out what killed that poor girl."

"Dammit, Meghan," he said quietly. "You're still hurt. You can't work right now. How can you not see that?"

"Davin. Please." My tone was quiet and pleading. "Please don't fight with me on this."

Anguish contorted his features. "How can I not? I love you, and you're hurt. *Really* hurt, Meg. It's not like a scratch that will heal in a few days. You *shattered* a rib. That's a serious injury. And even worse, the reason you're hurt is because of me. And now, you want to return to the Compound and start working every day of the week even though you're still not fully functioning."

He shook his head when he saw my expression. "No, don't give me that look. You know as well as I do what your schedule will be like if you want to find a cure. And you're asking me to say it's okay, but I can't. It's *not* okay."

My gaze dropped to the floor. I nodded and bit my lip tightly. "It's fine. You're angry. I get it. I probably would be too in your shoes, but I can't sit at home. I just can't."

Warm, large hands covered mine. "You don't have to sit at home forever. Just wait another month and then go back to work." He brushed a strand of hair off my cheek. "Please, babe. Don't put me in this position. I want to support you, but watching you kill yourself..." He shook his head and sighed harshly. "It kills me to see it."

"I get it. It's okay." Pushing awkwardly to a stand, I turned so he wouldn't see the pain that threatened to overwhelm me. "I'm still returning to work, but if you want to go back to Rapid City so you don't have to watch, I understand."

Inside, it felt like my heart was ripping to pieces. More than anything, I wanted Davin at my side, but I wasn't going to beg him. Especially if it would lead to more fights and arguments between us.

In a lightning-fast move, Davin was standing and blocking my path. My breath caught at the abrupt movement.

Tilting my chin upward, he cursed under his breath when he saw the fresh tears brimming my eyes. In a deft movement, he locked his arms around me.

My throat tightened. I wanted to sink into and lean on him, but I didn't. I hated that we were arguing right now, but I wasn't going to back down.

I needed to join Division 5.

It was the only way if I wanted a cure.

Davin's chest rose and fell heavily with each breath, but he didn't let go. It felt like he was warring with something inside himself from the tense way he stood.

Finally, he said gruffly, "I'm not leaving you. I can only imagine the state you'd be in if you try to do this alone."

I swallowed the lump in my throat. His words should have caused me to jump for joy, but I heard the anger in them, the quiet resentment.

That wasn't something I could handle right now. Having Davin at my side could be heaven or hell. And if it was hell, I didn't think I'd be able to bear it.

Fighting back more tears, I said quietly, "But I don't want to fight you, Davin. Not about this. If I join Division 5, I'll probably be working non-stop. I won't have the energy to fight you."

My breath felt shallow as I waited for his response.

At least twenty seconds ticked by.

"So I'm either with you or against you. Is that it?"

My head snapped up at the teasing tone in his voice. Relief flooded me when I saw the small smile tugging his lips up.

Laughing quietly, I shrugged. "Kind of. I want you by my side so bad it hurts but not if we're going to fight every day. I don't want us to turn into that."

He tenderly brushed a lock of hair from my face. "You're doing this one way or another, aren't you? It doesn't matter what I say. I can't talk you out of it."

"Yes. I'm going back to work."

Crushing me against him, his arms tightened even more. "Okay, then I'm coming with you. I couldn't bear to be apart from you, not again, but I won't lie. It's not going to be easy watching you work yourself to death, but I'd rather be by your side. At least then, I can take care of you. If the last year is any predictor of what's to come, I know you're not going to put yourself first."

My heart sped up at the thought of him staying. "Do you promise you're not going to fight with me about this anymore?"

His hands tightened around my waist for the merest second before he took a deep breath. "I can't promise, but I'll try."

AFTER DAVIN LEFT to retrieve our bags from the car and unpack, I picked up my phone and dialed Cate. Her voice had sounded so shaky in her message. So unlike her.

She answered on the first ring. "Meghan? Is that really you?"

"Yes, sorry. I just got your message."

Cate sighed heavily. "No, that's all right. I'm glad to hear from you. You're usually so prompt at replying."

Guilt crept up my neck at her worried tone. "I'm sorry. I was away for the week and turned my phone off."

Silence followed. When Cate finally spoke, surprise lined her words. "Your phone was off the *entire* time?"

"Yes. Dr. Sadowsky insisted I take some time off."

"How are you feeling? And more importantly, how are you healing?"

"I'm fine." I didn't mention my panic attack. Instead, I concentrated on the week Davin and I had away. "The… uh… last week has been pretty relaxing. I'm feeling a hundred times better."

Cate sighed in relief. "Good, because we're going to need you regardless of the restrictions Dr. Sadowsky placed on you. In fact, that may work to our advantage since you're not needed at Compound 26 right now. I'm sure you've heard of Zoe Mathison's death? Senator Douglas, that bastard, is using that family's tragedy to terrify the public. It's creating a public relations nightmare."

My stomach plummeted. "Does anyone know what caused her death?" I held my breath. It was silly. I *knew* it wasn't *Makanza*, yet worry still plagued me. Perhaps something had gone drastically wrong with the vaccine she'd been administered. All vaccine batches had been triple checked, yet the possibility of an error was still possible. As unlikely as that was.

In which case, more people will present with symptoms and die.

I shook that thought off before it could run away with me. Those safety measures had been put in place during the vaccine's creation for the sole purpose of avoiding something just like Zoe's death.

Tapping came from Cate's end, as if she were drumming her fingers on her desk. "As of now, it's still unclear why Zoe died. It doesn't help that the family is forbidding an autopsy."

"*What?* Why?"

"I know. It's crazy, but they're insistent we leave the body alone. They don't want her body cut into."

As much as my heart hurt for Zoe's family, I couldn't stop my next question. "But how can that be allowed when public safety is in question?"

"It can't. That's exactly why I've been called to look into it. Someone at Chicago Children's isn't doing their job despite the MRI's involvement, so I'm leaving for Chicago within the hour."

"Zoe died yesterday, right?"

"That's right. She passed away at 9:43 yesterday morning."

"So if an autopsy is allowed we could have answers within a day to weeks depending on what they find."

"Yes, which means the sooner the autopsy is started, the better."

Given Cate was traveling to Chicago, I knew she'd be busy, but as usual, she didn't leave me empty-handed.

"Will you help me handle the media? The public knows and trusts you. We need your face for this."

Sweat erupted along my brow. *Public speaking again?*

"Relax, it's not as bad as you think." Cate's soothing words strummed through the phone line. "I need you in Des Moines at ANN headquarters tomorrow for an interview. Can you get there by early afternoon so you're ready for their evening news slot? They'd also like you to spend the night so you can appear on their morning show the following day."

"Just two interviews? For the evening and morning show? That's it?"

"That's right. Only two. Even with your injuries, I figured it wouldn't be too taxing."

I took a deep breath. I'd do it for my friends. "Okay, I'll be there. Since it's only a four-hour drive to Des Moines we should arrive in plenty of time for the evening interview."

"Thank you." Cate's voice softened. "I always know I can count on you."

Hearing the relief in her words only reaffirmed that my reprieve from work had truly ended. As much as I knew Davin didn't approve of my plans, I couldn't sit at home while a public health crisis unfolded around us.

After Cate and I hung up, I called my parents to let them know I was okay, and then Amy to see how things were going at the Compound.

From there, I studied the unknown number on my phone. A voicemail waited from it. Frowning, I tapped the screen.

"Meghan, it's Makayla, Bethany's sister. We met when my sister came to you for help." She paused and sniffled. *"Sorry… it's been an emotional week, but would you please call me? Bethany… she did something she shouldn't have. Please call me if you can."*

She rattled off her phone number.

My heart rate accelerated as I peeked over my shoulder. Davin was in the bathroom taking a shower. The sound of running water filled my apartment.

With a shaky finger, I tapped in Makayla's number. She answered on the third ring.

"Meghan? Is that you?"

"Yes, it's me. I just got your message. Is Bethany okay?"

A quiet sob came from Makayla's end. "No, she's not."

I gripped the phone harder. "Why? What happened?

"After we visited you and talked to that doctor at the Compound, we drove back to Minneapolis. Your boss told us to go home since there was nothing to be done right now. I knew it could take a while before you found a cure, and I thought Bethany knew that too, but then the news started talking about that little girl in Chicago, and I think Bethany panicked. She…" Another sob came.

"What? What did she do?"

"She found some local doctor and asked him to do surgery on her. I didn't even know until the clinic called me yesterday from the operating room." She laughed hysterically. "And I thought she'd gone out to see some old friends."

My stomach dropped. *Operating room?*

Makayla sobbed again. "She almost died on the operating table, just like your doctor said she could."

"She really tried to have *surgery?*"

"Yeah, even though your doctor warned her not to!"

"Where is she? Is she okay?" My voice rose with each word.

"She's still in the hospital. They said it will take a few weeks for her to heal from the cuts they did trying to remove her wings. I guess they cut her pretty deep. But when she started bleeding, they called off the operation."

I closed my eyes. Blood pounded in my ears. *Why, Bethany? Why did you do it?*

But I already knew the answer.

She was desperate.

And when I couldn't help her, she'd taken matters into her own hands.

Movement in my peripheral vision caught my attention. Davin stood quietly in the hallway, a towel wrapped around his waist. His intense blue eyes burned brightly.

Bringing my attention back to the conversation, I said, "Tell Bethany that we're doing everything we can to find a cure, and she'll be the first to know when we do."

Makayla replied shakily, "Yeah, yeah, I'll tell her."

After we hung up, I dropped my phone at my side. I still had a few messages to listen to, but at the moment, I couldn't.

In a flash, Davin's arms were around me, and he was pulling me to his chest. Drops of water still clung to him, dampening my shirt.

He held me as quiet tears trailed down my cheeks.

"Bethany almost died, Davin. And all because we couldn't help her." I relayed what Makayla had told me, how Bethany had sought out a doctor willing to try surgery despite Dr. Fisher's warning.

"Shhh…" He ran a hand down my back. "You're not responsible for what she did. She knew the risk."

"But she's so desperate, and a cure would fix it. She wouldn't need surgery then."

He merely held me as my heart bled for all that Bethany had gone through.

I wasn't sure how long we sat like that, but as the minutes ticked by, my tears slowly dried. Taking a deep breath, I pulled myself back together. His arms loosened when I picked my phone back up.

"I better see who else called." I showed him the other messages waiting in my inbox.

He kissed me softly on the neck before gently picking me up and placing me on the couch. "I'll get dressed and start making dinner. It's almost five."

"Oh… right." Once again, I'd completely forgotten about eating.

In a blurred move, Davin was dressed and in the kitchen. From the sounds of it, his movements didn't slow during any of it.

I blinked when Davin appeared again. He sat on the couch, watching me. His azure gaze followed my every move. Delicious scents from the dinner he'd prepared carried from the kitchen.

I cocked my head at him.

He leaned forward. "It's in the oven. It'll be ready in an hour."

Once again, his sheer power and speed took my breath away. Only five minutes ago, he'd left to start dinner.

"I was just about to call the twins. Should we video call them?"

He smiled. "Yeah. We can talk to my mom too."

Sara answered the phone call immediately and quickly called for Sharon and Sophie to join her.

Since we used the video feed, Davin and I were able to see the three of them as they crowded around the twin's phone. Behind Sharon were the old oak cabinets in her kitchen. It appeared she and the twins had piled around the kitchen table while Sara held her phone in front of her.

Sharon's auburn hair was swept into a bun. Tendrils framed her face. Like Davin, her eyes were large and electric blue. But her normally warm demeanor was absent. Worry had etched itself into her expression.

The twins were no different. Forced smiles flashed across their blue-skinned faces. Silky, blond hair covered their heads, but each styled it differently. Sara's hair was pulled back in a ponytail while Sophie's was loose and hanging around her shoulders.

"It's good to see you're back. It's been a... uh... eventful week." Sara's smile grew even tighter.

"Yeah, I can imagine," Davin replied grimly.

Biting her lip, Sophie asked, "So what does Zoe's death

mean? Will we be locked up again?"

"No!" My reply was immediate and absolute. "It's impossible that *Makanza* killed Zoe."

The twins shared a worried look.

"But that's not what the news is saying." Sara frowned. "And that senator said we should be locked up again."

My heart pounded harder at the fear in her words. "He can't. It's against the law."

"But if they overturn the law…" Sharon pressed her lips firmly together. "But no, they can't do that. They just can't!"

I wanted to reassure them more, to tell them that this would all blow over and nothing would come of it, but the reality was—I didn't know if it would.

"I'm going to Des Moines tomorrow to appear on ANN. With any luck, I'll be able to help ease some of the tension this has caused."

"I hope you can." Sophie's words sounded small. "Because I can't go back to Reservation 1 or Compound 26, Meghan. I just can't."

10 – APPEAL

When morning came, I woke at my usual time as Davin slumbered beside me. I crept out of the bedroom so I wouldn't disturb him. With any luck, I'd be back not long after he woke.

I hadn't slept well during the night. Thoughts of Bethany kept plaguing me as did the twins' worry and Sharon's fallen expression. I needed to help all of them, and the only way to do that was to stop *Makanza* once and for all.

And while helping Cate with public relations was a step in the right direction, the only way I could truly stop *Makanza* was if I joined Division 5. And the only one who could grant that admission was Dr. Sadowsky.

My apartment door creaked closed as I snuck out. My plan was to find Amy and learn as much as I could about Division 5 before approaching my boss to see if he'd let me join.

The sky was still dark when I drove down the access road toward the Compound. I wasn't sure what to expect as I approached the main gates. Two weeks hadn't passed, and since Dr. Sadowsky stated I wasn't allowed to work until then, I wasn't sure if I'd be admitted.

Biting my lip, I rolled down my window apprehensively. Cold wind blew into my car when I pulled up to the first checkpoint. In the dark, the snow looked like gray mounds glittering in the moonlight.

An MRRA security guard stepped forward and bent down. A bulky parka covered him along with the standard hat and gloves that all MRRA officers wore.

When he pulled down his scarf, my eyes widened. "Sergeant Rose!"

"Dr. Forester!" Davin's former guard's surprise mirrored mine. "I didn't expect to see you here."

"I didn't expect to see you either." I shivered as another cold gust hit me. "I've never seen you at the perimeter. Did you transfer departments?"

"No. I'm just covering for another guard. It's been a while since I've done a perimeter night shift in the dead of winter. I think I'm too old for this." He laughed.

I smiled at his joke. "It's a bit different than the warm watch room."

"Or your lab." He cocked his head as the heat kicked on from my dash. Wrinkles lined his middle-aged face. "Speaking of which, are you supposed to be working in your lab right now?"

I ducked my head. "Technically, no."

"That's what I thought. I heard you were banned."

Crap. "Am I not allowed in?"

"Nothing that extreme, but we were directed to alert Dr. Sadowsky if you showed up."

Double crap. "How much time do I have before he knows?"

Winking, he replied, "Let's just say I won't send a message for another twenty minutes. That should buy you enough time to reach the lab."

He took my purse to search and then scanned my access badge. After he finished the admittance procedure, he leaned against the roof of my car. "You look like you're feeling all right, are you?"

"Yes, I'm much better. I haven't taken any pain meds today."

"I'm glad to hear that. I couldn't believe the news when I heard you were shot. I always thought Dr. Roberts was a bad guy, but I never thought he'd go that far. I'm just glad you're okay." Shaking his head, he added, "Speaking of that, have you heard from Davin? Do you know how he's doing?"

The curiosity in Sergeant Rose's tone was genuine. Since he'd been Davin's Monday through Friday daytime guard for almost seven years, he'd spent plenty of time with the Kazzie. And last year, when I'd desperately tried every means possible to break through Davin's walls, Sergeant Rose had been the one to help.

I shaded my eyes when I looked up at the guard. The bright perimeter lights above cut through the night. If anyone employed by the Compound cared for Davin, it was Sergeant Rose. I knew I could tell him the truth. "Yes, I've heard from him. He's… uh… actually at my apartment right now."

I expected shock or disbelief to roll across the guard's face.

Instead, his expression brightened. "That's the best news I've heard all year. So you two are together now?"

"Yes. As of last week, it's official."

"Good. If any two people are meant to be, it's you two."

"So you'll keep our little secret?" I still didn't know how the MRI would react if they knew I'd become romantically involved with my former research subject.

All joking left Sergeant Rose's demeanor. "I'll take that secret to my grave."

"I knew you would."

Shivering again, I was about to say goodbye and roll up my window when Sergeant Rose added, "Say, Meghan. Do you think Davin would be up for a visit from me? Maybe I could... I don't know, go and see him today?"

I smiled. "Yes, actually, I think he would enjoy that very much." I rattled off my apartment's address and how to get there. "When do you get off work?"

"The night shift ends in thirty minutes."

It was almost seven in the morning and considering Davin didn't know anyone in Sioux Falls except me, I didn't think he had plans to go anywhere.

"I imagine he'll still be in my apartment when you get off. I'll send him a message to make sure he stays there. I'm sure you two have a lot to catch up on."

"We do. Thanks, Meghan."

Sergeant Rose and I said goodbye, and I hastily typed in a text to Davin before pulling forward and hurrying to park and reach my lab. Even though the guard wouldn't report my admittance for twenty minutes, I knew it was only a matter of time before Dr. Sadowsky cornered me.

When I reached the lab, the door swung open with a hiss. I stepped onto the metal platform overlooking the lab below. Only Amy was working, but Charlie and Mitch would probably arrive within the hour.

Holding the railing, I took the steps easily but wasn't able to jog down them like I usually did. While I was getting better, running was still out of the question.

"Meghan!" Amy's red curls swished around her shoulders when she looked up from her lab station.

Our lab's twenty-foot tall white walls towered around us. Lab benches and equipment filled the area.

"What the heck are you doing here? You know you're not supposed to be back at work yet."

"I know." I dropped my purse on the bench. Considering I could be kicked out at any minute, I hadn't wasted time stopping at my office to drop it off. "Which means we need to talk fast. Tell me everything you know about Division 5."

Amy grinned. "I was wondering when you'd want to know more about it." She snapped her gloves off and propped her hip against the bench. "They've begun recruiting more scientists. Dr. Sadowsky asked if I wanted to be one of them."

My eyes bulged. "Really? Where are they stationed?"

"California. Compound 3 has been the main facility since the group began."

My eyes widened. "You're moving to California?"

Amy's smile broadened. "Yep, for a while at least. We're flying there in the MRI plane next week."

My heart beat faster at how quickly things were moving. "So who are the other researchers in Division 5, and why has it been kept a secret?"

Amy rolled her eyes. "From what I've heard, they didn't want the Kazzies or public knowing. If they *did* know, that could have prevented the Kazzies' release since the public may have insisted a cure be found first. As for who's involved… Compound 3 is where this all went down. They have a small team of MSRG scientists—only five of them, hence Division *five*. But now that the secret's blown, the team is drastically expanding. Those of us chosen to join the team are heading to California next week."

"And what have they discovered so far?"

"That, I don't know yet."

I bit my lip. *Two weeks will have passed by the time Amy and Dr. Sadowsky fly out.* "Do you think Dr. Sadowsky would be open to me joining Division 5 too?"

She arched an eyebrow. "That's a good question. I guess the only way to find out is to ask him."

FIVE MINUTES LATER, Amy and I were sailing down the halls on the way to see our boss.

"Do Mitch and Charlie know about Division 5?" My words sounded excited. Just the mention of the secret group created a hum of anticipation in me.

"Yeah, it's not classified anymore, so I told them the same day I told you." Amy's feet tapped on the floor as we trailed through the never-ending white corridors.

"Will Mitch and Charlie be involved? And do you have any idea how Division 5 will be run now that everyone in the MRI knows about it?"

"Nope, Mitch and Charlie weren't invited, and I don't really know any more than what I've told you. Maybe Dr. Sadowsky can enlighten us."

We rounded the corner to the elevators. For the most part, I'd walked at a normal pace. My chest didn't hurt except for a slight twinge when I reached for the elevator button.

Within a few weeks, I'll be back to normal.

Two other researchers waited in the elevator area beside us. I managed a thin smile when they eyed me curiously. When one leaned down to whisper to the other, I knew they recognized me.

I scoffed. *Everyone* in Compound 26 recognized me, even more so than the general public.

"Yeah, yeah." Amy rolled her eyes. "It's Dr. Meghan Forester. It's not like you've never seen her before or that we don't hear your whispers."

I smothered a smile. Leave it to Amy to call out the

elephant in the room.

Following Amy's comment, the researcher stood straighter and cleared his throat awkwardly. His co-worker smiled as his cheeks turned pink. The ding of the elevator saved all of us from further embarrassment.

"Gentlemen, have a lovely morning." Amy smiled sweetly as we stepped into the elevator.

I kept my gaze averted and joined her.

We took the elevators to the fourth floor. Dr. Sadowsky's office was on the south side of the Compound. Emma, his secretary, greeted us with narrowed eyes when we approached her desk.

"Dr. Forester." Her frosty glaze slid over me. "I believe you are supposed to be *off* work resting right now." Her tone reminded me of our first encounter—when I'd called Dr. Sadowsky repeatedly after being fired from the Compound last year. However, he'd never answered my incessant phone calls, Emma had.

"Hi, Emma." I subtly glanced at my watch. Over twenty minutes had passed since I'd been admitted. No doubt, Sergeant Rose had alerted the Director to my whereabouts by now.

As if on cue, the Director's door opened. Dr. Sadowsky shook his head when he saw me.

"Meghan, I see that you're once again defying my orders." He stood ramrod straight. As usual, he wore a business suit and silk tie—his tall, elegant manner was unfailingly intact. At over six feet with graying hair and sharp blue eyes, he was striking.

But while his words were direct, his gaze swept over my injury with worry. Despite his annoyed disapproval, I knew he had my best interests at heart.

I stepped closer. "I'm much better now, and honestly, I didn't come here to work today. I'd simply like to be updated on Division 5. It seemed talking to you and Amy in person would be more effective than a phone call. If you can spare a few minutes, I'll then be on my way."

His eyebrows rose. "You'll be leaving, as in *going home to rest* as soon as you're updated on Division 5?"

I twisted my hands. "Yes."

It wasn't a complete lie. I *would* be home for the rest of the morning before Davin and I left for Des Moines. And it wasn't like the interview with ANN was entirely work-related since it was to help Cate, not Compound 26, but it was still mostly work-related. Still, I knew the Director wouldn't approve, so I kept Cate's and my future plans to myself.

"Very well." He stepped aside and ushered us into his office. "I can spare a few minutes. Amy, I take it you're the one who informed Meghan about Division 5?"

"I did." She pushed a strand of red, curly hair behind her ear. Glittering green eyes, now filled with worry, shifted my way. "I was told it was no longer confidential."

Dr. Sadowsky closed the door behind us, thankfully. I could still feel Emma's piercing gaze needling into my back.

"That's correct. I was simply curious who'd informed her. I knew once you found out, Meghan, that you would inevitably be interested in returning to work, especially given the recent news stories." He gestured to the deep-seated armchairs in front of the bookcase by the large windows.

The Director's office was huge. It was easily five hundred square feet with floor to ceiling windows overlooking the snowy prairies below. The sun had finally risen. Gray clouds filled the sky, giving a heavy oppressive feeling to the land. The world outside appeared bleak, reminding me of old black-and-white movies set during the Great Depression.

After settling on the chair, I rested my hands in my lap. "So what can you tell me about Division 5?"

Dr. Sadowsky crossed his legs and steepled his hands. "It's comprised of a very small team of five MSRG scientists."

I bit my lip. "And what have they discovered to date?"

"I don't have the specific details, but the latest brief indicated the most recent generation drug is showing vast potential in the trials done on mice. It's possible they'll begin human trials within the month."

My eyes bulged at the same time Amy's mouth dropped.

"They're that close?" I asked.

"Perhaps. We'll know more when we arrive."

"About that..." I leaned forward in my chair. "I was wondering if I could join you. It will have been two weeks by the time you fly out."

My boss sighed. "I figured that's the real reason you came."

"I'll be fine by then, I'm sure of it," I said in a rush. "Already, I'm feeling a hundred times better, and I know the virus' makeup better than anyone. I'm sure I can be an asset to the team."

I held my breath as I waited for his response.

Dr. Sadowsky's brow furrowed. He leaned back in his chair. It squeaked quietly. "You do seem to be moving better from the report I was told..."

"I am, and I haven't taken pain meds in two days. I'll be 100% by next week, I'm sure of it."

He sighed heavily. "Very well, but I'll need a doctor's note stating that you're fit to return to work."

A grin spread across my face as I nodded emphatically. "Of course, whatever you say."

Amy gave me the thumbs-up sign when our boss glanced away. From her expression, I knew she was as happy as me. I bit my lip. *But will Davin be?*

When we stood to leave, my mind spun with everything that Dr. Sadowsky had revealed. If they were close to human trials, then they'd already made a breakthrough with their current drugs.

We're already months ahead of anything I could have hoped for!

There was a spring in my step when we walked through the door. My thoughts drifted to my Kazzie friends as Amy turned to shake the Director's hand. Dorothy had tried repeatedly to lose weight. For months, she'd cut calories and exercised daily, but none of it worked. Strain 8 would never allow her to be thin.

She'll probably want a cure. It's not just Bethany who isn't happy with the Changes made in her. I should tell Dorothy and Bethany about the human trials so they can participate if they want. They could be two of the first Kazzies cured!

I pictured the other Kazzies, the ones who looked different. *They may want the cure too.* Not everyone was as lucky as Davin. Nobody would ever know he was a Kazzie unless they saw his mind-numbing speed or inhuman strength. It was easy for him to hide and blend in.

But the others...

The vast majority of Kazzies had been physically Changed by their strains. They stood out like neon-vested hunters in the woods. Most likely, none of them could venture outside without being stared upon.

"Meghan?"

"Hmm... what?" I snapped my head up.

Dr. Sadowsky and Amy both looked at me expectantly. *Crap. I missed something.* It wasn't the first time that had happened. Whenever I became consumed in my thoughts it was like the rest of the world shut-off.

Dr. Sadowsky clasped his hands behind his back. "I was just saying that I'll need your doctor's note before you're allowed to board the plane."

"Of course, I'll be sure to get one."

Dr. Sadowsky nodded curtly. "Then perhaps we'll see you next week."

With that, he walked us to the elevators before we parted ways. Back on the main floor, Amy accompanied me to my car. Even though she didn't have a coat, she still braved the bitter wind outside.

"That would be fantastic if you joined us!" Her green eyes glittered with excitement while a strong gust blew red curls around her shoulders.

It would be the first time Amy and I had ever traveled together to another Compound for work.

"It *would* be fun," I agreed. "I'd love to work with someone there who I know."

Just the thought of all the new directors and Makanza Survivor Research Group scientists made my palms sweat. Even though I'd been learning how to better manage my social anxiety, I still had my moments.

Amy waved me off after I slipped into my vehicle. My grin didn't fade during the entire ride home. Come next week at this time, I could be in sunny California working with a dedicated team of scientists to find a cure.

The thought of Bethany's expression, when I invited her to the human trials, made my smile stretch even wider. But my smile disappeared as I remembered Zoe. If anyone else died before we found a cure, it could be too late—the public could turn completely against us and no cure would help that.

11 – THE INTERVIEW

The roads were mostly clear on our drive to Des Moines. Davin drove while I leaned back in the front passenger seat. Memories of our brief trip down south fluttered through my mind, like leaves falling on an autumn day. They brought a smile to my face.

"What are you thinking about?" Davin glanced over as we sped by snowy fields on the two-lane highway. As usual, he wore a t-shirt and jeans. Not even South Dakota's fiercest winters diminished his heat.

"Just our trip last week. Driving like this reminds me of it."

Strong muscles rippled in his forearms as he gripped the wheel. "You do know that was the first trip of many, right? As long as I stay free, we'll have years ahead of us to explore this country."

A chill settled over me, dimming my good mood. "It's not *as long as*. You *will* stay free."

The thought of him not being with me, of not having him at my side... I couldn't think of it. Just the idea of him locked up again… My hands shook.

Taking deep breaths, I gripped my knees.

He placed his large, warm palm over mine. It felt so good. Already, my fingers were ice. "Sorry. I didn't mean to worry you."

I shrugged the feeling off. "It's okay, but that's why we're taking this trip, right? To assure the public that Zoe Mathison couldn't have died from *Makanza*. Something else killed her."

Biting my lip, I stared out the window. When Davin began to remove his hand, I grabbed it and held it between the two of mine. I needed him close right now. As much as I wanted to believe that our future was secure, I wasn't naïve. Without a cure, every Kazzie was at risk of future imprisonment if public hysteria grew too strong.

At least he's coming to California with me. We won't be apart. I'd told Davin about my meeting with Dr. Sadowsky this morning. While Davin was resigned to me joining Division 5, I knew he still wasn't happy about it. *But he's going to come. He'll be at my side.*

When my heart finally felt like it beat steadily, I let go of Davin. "So how was your visit with Sergeant Rose?"

A hint of a smile ghosted his lips. "Good. Really good, actually. It was nice to see him again."

"You two certainly spent a lot of time together." As Davin's Monday-Friday daytime guard, Sergeant Rose had been with Davin consistently during his seven-year imprisonment within Compound 26.

"We did. Too bad I spent so many of those years ignoring him." He laughed.

The sound warmed me. It was good to see that Davin had let go of the rage that had consumed him when we'd first met. I knew Sergeant Rose had helped with that. It seemed at times that the middle-aged guard and I were the only ones within the MRI who truly cared about Davin's well-being.

"He has a lot of respect for you."

Davin glanced over as we sailed around a turn in the road. "I have a lot of respect for him too."

His gaze grew distant, and I could only imagine what memories he was reliving.

Since he seemed lost in his thoughts, I pulled out my phone and tapped in a familiar number.

Cate should be in Chicago by now. With any luck, she'd give me an update on how progress was coming with the autopsy. Once the autopsy started, it was only a matter of days, possibly longer, before we knew what really killed Zoe Mathison.

"I was wondering when I'd hear from you."

Cate's brisk tone made me smile. "You're in Chicago?"

"I arrived last night. I'm at the hospital now and am about to meet with the family."

I sat up straighter. "Do you know yet why the autopsy hasn't been conducted?"

She made a guttural noise, almost like a growl in frustration. "The coroner said he was specifically instructed by the CEO of the hospital to not conduct the autopsy against the parent's wishes. As for why the CEO would instruct that, I have yet to uncover."

"So does this mean the autopsy is now underway?"

"It will be shortly. I'm going to talk to the parents first, but we'll start it this afternoon with or without their consent."

I rested my head back against the seat. "I hope they take it okay."

"They'll have to," Cate replied grimly. "Whether they like it or not, they don't have a choice in the matter."

WE REACHED DES Moines an hour later. America News Network's headquarters was located on the south side of the city. The building was large yet simple. Glass windows interweaved the steel structure. The modern design contrasted with the older brick buildings across the street and the ancient diner on the corner.

Davin glided the car into a parking spot. Biting my lip, my gaze traveled across the snowy lot. Around thirty other cars filled the spaces—evidence of the network's small size. While ANN was our national news station now, after the fall of the major networks during the First Wave, it was by no means a powerful corporation. Most nights and mornings, it was one of two newscasters. And the correspondents who traveled to areas of the country for news coverage weren't more than half a dozen.

So much had changed in the past ten years.

"Who do you check in with?" Davin asked after cutting the motor.

"I'm supposed to go to the main desk by three this afternoon."

It was just after two.

"We're early." Davin rested his elbow on the windowsill. "Do you want to check into the hotel first?"

"No, I'd rather know what I'm getting into. Let's see if they can provide a list of questions I'll be asked. With any luck, I can have rehearsed answers for the segment tonight."

"Do you want me to come in with you?"

My hand stilled on the door handle. We were about to enter the largest news station our country now had. Davin was a Kazzie. It was inevitable some of ANN's reporters had seen him before when reporting on the reservation.

He leaned closer and tucked a strand of hair behind my

ear. "I can see those wheels churning in your mind. I'm guessing you're also debating if it's wise for us to be associated together here."

I relaxed under his feathery touch as my eidetic memory roared to life. Memories flashed through my mind with images of reporters that had traveled to Reservation 1. Scenes filled my mind, like snapshots from a camera. With lightning speed, my brain filtered through them.

When I felt confident that I'd identified each ANN reporter to have ever seen Davin and me at the perimeter, I smiled. "Only two were present on the occasions we were together near the fence. Neither is local. Both are affiliates who only report on long-distance news stories."

He shook his head in amazement. "Unbelievable. How did I snag a genius for a girlfriend?"

I laughed as cold wind blew into the car when I opened my door.

He unbuckled his seatbelt and stepped out of the car.

It was a briskly cold walk to the door. I kept my head down and scarf pulled up.

Davin hurried ahead. While he moved fast, he didn't turn into a blur. Who knew if anyone inside was watching.

He had the door open when I reached the entrance. Gliding into the entryway, he stepped ahead of me at the last moment and opened the second set of double doors.

ANN's entry opened to a high-ceilinged spacious lobby. Black tiles covered the floor, a curved desk waited directly ahead, and potted ferns filled the shaded corners. A hint of fresh paper smell hung in the air, while a subtle hum from the heating system reached my ears. The adjacent walls were covered with windows, allowing natural light to spew in.

At the curved desk, two receptionists worked. Directly

behind them was a solid, freestanding wall with the large letters *ANN* printed on it. Several awards hung below it.

Each woman wore headphones with attached microphones. Their fingers flew across their keyboards while they stared at computer screens. A shrill call rang on the main line, getting a jump out of me. One absently reached for it and clicked a button before bringing her hand to her headset.

The other continued tapping away on her keyboard.

Since both seemed busy, I hovered a few feet back and waited patiently.

Davin, however, boldly stepped forward and rested his forearms on the tall receptionist desk. He then drummed his fingers, the tapping loud enough to be heard over the receptionist's voice as she spoke to the caller.

The other woman glanced up. Her eyes widened when she saw Davin.

Davin still didn't seem aware of how he affected women. Since being freed from the reservation, and mending things with me, a new, playful side had emerged in him.

It was a side I loved since he didn't seem as dark or angry anymore. Instead, he was a tall, broad shouldered, devilishly handsome man who smiled much more readily. Couple that with cobalt blue eyes, raven black hair, and honey-hued skin tinged with fire, he was also drop-dead gorgeous.

Despite his looks, the most alluring aspect about Davin was that he had no idea how attractive he was. Right now, I imagined the receptionist's heart was fluttering inside her chest as she reached a hand up to smooth her hair.

An ache filled my belly at how much I loved him. It didn't occur to me to be jealous. I knew he was all mine, but it didn't stop me from wanting him as much as I did. Wanting him in a way that we hadn't experienced yet.

No sense in thinking about that. He may be more carefree now, but he's still just as stubborn. Until I'm fully healed, nothing is going to happen in that department.

The receptionist finally took her headset off and smiled brightly while her co-worker continued to take calls and work on her computer.

The woman's gaze stayed on Davin, never once shifting my way. "Yes, sir? How may I help you?"

Davin raised his eyebrows and gestured toward me. "I believe you should be asking Dr. Forester that question."

With a startled glance, as if just realizing someone else stood beside the tall, half-Lakota Sioux, her head turned my way.

Holding out my hand, I stepped forward. "I'm Dr. Meghan Forester. I'm a bit early, but I'm supposed to meet Rob Hansen this afternoon. I'm on the evening news show tonight."

The receptionist's eyes turned to saucers as she shook my hand.

"Yes, of course, Dr. Forester. Forgive me for not recognizing you right away. We're so pleased to have you join us. I'm so sorry I didn't attend to you immediately. Would you like a drink? Or may I take your coat?"

I shook my head. "No, that's fine."

The receptionist stood and smoothed her skirt. Her dark hair was pulled back in a bun. A clean, yet old business suit adorned her frame. I imagined it had been manufactured before the First Wave. However, it was in pristine condition, and from her groomed manner, she appeared to take care of her things.

Smiling politely, she said, "My name is Ms. Parkinson. I'll be happy to help you in any way I can. Now, if you'll follow me."

She handed me a pass to wear around my neck and then turned on her heel, gesturing to the airy, black-tiled walkway behind the receptionist area. "I'll show you to the room we have ready for you. You can make yourself comfortable there until the segment tonight, or you can leave and return later. That pass," she waved at what I wore, "gives you access within the building. Just make sure you're in your room by 3:30 p.m. Rob will stop by then."

We followed her around the curved desk and down the expansive hall to a set of stairs. Glass railings ran alongside the steel-beamed floating slabs. I gripped the railing tightly. The stairs gave the feeling that we were ascending on air.

Clearing my throat, I asked, "Will I be given the list of questions I'll be asked on the show tonight?"

The receptionist glanced over her shoulder just long enough to make eye contact. "Rob will be able to answer that for you. I'm afraid I don't have those details."

We reached the second floor. To our left ran another glass railing that opened to the main floor below. The sound of trickling water reached my ears. A fountain sat in the corner on the far end. It suddenly struck me that the entire building was eerily quiet. I also didn't see anyone else around.

"And if questions are asked that Meghan doesn't want to answer, how will that be handled?" Davin's deep voice held an edge to it. His hand rested on my lower back as we walked down another hall.

"Dr. Forester may refuse to answer any questions she's not comfortable with. We're extremely pleased that she agreed to our interview during this tumultuous time."

Or stupid enough. I imagined they'd grill me like no other. While I'd grown used to questions from fearful crowds, being one-on-one with a skilled journalist was another matter entirely.

I gripped my purse strap and pushed that worry aside. "Of course, I hope to set the record straight once and for all about poor Zoe Mathison. The virus didn't kill her."

The receptionist merely nodded.

Our footsteps turned mute when we rounded a corner and the tiles fell behind. Carpet lined this corridor.

We followed the receptionist through a set of double doors to a large studio. My eyes widened as the set for the ANN evening show appeared. Unlike the vacant hallways, this room was bustling with activity.

About a dozen behind-the-scenes workers were fiddling with cameras or sitting in front of multiple TV screens. All of them wore headsets. A few glanced up when we walked by and nodded in my direction. The MRI had done well at making my face easily recognized.

"We have you in guestroom B." Ms. Parkinson's heels tapped on the hard floor as we traveled through the room. "If you need anything between now and the show tonight, simply press the black button by the door and someone will attend to you."

After hopping over electrical cords and smiling at people we passed, Ms. Parkinson led us into another short hallway before stopping at the second door. The letter "B" was stenciled on it.

She opened the door with a flourish. "I hope this will do."

Inside were two couches, a small table sporting beverages and refreshments, and a large window that overlooked the snowy parking lot below. I felt certain it was a far cry from the suites the large networks had once furnished. Regardless, the room appeared clean, comfortable, and was more than I expected.

"Thank you, this is very nice." I dropped my purse on the couch and gripped my shaky hands together.

All of a sudden, it felt like a dozen butterflies flapped around in my stomach as icy cold sweat erupted on my brow. In a few hours, I'd be on national TV. *Deep breaths, Meghan.*

Davin stepped closer. His subtle scent of soap and aftershave drifted toward me. Circling his arm protectively around my shoulders, he pulled me to his side.

"Thank you very much, Ms. Parkinson. We'll be sure to push that button if we need anything." Davin's tone left no question that he wanted us left alone.

The receptionist nodded and discreetly closed the door behind her on her way out.

When it was just Davin and me, I sagged onto the sofa and dropped my head in my hands.

Davin kneeled down. "Meghan, look at me."

Liquid sapphire irises blazed into mine. "You're an experienced speaker, a gifted scientist, and the founder of the vaccine. Never forget who you are or all that you've accomplished."

I straightened and took a deep breath.

Hot palms closed over mine. Since his hands were so warm, that meant mine were ice. "You can do this. I know you can."

"Thank you for being here." His unwavering faith in me made my anxiety melt away like icicles in the springtime sun. Already, my hands felt warmer.

He squeezed. "Always. Although, it's a good thing nobody knows me here." He winked which got a chuckle out of me.

He shifted to sit beside me and place his arm around my shoulders. "I'll stay as long as you want. Just tell me what you need me to do."

"In all honesty, it'll probably be best if Rob doesn't see you. I don't want him asking questions about who you are. Now that I'm settled, and I don't feel like I'm going to freak out, do you want to go check us in to the hotel?"

"I can do that." He leaned closer and pressed his lips against mine.

I closed my eyes and instinctively tangled my fingers through his hair. It was silky soft and thick. Curling a few locks between my fingers, I pulled him closer. Only a small twinge from my injury followed.

He growled and deepened the kiss. He tasted as sweet as honey.

Despite our circumstances, desire flowed through my veins. For a moment, I let myself become lost in the kiss. The world around us disappeared. The feel of his hard chest pressed against mine made me ache on so many levels.

By the time he pulled back, his breathing was ragged. "Damn, woman. You're going to be the death of me."

I trailed my fingers across his chest. "Text me when you get to the hotel?"

He nodded and with one last peck on my mouth, whispered goodbye before leaving the room. A breeze from the door opening and closing rustled the tablecloth on the refreshment buffet.

Leaning back on the couch, I tried to distract myself with potential questions I'd be asked. Since it was only midafternoon, I still had several hours until the evening program. Ignoring the urge to stand and pace, I crossed my legs and pulled out my cell phone to call Cate.

She answered readily. I knew that meant her meetings were either over or she was in between them. "Meghan, how are you? Are you in Des Moines?"

"Yes, I arrived about twenty minutes ago. I'm currently in a guestroom in the ANN building. Rob Hansen should be arriving shortly to discuss our interview. How's everything in Chicago?"

"Well… it's been interesting. I met with Zoe's mother, but her father is nowhere to be found. Mrs. Mathison was upset and hard to console, but after I explained the importance of discovering what killed her daughter, she agreed to the autopsy."

I breathed a sigh of relief. "So you never had to force it upon her. I'm so happy to hear that."

"Exactly. She still believes that we would never have conducted it without her consent, and I'm happy to let her continue that belief."

I leaned forward as people walked by in the hall outside. Muffled voices came and then disappeared. *Obviously, not Rob Hansen.*

"So where's Zoe's father?" I asked.

Cate made a noncommittal noise. "No one knows. He was last seen yesterday evening. Even his wife doesn't know where he's gone. It's possible he's disappeared to avoid the public eye. It wouldn't be the first time a parent needed to distance themselves from a child's death."

Since I'd never lost a child, I couldn't relate, but I'd certainly witnessed enough families torn apart by death.

"Should we be worried that he's disappeared?" I asked.

"His wife said he did something similar during The First Wave after his brother died. He came back after a few days, so right now, I don't think there's cause for concern."

We spoke for a few more minutes as Cate filled me in on her agenda. I also told her about my plans to join Division 5 next week.

"That's excellent! They'll need you." Cate sounded as excited as I felt.

We hung up a few minutes later just as a text from Davin buzzed on my phone.

At the hotel and checked in. How's it going?

I tapped in a quick reply.

Fine so far. Just got off the phone with Cate. They began the autopsy in Chicago.

That's great news. Let's hope for some answers soon.

Exactly. I'll call you when I'm done here. Love you.

Love you too. x

My heart flipped at those three little words. I slid my phone back in my purse. As I was zippering it closed a knock sounded on the door.

Before I could reply, Rob Hansen strode in. A whiff of cologne came too.

He held out his hand and grinned. "Dr. Meghan Forester, it's a pleasure to finally meet you."

I hastily stood and grasped his large palm. He was even bigger in person. "Thank you. I'm glad to be here."

Rob pumped my hand. Thankfully, it didn't hurt.

With a smooth complexion, sandy blond hair, warm

brown eyes, and the all-American look, I could see why he'd risen in the ranks at ANN. Natural charisma practically oozed from him.

"Our receptionist told me that you'd like to know the questions I'll be asking you tonight." He waved toward the sofa. "Should we sit?"

Smoothing my pants, I sat back down.

He joined me, the cushion sinking beneath him. Looking around the room, he raised his eyebrows. "I hear that someone accompanied you here. Did he leave?"

I should have known that Davin's presence wouldn't go unnoticed. "Yes, he left to check into the hotel. It's just me now."

"A friend of yours?"

"Yeah. A friend." From Rob's expression, I knew he wanted to ask further questions, so I jumped in. "Can you tell me what I'll be asked tonight?"

He interlocked his fingers. "Tonight, I'd like our interview to be more like a discussion than a question-answer session. We'll review the virus, and the vaccine that you and the other scientists created. I'd then like to delve into Zoe Mathison, who she was, what happened to her, and why people believe the virus killed her."

I flinched. "The virus didn't kill her."

He raised his hands in surrender. "Whatever the truth may be, the public wants to know more about her exposure. I'd like to touch on that subject."

"Of course." I couldn't blame him. It was why I was here after all.

"The network's given us sixty minutes for this segment. If we don't need it all, we can fill in gaps with commercial breaks." Shifting closer, he smiled warmly. "The best thing you can do is stay relaxed and be yourself. Just think of me as an old friend that you're having coffee with, and I'll do my best to make you comfortable."

I nodded and forced a tight smile. Staying relaxed and acting natural were *not* my strong points, but this wouldn't be the first time I'd done something out of my comfort zone. *I can do this!*

We spoke for a few more minutes before he stood to leave. It was only when the door closed behind him that I realized he never provided me with a list of concrete questions.

For a moment, I debated pushing the black button but then decided against it. Rob seemed friendly and engaging. I would follow his lead and try to take his advice. Relax. Get comfortable. Try to think of him as an old friend.

Here goes nothing.

WHEN IT WAS time for me to join Rob on the evening show, a young woman came to my room to lead me out. I felt a bit like a doll following her. Hair and makeup had just visited. Consequently, my face felt like caked plastic. They'd applied so much concealer and powder, yet I had to admit they'd done a good job.

My skin looked flawless, while my eyes popped with the shadow and eyeliner they'd applied, and my lips were a dark berry red.

It's too bad Davin didn't stay. He probably wouldn't recognize me.

Using that thought to distract myself, I tried to ignore my fluttering stomach as we entered the studio. Two chairs sat on a raised section to the left of the main desk. Rob already sat on one as several workers fluttered around, powdering his nose and going through last minute notes with him.

When he saw me, he stood and pulled off the white paper from around his neck. "Dr. Forester. You look fantastic. How are you feeling?"

His warm hand closed over mine as he gestured to the vacant chair.

"I'm fine, Rob, thank you." My voice was steady and even. Pushing my remaining insecurity away, I sat down and smoothed my pants.

"We're starting in three minutes." One of the workers fumbled with her headset while checking her watch.

"Now, remember. Just relax and be yourself. You'll be fine." Rob grinned again and brushed off the remaining workers around him.

I folded my hands in my lap and took another deep breath. The chair shifted beneath me as I fidgeted. *Just relax, Meghan. It's just another interview.*

Three minutes passed as if it were seconds.

"And we're on in... three... two... one!"

The cameraman pointed at Rob as the light on his camera flashed red. Bright lights above filled the stage as Rob turned, a grin plastered on his face.

"Good evening, America and welcome to America News Nightly Show. I'm Rob Hansen." He angled his body to face a different camera. "Tonight I bring you an exclusive edition to our nightly show, featuring someone we've all come to know and trust during the previous months. Dr. Meghan Forester, renowned scientist and founder of the *Makanza* vaccine has joined us to discuss the tragic death of Zoe Mathison and what this unforeseen event means for our country."

Rob turned his somber expression toward me. "Welcome, Dr. Forester. We're so pleased to have you here to discuss these events during this tumultuous time."

I nodded tightly as sweat erupted on my brow under the harsh lights. "Thank you. It's my pleasure to be here."

Rob clasped his hands and leaned forward. "To start with, tell me more about the vaccine. How was it created, and why is the MRI so convinced it's 100% effective?"

My heart rate slowed at the familiar territory we approached. "As you probably know, the vaccine was developed after years of exhaustive research conducted by thousands of MRI scientists. Once we unlocked the secrets of *Makanza's* genome, we were able to formulate a vaccine using standard methods. Numerous trials were undertaken to assure its safety and effectiveness. And as you probably know, I along with hundreds of other MRI scientists, exposed ourselves to the virus long before the public was vaccinated. Our trust in the vaccine hasn't altered. I feel confident saying that Zoe's death was *not* linked to *Makanza.*"

Rob nodded, his expression contemplative. "But doctors have confirmed that Zoe was exposed to *Makanza*. How can you be so sure the virus didn't contribute to her death in some way?"

I frowned, debating how to word my answer. It was possible Zoe's immune system had been slightly compromised after being exposed to the virus. However, it wouldn't explain her death.

"Every drug trial we conducted assured us the vaccine is effective. Right now, we're working to determine the real cause of Zoe's death, and I'm sure once we do, the American public will see that the virus wasn't a contributing factor."

"That's interesting that you say that." Rob leaned back in his chair and steepled his hands. "Those who opposed the Kazzies being released say many Americans have fallen ill since being exposed, not just Zoe. Some even say that Zoe's death is the first of many, and that we should confine the Kazzies again before mass casualties ensue. What is your response to that?"

I bristled and sat up straighter. "While a mild flu-like response is to be expected after being exposed, the rest of those accusations are false. They're nothing more than vicious rumors from people with specific agendas that do *not* have the public's best interest at heart. I'd rather not fuel those inaccuracies by discussing them tonight."

His contemplative expression didn't waver as he asked me more questions about the vaccine. He grilled me on the drug trials and made me explain several times why the vaccine was so effective. And while I felt that he was genuinely interested in hearing about the vaccine's creation, I also had the subtle feeling that he was looking for a weak point. As if he wanted me to stumble and admit that we hadn't been as diligent as we'd claimed.

"I can assure you that every safety measure was considered during the vaccine's creation and the public's inoculation. We're all safe—I can promise you that."

Rob shifted in his seat and frowned. Just as he did, an ANN worker dressed entirely in black rushed onto the stage and placed another chair at my side. The worker was there and then gone, like a shadow in the night.

I eyed the empty chair and turned to Rob, my eyebrow arching in question.

But instead of telling me what was going on, Rob merely smiled wanly. "As much as I respect the work you've done for the MRI, I have to honor the public's wish to hear both sides of the story. That's why I'm now welcoming a new guest to the stage. Senator Douglas of Arkansas, please join us."

My eyes widened as my biggest rival stepped onto the platform. His heavy jowls jiggled when Rob shook his hand.

When he turned toward me, malice glowed from his narrowed eyes. "Dr. Forester. We meet again."

My mouth refused to work as a grin spread across his face.

12 - SURPRISE

The cameras stopped as they went to a commercial break. It didn't matter. I sat frozen in my chair. It was only my second face-to-face encounter with the senator—the first time being at the Summit in Washington D.C. last summer. At the Summit, the senator had sat in the audience and gloated over his ability to manipulate me during my speech.

His presence now only reminded me of that awful encounter.

My heart beat wildly, and my hands clenched into fists. The sharp edges of my nails cut into my palms.

I had never been told that Senator Douglas would be joining us tonight. Rob Hansen certainly had plenty of opportunities to inform me, but he hadn't.

So, not surprisingly, Rob Hansen wasn't helping matters now. He currently sat forward in his seat while talking to the Senator, ignoring me completely. Rob acted like nothing was remiss as they chatted easily. From how each joked and laughed, they seemed like old frat buddies who'd only just been reunited.

I knew if Cate was watching the program she'd be as angry as me. I moved my hands to grip the chair arms tightly. My knuckles cracked from the force in which I dug into the wood.

I'd been sabotaged on purpose.

Rob had obviously chosen to leave me in the dark about Senator Douglas' appearance. It was clear he had wanted to catch me unaware.

My knuckles cracked again.

A surprise like that was not only unprofessional but disrespectful. However, instead of my anxiety getting the best of me, I used the anger swirling inside of me as my focal point.

I won't let either of them win.

Just as that thought solidified in my mind, the Senator turned to me. His jowls jiggled as his large potbelly strained against his suit. A giddy triumphant light shone in his irises. He knew he'd caught me unaware and unprepared, and that knowledge clearly delighted him.

"Dr. Forester. It's a pleasure to see you again."

I smiled tightly. "It's a pleasure to see you too, Senator."

"Sorry if my appearance is a surprise. I thought Rob would have told you."

Rob was busy having his nose powdered. Two makeup artists swarmed around him like bees at a honeycomb.

My smile was so tight now it felt like my face would crack.

"But since you're the famous *Dr.* Meghan Forester, I'm sure you'll be just fine explaining to the American people why you allowed a Kazzie to infect and kill that poor girl."

His insincere tone dripped with mock concern. And at that moment, something Cate said flashed through my mind. *"The coroner said he was specifically instructed by the CEO of the hospital to not conduct the autopsy against the parent's wishes."*

It was like a lightbulb went off.

Narrowing my eyes, I replied, "I think we both know the virus didn't kill Zoe. Tell me, Senator, how did you convince the CEO of Chicago Children's to interfere with Zoe Mathison's autopsy? You do realize that interference is illegal since it breaches the Public Health Protection Act?"

I held my breath as I waited for his response. I had no proof he was involved, but logic deemed he could have something to do with it.

His smile disappeared.

My heart hammered. *Perhaps he does have something to do with it!*

The Senator's gaze turned glacial when he said, "I don't know what you're talking about."

"I think you do." My voice was so sweet it was honey.

Heat crept up the Senator's neck, causing his jowls to turn as crimson as a sunset. "You better watch what you say, little girl."

His threat was quiet. Deadly. I knew only I had heard it.

Ignoring the shiver that threatened to wrack my body, I replied, "Threats won't help you when the law comes knocking."

He sneered and leaned closer until I smelled his foul breath. "Neither will messing with someone who has my connections."

With a swift turn, he shifted back to face Rob just as the makeup crew hopped off the stage. Neither Rob nor the crew appeared to have heard the senator's and my exchange. A large, fake smile spread across the Senator's face.

My heart pounded so hard, I thought I'd pass out.

Keep it together, Meghan. If you faint now, the entire country will see.

The Senator's look and words said everything. I was now *certain* he was the reason Zoe's autopsy had been delayed. Still,

I had no proof.

Without proof, he won't be charged with anything.

And if I was going to stop him from wreaking havoc on the fragile truce this country had begun to build with the Kazzies, I was going to have to find out *how* he was involved before he could use his political power to silence me, or worse, imprison my friends again.

"And we're back, thank you for joining us tonight as we continue our discussion with Dr. Meghan Forester, a prestigious scientist from the MRI, and Senator Douglas of Arkansas, a well-known opponent to the Kazzies' release." Rob's voice boomed through the room. "If you're just tuning in, we've been discussing Zoe Mathison's death, the role the virus played in that, and where our country should go from here to ensure no further deaths occur."

Rob turned in his chair to face Senator Douglas. "Senator, tell me more about what you've learned regarding Zoe Mathison."

The senator puffed up in his chair, like a peacock strutting with his feathers out. "As you know, it's been confirmed that poor, little Zoe became infected with *Makanza* after encountering a Kazzie. Her parents are devastated by their loss. She was their only daughter."

His words were so thick and full of remorse, that if I didn't know him, I'd have believed he actually cared.

Clearing my throat, I cut in just as Rob opened his mouth to reply. "But that *doesn't* prove that Zoe died from *Makanza*. As of now, there has been no definitive conclusion for the cause of her death. I think it's best to remember the science and not instill panic in our country. The vaccine has proven it's 100% effective, time and time again."

The senator's beady eyes turned on me. "I wish I could

agree with you, Dr. Forester, but my loyalty lies with the American people. I swore an oath to serve and protect. And since it's my duty to do what's best for the American people, I can only advocate for the Kazzies return to Reservation 1."

I gritted my teeth. "And it's my duty, as a scientist with the MRI, to also protect the public. Do you really think any of us would have voted to free the Kazzies if it put anyone in the public at risk?"

"Given how you care for Kazzies more than your friends and family, I can't say I'm sure, Dr. Forester." The senator's words dripped with mock concern.

Annoyance flared inside me just as Rob smiled brightly and asked the senator another question.

Rob's warm brown eyes stayed guileless as he volleyed questions between me and Senator Douglas. I didn't bring up my suspicions about the senator's interference at Chicago Children's. It was too risky. I didn't have proof, and the senator would clearly pursue legal action if I smeared his name.

Somehow, I managed to keep my cool and answer each question objectively during the rest of the interview, even when the Senator baited me for a more emotional response.

Luckily, it wasn't the first time I'd been cornered. I called upon my experience during the summer when Cate and I had toured the country.

It was the only thing that saved me.

When Rob concluded our interview, I managed to smile and shake hands with both of them, as if we were all old friends who'd shown up for a friendly debate. However, once the red light disappeared from the camera, I stormed off the stage.

"Meghan!" Footsteps sounded behind me as ANN workers shifted out of my way.

I didn't stop. Once I collected my purse, I'd be gone.

"Meghan..." A hand touched my upper arm.

I spun as Rob smiled down at me. "Why the rush to leave?"

"*Why* the rush?"

I didn't know what it was—perhaps it was how he'd tricked me and didn't seem to have any intention of apologizing for that. Maybe it was because he used my first name versus the title I'd spent years working to earn. Or maybe it was how Senator Douglas had referred to me as *little girl* while he and Rob seemed in cohorts about this interview from the beginning.

Whatever it was, every ounce of Midwestern politeness vanished. Standing up straighter, I replied, "It's *Dr.* Meghan Forester, and if you think I'll speak to you for one more second after the stunt you just pulled—you're wrong."

I spun on my heels and continued striding away, but he quickly fell into step beside me. "Dr. Forester, please, you have to know that the public wants *both* sides of the story. You can't expect only your voice to be heard."

I kept walking and exited the studio. Suite B was only steps away. When I reached the door, I turned to face him.

"I think you and I both know what truly happened here today. Yes, you're right, the American public does deserve to hear both sides of the story, but when a well-known journalist intentionally sabotages one of his guests, that's another matter entirely. You had ample opportunity to tell me that Senator Douglas would be joining us, but you chose not to."

I paused to take a breath. My chest was rising and falling so fast I thought I'd pass out. "I'll be reporting your unprofessional behavior to not only the Directors at the Makanza Research Institute but also your superiors. If ANN wants to continue its good-standing relationship with the MRI, I have no doubt they'll listen to how I was treated today."

His easy-going smile faltered. "Dr. Forester... There's no need to take it to such extreme measures. I was simply doing my job."

"Last time I checked, doing *one's job* didn't involve sabotaging a guest on your show. And if you think I'll be fooled—you don't know me at all."

He stepped closer, the warmness leaving his expression. He towered over me, his eyes sparkling with fury.

When he opened his mouth to speak, I beat him to it. "Don't say another word. Do you really think you're the first male in a position of power who's tried to intimidate me?" Images of Dr. Roberts flashed through my mind. "If you're smart, you'll stop right now. I'd hate to add anything else to your list of unprofessional behaviors."

Despite him standing less than a foot away, I held my ground.

Anger filled his eyes as his jaw clenched. I could tell he wanted to lay into me, to put me in my place, but something held him back. Without saying another word, he turned on his heel and strode swiftly down the hall.

Senator Douglas was visible in the studio, talking to another anchor that typically covered the morning program. The senator eyed me and smirked before turning back to the anchor. Rob Hansen approached them, a grin back on his face, as if our conversation had never taken place.

Now that I was alone, my façade crumbled.

My hand shook when I gripped the door handle. It took three attempts before I was able to open it.

With a strong push, I burst into the guestroom and closed the door behind me. It was only then that I leaned against it and sank to the floor.

My heart beat wildly as I closed my eyes and covered my face.

A second later, rapid knocking came from the back of my mind. Sara. No doubt she'd felt my surge of adrenaline.

I opened our telepathic connection, glad for the distraction. *Hi.*

Meghan? Are you okay? Sharon, Sophie, and I just watched the program you were on. It seemed to go okay, but I just got a strong emotional push from you. Did something happen after the cameras stopped rolling?

I sighed. *You could say that.*

I summed up what had just transpired between the Senator and Rob Hansen. *It definitely felt like an ambush. And I think because I'm young and a woman, they didn't think I'd fight back.*

Sara seethed. I could feel it—like a swirling tornado of indignation. *What scumbags!*

That's putting it mildly.

So now what?

I rose from the floor and collected my purse and coat. My hands still shook. *Now, I call Davin and get out of here. If ANN thinks I'm coming back in the morning following a stunt like that— they're wrong.*

Oh, Meghan. I'm so sorry that happened. Have there been any updates on Zoe's death?

The autopsy was approved. They started today.

Sara breathed a sigh of relief. *So we'll have answers soon and will know if the virus killed her?*

We'll have proof the virus didn't kill her.

The nerves strumming through Sara carried over to me.

I softened my voice. *It's going to be fine. I promise. The vaccine is effective.*

I hope you're right.

I took a deep breath as we both tried to calm our nerves. When my heart rate finally slowed, I said, *There's something else I should tell you. I'm going to be working out of state for a while. I've been invited to join a group in the MRI that's working on a cure.*

Sara's breath sucked in. *Out of state? Where are you going?*

California.

For how long?

As long as it takes. But I didn't tell her that. *I don't know. It may be for a while.*

Do we get to see you before you leave?

Of course. This will be my last weekend in Sioux Falls for a while. Do you all want to visit?

Yes! I'll talk to Sophie and Sharon about it tonight.

We shut down our connection after promising to see each other soon. The weekend was rapidly approaching, and it was possible it would be the last time I'd see the twins or Sharon for a while. If I traveled to California next week to join Division 5, it could be months before I'd see them again.

DAVIN LOOKED AS happy as someone who just drank turpentine when he pulled up to the main doors at ANN. I already stood outside waiting in the cold. I didn't care that the windchill was below zero or that I'd left my gloves in the car.

Spending another second in ANN's headquarters was more than I could bear.

"Are you okay?" were Davin's first words when I slipped into the passenger seat. Warm air from the dash heated the cab. I held my chilled fingers to it.

"As well as I can be. That's not an experience I'd like to repeat."

His chest rose up and down as rage coated his eyes. "If I

ever see that guy—"

"You won't do anything to him." I laid a hand on his thigh.

Strong muscles bunched under my light touch. I hadn't seen Davin this angry since my encounter with Dr. Roberts. Rage practically ignited off him.

He angled his body to face me better. His broad shoulders brushed against the window. "Those bastards ganged up on you! And you were never informed that the Senator would be in the interview. They purposefully manipulated you!"

"Yes, they did. I've already reported Rob Hansen to his superiors at ANN. I plan to do the same within the MRI. And while that doesn't guarantee he'll never do something like that again, it does complicate ANN's relationship with the MRI. We've always willingly given interviews when asked, but if MRI's upper management is alerted to how I was treated—that may change."

Davin's nostrils flared, and the steering wheel cracked menacingly when he gripped it tightly. "I should have been here."

I moved my hand to cover his. "There was nothing you could have done, and please don't break the steering wheel. If you do, we'll be stuck here."

My gentle, joking words seemed to help.

His grip loosened as he took a deep breath. "Sorry, but when I saw that bastard come up on stage, and I knew you didn't know he'd be there…" He shook his head. "I almost tore the hotel room apart."

"I'm glad you didn't. That would have been an expensive bill."

His shoulders relaxed more as a chuckle escaped him. Capturing me in his azure gaze, he tenderly brushed a finger along my cheek. A smile threatened to spread across his face. "Should we get out of here?"

I nodded. "Please."

WE SPENT THE night at the hotel. Since I had no intention of conducting an interview at ANN in the morning, we could have driven back to Sioux Falls, but we'd already paid for our room and it was late.

There was another advantage to staying in Des Moines. The hotel kept us safe from further harassment. If ANN reporters went looking for me again after tonight's controversial show, they wouldn't know where to find me. We had made sure to only put Davin's name on the hotel bill.

As soon as we reached our room, I called Cate. She fumed as hotly as Sara when I explained what happened. She then promised to lodge complaints against Rob Hansen within the MRI. But her response when I told her my suspicions about the senator interfering with Zoe's autopsy was even more explosive.

"That conniving, evil bastard! If he's the reason for the delay in her autopsy, there'll be hell to pay."

Even though neither of us knew how we could prove the senator's involvement, it didn't stop our resolve. "I'll start asking around," Cate concluded with, "and I'll see if I can find anything on him."

After we hung up, my shoulders sagged in relief. It was only then I realized I'd gone the entire day without taking pain meds or being bothered by my injury.

I rolled my right shoulder as I sat on the hotel bed. A slight twinge of pain followed, but for the most part, I felt fine.

Shifting on the mattress, the worn bedspread bunched together. Our room was simple with a queen-sized bed and threadbare carpet. It was a far cry from luxury, but it was clean. Clean was the best one could hope for in paid accommodations these days.

When I tested my arm a second time, Davin turned into a blur from where he'd been standing by his suitcase. He was instantly at my side.

"Are you okay? Is your injury bothering you?"

"Surprisingly, no. It's felt fine all day."

He joined me on the bed, and I lay down so we could face one another. Davin's fresh, familiar scent washed over me.

Even though all I wanted to do was sink into him and forget about the world, I didn't. Instead, I opened my mouth to talk more about Zoe, the virus, and where we could go from here, but he brought a finger to my mouth. "Shh."

He then replaced his finger with his lips.

I automatically locked my arms around him. Our bodies pressed tightly against one another's. His hard to my soft.

Groaning, he pulled me even tighter to him until I was fully enclosed within his embrace.

The all-too familiar ache began low in my belly as we kissed and explored one another. I shifted even closer until his hard thigh parted my legs.

"When?" I whispered when he moved to kiss along my jaw and down my neck. His kisses burned, leaving a trail of fire, making me want to beg for more.

He didn't stop and only paused long enough to reply, "When you're fully healed."

"Isn't that now?"

He chuckled and nipped my earlobe. "No. I'd probably hurt you if we did it now."

"But I've felt fine all day!"

He moved to lie on top of me but kept his upper body

positioned above. All of his weight rested on his forearms.

Even now, while desire swam through his gaze, he was still conscious of my injury—he held back just enough to not put any pressure on my healing ribcage.

"The doctor said it will take several more weeks."

I groaned and threaded my fingers through his silky soft hair. "That's so long."

He chuckled and lowered his head to nibble my lower lip. "You're worth waiting for."

When it became obvious no amount of pouting would sway his decision, I settled with his compromise to order a pizza to take our minds off one another. I also noticed that Davin was once again making sure I ate.

Half-an-hour later, we were sitting cross-legged atop the bed with an open pizza box in front of us. Biting into a slice of thick sausage and mushroom that cost half of what our hotel room did, I closed my eyes and savored it. During the past few months, when anxiety had ruled my life, I'd neglected to notice how food tasted or how comforting a full belly was. Now, those small pleasures were slowly becoming the norm for me again.

"You look like you've died and gone to heaven." Davin's eyes twinkled.

I laughed and finished swallowing. "This is quite possibly the best pizza I've ever had."

He ripped off his third piece and ate half of it in one bite. "I think you may be right."

I WOKE THE next morning to the feel of Davin's arms around me. We didn't waste any time packing and getting ready to go. Sharon and the twins would be arriving in a few days. And since I was still banned from the Compound and we'd both be leaving for California next week, I wanted to make the most of their visit.

"We'll have to find a way to buy more food during their stay." I shoved my dirty clothes into my bag and zippered it closed. A slight twinge in my shoulder followed.

As much as I hated to admit it, Davin was right. I still needed to heal.

"My food allowance won't accommodate five people, even if we eat like birds, and eating out would be so expensive." I bit my lip as I tried to figure out how to house all of them through the weekend *and* feed them.

Davin lifted his suitcase off the bed. "What if I apply for a SDFDC card?"

"But you live in Rapid. They won't give you one for Sioux Falls."

He stepped closer, his blue eyes bright. "What if I lived in Sioux Falls?"

My breath stopped at what his question implied. "You mean… you want to move in with me?"

His gaze softened as he brushed the hair from my shoulder. "I've spent over a year waiting to be with you. Is it that shocking that I'd like to live with you?"

"No… of course not, I just…" A smile parted my lips. "I'm glad you want that. I want that too."

I WAS STILL beaming like a giddy high school girl when Davin disappeared from the room with the bags. We'd planned for him to pack the car while I checked us out.

A smile played on my lips as I idly walked down the carpeted hall to the stairs. I took them down to the lobby at a normal pace. Still not a run, but faster than I'd been moving even a few days ago. Only the last jump jostled my injury.

The receptionist glanced up when I approached. I dug into my purse for my wallet. Davin and I had cracked the minibar so I knew there'd be an extra charge. Just as I pulled out my money a growl came from my right.

Stopping, I turned to see a man standing only feet away. He was wild-eyed and looked a bit unhinged. Another guttural sound came from him.

I instinctively took a step back.

"Meghan Forester?" His question was low and fierce.

I opened my mouth to deny it, instinct telling me to run.

"It *is* you. You look just like you do on TV."

I was vaguely aware of the hotel's receptionist picking up her phone and hurriedly talking to someone on it, but my gaze stayed on the man. He appeared to be in his forties with a full head of brown hair.

"I'm sorry…" I took another step back and clutched my purse tightly to my chest. "Do we know each other?"

"We should know each other. You're the reason my little girl is dead."

And then he lunged at me.

13 - ATTACK

One second the man was a few feet away, the next he was on top of me.

I screamed when I hit the ground. Pain seared through my arm.

The man pinned my wrists on either side of my head. A ripping sensation tore through my chest as I thrashed beneath him.

Spittle flew from his mouth. "You killed her! You killed my little girl!" Tears sprouted from his eyes like giant raindrops. They poured down his face as his mouth twisted in rage. "My baby Zoe..." A sob wracked his chest. "She's dead because of you!"

My thrashing movements stopped as I gazed at him in disbelief.

Zoe's father. The man who'd gone missing, that Cate assumed had wanted to escape the public eye, had just attacked me.

He purposefully left Chicago to find me.

That crazy thought sped through my mind and then

disappeared as he lifted my wrists and slammed them back on the floor. "You killed her!"

I screamed.

His tears increased and his grip suddenly loosened.

"She's dead..." His voice grew weaker as more tears came.

Shouts reached my ears as the hotel receptionist pointed toward me. "Help! Help us! He's attacking her!"

The sound of rattling chains on belts came next as two security officers appeared. They grabbed Zoe's father by the shoulders and tried to pull him off, but his grip tightened.

"No!" He hunched closer to me. Tears fell from his cheeks onto my face. "She needs to pay for what she did!"

A roar emitted from somewhere else in the lobby. The air rustled around me and then Davin was there. Large veins bulged in the side of his neck as he ripped the security officers away. Both men stumbled back, but before they could protest, Davin reached for Zoe's father and with one swift move threw him across the lobby, a guttural sound emitting from his throat.

Zoe's father landed with a crash against the wall by the main doors. He didn't move when he hit the floor, and his arm lay at an unnatural angle.

I lay frozen, as if my brain was no longer connected to my body. I told myself to move, but nothing happened. Rapid knocking came from the back of my mind. *Sara.*

I didn't open our connection. My gaze stayed on the ceiling above. It was an old-fashioned popcorn ceiling with a rickety fan spinning in its midst.

They have a fan running in winter. How odd.

The next thing I registered was Davin hovering directly in my vision. His cobalt eyes glittered with worry, but something else coated them.

Fear.

"Meghan? Babe?" He smoothed the hair from my face while his gaze rapidly assessed me. "Can you hear me? Where does it hurt?"

I tried to open my mouth to respond but couldn't. A shiver struck me, then another.

"Can we get some help here?" Davin yelled at the receptionist.

The two security guards stayed away, numbly watching us.

"I... I already called the police," the receptionist responded, her eyes wide.

Just then a commotion sounded at the main doors. Two police officers strode in, their radios crackling on their shoulders.

When they saw Davin leaning over me, they rushed to our sides. The first kneeled down and quickly looked me over. The other stood over him assessing the situation.

"That psychotic guy over there attacked her." Davin nodded at Zoe's unconscious father. "This is Dr. Meghan Forester. She's a renowned scientist at the MRI, and it seems he specifically came to this hotel to attack her."

"We know who she is," the standing police officer replied, his eyes hard.

"Are you all right, Miss? Are you able to move?" The other officer gripped my arm.

I winced as he helped me sit up. My hand instinctively went to my wound.

"She's bleeding," the officer called to his partner.

I glanced down. Blood soaked through my shirt on my upper chest.

As if on cue, sirens from an ambulance wailed outside as flashing lights penetrated the hotel's front windows. Several paramedics rushed in with stretchers. Two came to me, the other two went to Zoe's father.

The police officer helped me to stand and then began issuing orders. Before I knew what was happening, the medical personnel swarmed. They assessed me, asking me questions that I didn't fully comprehend, before loading me onto the stretcher.

Davin stood helplessly behind them, but his eyes watched their every move. When our gazes locked, I drew strength from him.

I held out my hand.

He grabbed it and came to my side.

"Don't leave me," I whispered.

He shook his head. "Never."

I SPENT THE rest of the morning in Des Moines' hospital. I was given intense painkillers, and the doctors ordered a barrage of tests. Despite the chaos, only one thought kept swirling in my mind.

What if this attack prevents me from joining Division 5?

My wound had re-opened, the fall to the ground had jarred my healing ribs, and all of that could mean I was no longer fit to return to work.

Dr. Sadowsky had insisted that I present a doctor's note before I boarded the plane for California. Now, that requirement seemed impossible.

While we waited for the results, a young resident bandaged my wound. The thin tissue that had covered it was torn right through.

"It should heal back up in a few days." The doctor's eyes were kind as he applied a cool salve. In the small ER room, he sat only two feet away on his stool. "I'm afraid you'll have a nasty scar, and you may need physical therapy to regain complete movement after you've healed, but in the long-run, you should be fine."

Physical therapy?

I met Davin's worried gaze from where he stood in the corner.

"Do you really think I'll need therapy?" I rolled my shoulder after he finished with the bandage.

"Most likely. The scans indicated you have new soft tissue injury around your ribs. Your muscles and tendons won't be as flexible or as strong as they used to be."

I nodded numbly. *I can't believe this is happening.*

"And the x-rays you took?" Davin placed his hands firmly on his hips. "Can we see them?"

The resident's eyes turned wide when he glanced at the large Kazzie. "Let me pull them up."

He wheeled over to the computer in the corner. Davin stood with crossed arms just behind him.

The resident's Adam's apple bobbed. "Well... um... as you can see here," he lifted his finger and pointed at the x-ray, "her upper ribs seem to be stable. The surgeon that repaired them after her gunshot wound did a good job." His gaze traveled across the screen. "I don't see any new fractures. However, you'll still need to be careful, Dr. Forester. Those bones are still healing."

"But I can still work, right?" Davin's eyes narrowed at my question. He opened his mouth to say something, but I cut him off before he could interfere. "I mean, overall, I'm fine, so I should still be able to work."

The resident cocked his head. "If you have a desk job, yes, you can work."

"And if I don't?"

He frowned and crossed his arms. "Then you'd probably need to be off work for a few more weeks."

My stomach plummeted. "But I *can't* miss work for a few more weeks. I need a doctor's note that states I'm fit to work next week."

His Adam's apple bobbed again. "Well... I could write you a note, but I can't state that you have full capacity to work right now. It wouldn't be ethical."

"But what if I don't lift anything and I make sure to take frequent breaks. Could you then?" My tone sounded desperate, but that was exactly how I felt. "Please write me the note. It's a matter of public safety. If I don't—" I stopped myself before I revealed anything about Division 5. While the secret group was no longer confidential to MRI employees, that didn't mean they wanted us sharing everything with the general public.

"Just, please. Write me a note and say that I can return to work. I won't lift anything. I'll take frequent breaks, and I'll sit down when I'm tired. I promise."

Silence followed as the resident and I stared at one another.

He eventually broke eye contact. "Um, sure. I suppose I can write you a note to return to work for six hours a day, but I can't do more than that."

I bit my lip to stop my further pleading. It was possible I wouldn't get a better note than what he was offering.

"Okay. Thank you."

After the resident left, a radiologist joined us to better review the images from the numerous scans. I listened numbly as she described the further damage in my upper chest.

When we finally had the room to ourselves, Davin sat at the edge of my bed. Bright sunlight from the cold winter day outside streamed through the window. I was still in a makeshift bay in the Emergency Department. Luckily, I wouldn't need to be admitted to the hospital.

The smell of antiseptic hung in the air, and every now and then conversations could be heard as people walked by on the other side of the curtain.

I had no idea where Zoe's father was. The paramedics had taken him away, and so far, nobody would tell me what had happened to him. As for Sara, I'd finally opened up our connection and apologized for not being in touch sooner. She was worried, obviously, by the intense feelings I'd given off after the attack, but I didn't tell her about Zoe's father or what he had done. Quite simply, I didn't want to talk about it. Not yet, at least.

Once I closed down the link with Sara, I met Davin's gaze.

He shifted. Worry emanated from him, like electricity from a storm cloud. "Meghan, how can you work—"

"Don't." I held up my hand. "Just don't. Please."

His jaw clenched, the muscle in it ticking. Finally, he nodded.

Softening my gaze, I scooted over on the small bed to make room for him. I patted the spot beside me.

In a flash, he was at my side and reaching for my hand. Deep emotion swam in his gaze. Absentmindedly, he traced a finger on my palm.

"I should have been there. I should have stopped him." His voice was quiet, but pain lined his words. "Then you wouldn't be in this position."

"You couldn't have known. None of us could have. Unfortunately, events like this seem to come with the territory."

Davin snorted. "Nobody should be harmed for doing their job. Besides, all you've ever tried to do is help others."

"Some don't see it that way. Some think I'm trying to harm them." I swallowed tightly.

That thought stung as it always did. A good portion of this country felt I was putting the Kazzies' well-being before their own. So many still believed the vaccine wasn't effective and that *Makanza* would once again sweep through the country, killing those of us that had survived the First and Second Waves.

Seeing the pain on Zoe's father's face only made it worse. "He blames me for her death. He believes *Makanza* killed Zoe even if it didn't. And he thinks that if I'd never helped free all of you that she'd still be alive." I squeezed my eyes tightly shut. *Please don't let that be true!*

More than ever, we needed the results of Zoe's autopsy.

"Have you heard from Cate?" Davin traced a finger up my forearm.

"Not yet." I pushed to sitting and swung my legs over the side of the narrow ER bed. "I just want to go home. I'll call her later to get an update."

Davin stood to give me room.

I tentatively moved my limbs. My shoulder felt sore, and the fragile skin over my wound was tender, but for the most part, I felt okay.

Unfortunately, leaving wasn't that easy. Not only did I need to wait for the discharge papers from the Emergency Department, but there was also the small matter of Zoe's father assaulting me.

I had to file a report with the police. That took another few hours even though I insisted that I didn't want to press charges.

When I made that declaration, Davin's mouth thinned into a tight line, but he didn't say anything.

I knew he wanted Zoe's father locked up, but I couldn't do that. Her father's anger stemmed from pain. It didn't make what he'd done to me acceptable, but locking him up wouldn't help anything.

"What if he attacks you again?" Davin leaned down and spoke quietly into my ear after the police officers left.

The nurse had also come and gone. We'd finally been given the all-clear to leave.

I sat down on the wheelchair Davin held out. Squeaking from the wheels ensued when he began pushing me out of the makeshift room down the hall.

"He won't."

"You don't know that." His words were tight.

We passed hospital personnel and other people in the hall. Some stopped to watch us.

The exit doors couldn't come fast enough.

"You're right. I don't know that," I said in a low voice. "But I'm going to take my chances. And if he does attack me again, then I *will* press charges. I'm willing to forgive him for this one occurrence. His daughter just died, he's hurting, and he's looking for someone to blame. And I also think other voices have put ideas into his head. I don't think he would have come here on his own if higher powers weren't involved."

"Senator Douglas?" A cold gust of winter air quieted Davin's words as he pushed me through the main doors.

"Yes. Senator Douglas."

More than ever, I was convinced the senator was somehow involved with Zoe's parents. He had the power to find which hotel I'd stayed in, despite Davin and me taking precautions. I imagined Zoe's father wouldn't have been able to acquire that information alone. It would explain how he'd found me.

However, I still had no proof that Senator Douglas was connected to Zoe Mathison or her parents. And while I still didn't have proof that the senator had also manipulated the hospital's CEO in Chicago—I firmly believed he'd done that too.

With a CEO bending the rules and Zoe's parents not complying with the MRI—well, it played right into the senator's agenda to convince the public Zoe had died from *Makanza*. It also fueled his case for locking my friends up again.

I pulled my coat tighter around me as Davin pushed me across the parking lot. "He got to them, Davin. I'm sure of it."

It was already late afternoon and the sun was setting. Clouds drifted above when we reached Davin's car.

Opening the door for me, Davin cocked his head. "What do you think he said to them?"

"I'm not entirely sure, but he did *something* to convince them an autopsy wasn't necessary. He may have also instilled beliefs in them that *I* was to blame for their daughter's death. It would explain why her father singled me out. Or," I paused and shrugged, "her father decided that entirely on his own, and Senator Douglas had nothing to do with it."

I slid ungracefully into the passenger seat.

Davin clicked my seatbelt in place before I could protest.

In a blurred move, he vanished from my side. The next thing I knew the wheelchair was back at the hospital door and Davin was inside the vehicle. As usual, it was like he disappeared and then reappeared beside me. Luckily, there was no one around to see.

I spent the drive back to Sioux Falls either biting my lip or staring out the window. The attack could prevent me from joining Division 5. If Dr. Sadowsky caught wind of it, he'd not only use my injury as an excuse to keep me from work, but my safety as well.

"I don't want anybody knowing what happened in Des Moines." I uttered the words just as Davin pulled into my apartment's parking lot.

He cut the motor and angled his body to face me. "Why's that?"

I explained my fears to him. With every word that left my mouth, his expression grew darker and darker.

"Meghan, maybe it's best if we disappear again. You're right about what could happen. This could just be the beginning. If others fall ill, more people will blame you. More could come looking for you, and if I step away and am not there to protect you—"

"But people *will* fall ill. That can't be prevented. That's part of the process when one is exposed. We've told the public that over and over, but that initial feeling of being unwell won't last. They may feel sick for a few days, but then they'll feel fine."

Davin nodded. "I know that. You know that. But logic doesn't necessarily mean that others will believe it. You of all people should understand that."

I slumped against the seat. He was right. Fear still ran rampant in our country. It didn't help that our opponents were actively trying to wreak havoc.

"It just needs to blow over. I've been saying that from the beginning, and I stand by that. This first month is going to be the hardest as people become exposed. And over the years it should grow less and less." I grabbed his hand and squeezed it tightly. "There are only twelve-hundred of you. Most people will never encounter a Kazzie in their lifetime. I don't understand why people don't see that."

He squeezed me back. "I still think we should leave. You've done enough for the MRI and this country. And you're still not fully healed. Let somebody else fight this battle for a while."

I met his gaze. Fear still lined it. I understood his fear of losing me since I was terrified of losing him, but I wasn't willing to back down.

Not yet.

"I'm going to California, Davin, and I'm going to join Division 5. We need a cure."

14 – WEEKEND VISIT

Davin and I spent the next few days at my apartment. Thankfully, my wound had closed by the time Sharon and the twins' were due to arrive, but that didn't stop my worry over what I was seeing on the news.

It seemed each time I turned on the TV, opened a newspaper, or pulled up the internet, some story flashed across my vision about people becoming sick and blaming the Kazzies, or a Kazzie attacking an innocent bystander for no apparent reason—which I didn't believe. It was all so absurd.

But what was extremely surprising was that my attack in Des Moines was never mentioned anywhere. Not once.

I bit my lip as I scanned the internet. *Only one person I can think of has the power to keep a story like that from spreading.*

But... Division 5 loomed which meant this could all go away.

If we find a cure.

Snapping the lid of my laptop closed, I joined Davin in the bathroom. He was helping to clean my small apartment for our impending visitors. After pulling on my cleaning gloves, I got to work on the toilet which wasn't easy with my injury.

Davin peeked his head out of the shower. A lock of dark hair fell across his forehead. "I've got this. You don't need to help."

"I can help. My arm may be injured, but it's not broken."

He grumbled a response before closing the see-through curtain. Behind it, he turned into a blur just as my cell phone rang. Cate's picture flashed across the screen.

My heart jumped into my throat. Ripping off my glove, I brought my phone to my ear. "Hi. Any news on the autopsy?"

"No," Cate replied. "That's not actually why I'm calling. I just thought I'd fill you in on Zoe's family. Her dad finally turned up."

I dropped the sponge I was holding into the toilet water. "He did?"

Since I'd asked Cate about him daily since the attack in Des Moines, I wasn't surprised she was calling to fill me in. However, I still hadn't divulged the attack to Cate. I knew she'd agree with Davin and say that I should have pressed charges, but I knew in my heart that would have distracted everyone from the *real* problem in front of us.

Senator Douglas.

After seeing the lack of news coverage on my attack, I firmly believed that if Zoe's father had truly acted on his own with no outside manipulation, the story would have made national headlines, the MRI would have been informed, therefore, Cate would have known. But if the senator was involved, he wouldn't want to be implicated in any way, and he'd use his power to keep my attack hushed.

I hung my head. *How am I ever going to prove that he's involved?*

"He arrived back in Chicago last night and came to the hospital to take his wife home." Cate's words snapped my attention back to our conversation. "He was acting a little odd. He wouldn't speak to anyone, and he kept his head down. He also seems to have broken his arm, since he had a cast on."

"Oh. Really?" I played dumb. I didn't tell Cate that the cause of his broken limb was probably from Davin throwing him across the room. Clearing my throat, I added, "Well, I'm glad he's back. His wife must be relieved."

"She is. I think she needs his support."

Cate and I hung up a few minutes later with her promise to call me if anything was revealed in the autopsy.

I retrieved the sponge floating in the toilet before snapping off my other glove and washing my hands. Davin stepped out of the shower. I was pretty sure my shower was now the cleanest it had ever been.

"Any news?" he asked.

"Not about the virus or Zoe, but Zoe's dad turned back up in Chicago."

Davin's mouth tightened. "Have you told Cate yet what he did? How you're more injured now?"

I shook my head.

His jaw clenched, but he didn't argue.

We both moved into the living room as scents of the dinner Davin made wafted in from the kitchen. Luckily, Davin had acquired a South Dakota Food Distribution Center card after using my address as his own. He'd also changed his driver's license to show his permanent residence being here. So while the event in Des Moines had been scary and wasn't one I wanted to repeat, one good thing had come out of it.

Davin and I were officially living together.

I sat down on the couch and only winced slightly. I'd taken pain meds again this morning, but I was moving better, and I'd finished my course of antibiotics. Still, a few days ago I'd been pain pill-free. The attack in Iowa had definitely pushed my recovery back.

Sitting beside me, Davin interlocked his fingers. "Are you sure you're up for this?"

"Yes. I can't wait to see them. It's exactly what I need."

I lifted my lips to him and he kissed me softly. His lips felt so smooth and firm. He tasted like honey and chocolate. The familiar tingling began deep in my belly. Wrapping my uninjured arm around his neck, I pulled him closer.

He deepened the kiss, his tongue flicking into my mouth.

A knock sounded on the door.

Davin pulled back. "Damn visitors. Couldn't they have waited another hour?"

I smiled and smoothed my hair back. "Perhaps we can finish this later?"

He growled and pulled me closer. "I'm holding you to that."

In a blurred move, Davin was at the front door. Squeals of joy and Sharon's laughter followed when the twins and Davin's mother spilled into my tiny apartment.

Sara's eyes crinkled in the corners when she saw me. She looked exactly as I remembered her. Blue skin as beautiful as a robin's egg, shiny blond hair, and eyes bright with happiness.

"Meghan!" She barreled into me.

I groaned.

"Oh, shoot! I'm so sorry! I'm such an idiot!" She pulled back and looked at my shoulder. "Did I hurt you? Are you okay?"

I laughed and pulled her back into a hug. "I'm fine, really. The doctors said in a few weeks I'll be back to normal."

I left out the part about how I'd probably now need physical therapy to regain full movement in my arm. Neither

Sharon nor the twins knew about the attack in Iowa, and I intended to keep it that way.

"Oh, good. I'm so glad to hear that!" She grinned again and hugged me more tentatively.

Sophie hovered at my side when Sara pulled back. The *Sara* tattoo flashed on Sara's wrist when she lifted a hand to run through her hair. Beside it was a thin scar from where they'd implanted a tracking device in her during her time on Reservation 1. Sophie had both too.

The tattoos had been forced on the twins during their time in Compound 26. They were like concentration camp markings inflicted into their skin. And it had all been Dr. Roberts doing. Whereas, the tracking devices had been implanted when they arrived on Reservation 1. They had been removed before the twins left the reservation, but still...

I forced down my anger. Those tattoos and scars symbolized so much more.

"How are you?" Sophie smiled shyly and shoved her hands into her back pockets.

She looked just like Sara but carried a different air to her. Whereas Sara was outgoing and bubbly, Sophie had always been more reserved and shy. More like me.

"I'm good. How are you?" I stepped closer and pulled her into a hug.

A year ago, I never would have done that, but when it came to the Kinders and now the twins, I didn't balk at being touched or showing affection.

Sophie stiffened for a second, but then she softened and wrapped her arms around me. Her hair carried the same floral scent as Sara's.

When she let go, Sharon stepped forward and embraced me. "Meghan, sweetie. How are you?" Her auburn hair was swept back in a loose ponytail. As usual, a few stubborn tendrils escaped to frame her face. She had eyes just like Davin—electric blue and bright. They were the only people I'd ever met with eyes like that.

"I'm good. I've missed you."

She smiled tenderly. "I've missed you too."

Just behind them, Davin lounged against the wall with his arms crossed and a content smile on his face. My heart filled at the sight.

Everyone I loved was in this room.

Except for your parents.

My head cocked at that thought. *Yeah, except Mom and Dad.* I suddenly had the crazy idea to call them and ask them to join us, and then I realized that thought wasn't entirely crazy. The twins were my best friends, and Sharon was like a second mother to me. *Why shouldn't my parents be here?*

As the four of us stood in my tiny apartment, my spirits rose. "It's so good to have you all here."

Sara did a little happy dance. "I've been wanting to visit you for ages. And this is where you live, huh? So, do we get a tour?"

I grinned. "Sure, but don't blink or you may miss it."

Sophie giggled as I led them down the hallway to show them my bathroom and bedroom. The tour literally took twenty seconds.

Back in the living room, I shrugged. "I told you not to blink."

Sara glanced out the window to check out my unimpressive view before plopping down on the couch. The couch springs squeaked. "I love it! I can't wait until I live on my own when Sophie and I are done with school and have jobs."

Sophie sat in the middle of the sofa just as Davin brought out glasses of water for everyone. He handed them out before going back to the kitchen.

"So you have a house husband now?" Sara watched Davin's retreating form.

Sophie giggled.

"I heard that!" Davin called.

"Well… we've uh…" Heat rushed up my neck.

Sara angled her body toward me. "You're blushing!" She grinned. "Okay, spill it. What's going on?"

Sharon also leaned forward from where she'd sat on the lone chair.

"Meghan and I are living together." Davin's deep voice rang again from the kitchen. Whistling sounded from the tea kettle. "I've officially moved to Sioux Falls."

Sharon's eyes widened.

I wrung my hands. "I know you wanted him home with you since you haven't seen him for almost seven years. Please know you're welcome here anytime."

She nodded acceptingly. "I knew I wouldn't have him for long, and I'm thrilled things have worked out between you two."

THE REST OF the weekend flew by. My parents came up on Sunday morning to spend the day with all of us.

A part of me worried it would be awkward, but since my parents had already met the twins and Sharon following my injury and time in Reservation 1's hospital, it was anything but.

Sharon greeted my mother in her typical fashion while my dad pumped Davin with questions about how he was adjusting to life on the outside.

The twins and I spent every minute together. It was crazy

how much they felt like the sisters I'd never had.

By the time Sunday evening rolled around, it was time for everyone to go. Sharon and the twins left first since they had such a long drive, but my parents lingered.

When it was nearly nine at night, they finally made their way toward the door. I wrung my hands as they shrugged their coats on.

I'd already told Sharon and the twins about my and Davin's plans to fly to California, but my parents still didn't know.

"Um, I suppose I should tell you guys something."

My dad looked my way as my mother picked up her purse.

"What is it, kiddo?"

I felt Davin approach me from behind. He laid a hand gently on my uninjured shoulder.

"Davin and I are moving to California temporarily. It's for work."

My mother's eyebrows rose. "Who's work? Did you get a job there, Davin?"

I quickly shook my head. "No, *my* work. I'm going to be working at Compound 3 for a while." *I hope.* I didn't add that my position still wasn't a guarantee. While I had the doctor's note Dr. Sadowsky insisted on, it still held the work restriction. "But it's temporary," I rushed to add. "It's just short-term for a project."

My dad exhaled in relief. "That's good to hear. You scared me there for a minute. I thought we may be losing you forever."

The meaning behind his words wasn't lost on me. I could have died from my gunshot wound.

"No, Dad. You're not losing me. Most likely, I'll be back in a few months."

My mother's lips pursed. "You're still injured, Meghan."

"I know. I am resting. Really, I swear."

Davin stepped to my side. "I'll make sure she's taken care of. That's a promise."

Relieved expressions crossed both of my parents' features at Davin's words. Apparently, my track record wasn't the best for personal care.

"Well, in that case…" My mother stepped forward tentatively. Lifting her arms, she wrapped me into an awkward hug.

It was nothing like hugging Sharon, but my mother wasn't nearly as practiced in touching people. Closing my eyes, I squeezed her in return before she awkwardly stepped back.

It's not natural yet, but maybe in time, it will be.

My dad also embraced me which was equally as embarrassing, but a warm feeling still rushed up inside me. It was crazy how much I'd wanted my parents' support in this matter.

"Bye, kiddo." My dad waved as he and my mother departed.

When the door closed behind them, I sank against it.

"I suppose I better start packing for California." I gazed up at Davin.

"I'll do it. I'm a bit faster than you." He winked.

In a blur, he was gone.

I used the time to tidy up the kitchen. Not even five minutes passed before Davin was back at my side.

"That's done." He held my laptop in his other hand. "We better follow up on those properties I found. I have appointments with two landlords the morning I land."

Davin had spent the past few evenings searching the internet for rental properties while the twins and I acted like school-girls. He had already been in touch with several landlords.

"Good idea." I sat on a kitchen chair as he pulled the rentals up on my laptop. Even though there was no official MRI policy against dating Kazzies, I still wrung my hands. I had a feeling there may be a policy if it was discovered I'd become involved with Davin, but then I cocked my head. *The MRI has relaxed their rules on dating. It's quite possible they wouldn't care about this either.*

Still I decided it was wiser to err on the side of caution. For the time being, I had no intention of telling Amy or Dr. Sadowsky about Davin joining me.

15 - COMPOUND 3

The doctor's note I carried fluttered from my hand in the winter breeze like a beckoning white flag. I clutched it tightly so it wouldn't fly away as I walked toward Sioux Falls' airport.

Davin had discreetly dropped me off before leaving. He was currently driving to Omaha, the only open airport in our region, to catch a commercial flight to California. Family and friends weren't permitted to travel with the MRI, and since Davin and I were still trying to keep our relationship under wraps, it made the most sense to travel completely separate.

Ahead, I could just make out Amy and Dr. Sadowsky's outlines through Sioux Falls airport's dirty terminal windows.

Someone obviously let them in.

The local law enforcement must have unlocked the doors so we wouldn't have to wait in the freezing cold. Every other time I'd flown from this airport I'd waited outside on the tarmac. I guessed that it was at Dr. Sadowsky's request that the terminal was open.

Normally, this place was a tomb. Sioux Falls' small regional airport had died along with millions of Americans during the First Wave. It had been abandoned ever since.

When I reached the ancient sliding doors, I dropped my suitcase handle and pushed the doors open. They squeaked sharply in protest. Inside, the terminal was dark and bleak. Dust lined the floors and bird poop splattered the numerous windows.

Amy's eyes brightened when I pushed open the second sliding door to get inside.

"Meghan! Here, let me help you." She rushed over and pushed the doors closed behind me and then grabbed my suitcase. Thankfully. My arm already hurt from wheeling it while carrying my purse and laptop on my good shoulder, and then having to wrestle the unoiled sliding doors had only aggravated my injury more. But I couldn't let either Amy or Dr. Sadowsky know that.

Standing up straighter, I ignored my throbbing wound.

"Dr. Forester," my boss said appraisingly. He wore a long wool coat over his suit. His gaze slid over my form as if assessing if I was healthy enough to join them.

"Good morning." I thrust the doctor's note toward him and held my breath.

He took it and scanned it with narrowed eyes. A few seconds passed before he said, "Six hours."

My heart stopped.

Glancing up from the note, he sighed. "This says you're only fit to return to work for six hours a day and that you're not supposed to lift more than ten pounds." He raised an eyebrow at my heavy suitcase.

"I know, but six hours is long enough, isn't it?" I avoided the urge to twist my hands and purposefully ignored the lifting restriction.

"I expect we'll be working a *minimum* of eight hours a day.

Most likely, many more."

Crap. I glanced at Amy for help.

"But there's no reason Meghan can't continue working once she leaves the Compound," she said in a rush. "With her laptop, she'll be able to work remotely from the comfort of a bed while continuing to rest. We can leave most of the conceptual work to her."

I nodded emphatically. "Exactly, but I'm sure I *could* work more than six hours. The doctor stated six hours only to follow hospital policy. But every day, I grow stronger, and in less than a month, all of my restrictions lift."

The Director's eyebrows knit tightly together. "I don't see how—"

"Honestly, I feel great," I cut in. "I'm more than ready to return to work." I held my breath after that admission.

"Please?" Amy added.

An aching minute passed as Amy and I stared up at him with pleading eyes.

Sighing in exasperation, Dr. Sadowsky folded the note and placed it in his pocket. "Fine. But if I see any sign that you're not up to the task, you'll be flying back here... on your own dollar."

In other words, not on the MRI plane. "That's absolutely fine with me." I bit back a smile.

Amy grinned and clapped her hands. "You're coming!"

I swear Dr. Sadowsky rolled his eyes before pulling up his coat sleeve to glance at his watch.

A few minutes later, the jet appeared in the distant sky. I pulled my phone out to check my messages one last time.

Nothing new. In other words, no updates from Cate.

Cate had called last evening to fill me in on the progress. So far, she hadn't found anything incriminating on Senator

Douglas, unfortunately. As for the autopsy, it showed that Zoe had indeed been infected with *Makanza,* but no DNA within her cells had actually Changed. That meant her immune system was fighting it off since she wasn't turning into a Kazzie. In other words, *Makanza* hadn't killed her. Something else had.

"Do they have any hypotheses for what really caused her death?" I'd asked Cate.

"What we do know is that she wasn't feeling well in the days before she was admitted. Her parents stated she was having a hard time sleeping and at times seemed confused. And in the hours before her death, she experienced paralysis in her lower body."

"That doesn't sound like *Makanza.* "

"No, but it does sound like a virus. Now, it's just a matter of figuring out *what* virus."

After we'd hung up, I had nibbled my lip. In a way, what they'd discovered was relieving. So far, there was no scientific evidence that *Makanza* had killed her. It only solidified in my mind that the vaccine was 100% effective.

"Touch down!" Amy's comment pulled me back to the present. My co-worker's red hair dropped over her shoulders when she bent to pick up her bag.

We quickly clambered out of the terminal to meet the jet on the runway. Amy tried to carry my bag, but Dr. Sadowsky was watching, so I forced a grin and gritted my teeth against the exertion.

Once onboard, I breathed a sigh of relief that I was actually *on* the plane. After sending Davin a discreet text that we were about to take off, I tucked my phone away.

Several other researchers occupied the seats. I didn't recognize any of them. My heart rate increased at the site of so many new faces. At least ten other people stared back at us while we found places to sit.

Amy walked to the back and slid into a row with two open seats. "Is this exciting or what?" She tightened her seatbelt and gazed out the window before turning back to me with a grin. "Was it always like this when you traveled?"

"More or less. The plane usually wasn't this full, though."

I'd never told Amy about my social anxiety. I felt certain that she'd picked up on it a few times. Between my sweaty skin, ice cold hands, and eyes widened with fear, anybody with half a brain could see that crowds affected me. However, she never seemed to judge me for it. If anything, she stuck up for me when fear paralyzed my tongue.

Within minutes, we were in the sky. Clouds drifted beneath us.

"Charlie and Mitch are pretty jealous that they can't join us." Amy's green eyes glittered as she sat back in her seat.

"It's too bad they can't."

Amy chuckled. "What fun would it be if I couldn't tease them about all of the cool things we're going to see? If they were here, I wouldn't have that leverage."

I laughed. Amy, Mitch, and Charlie were more friends to me than co-workers. We'd worked so closely with one another over the past year that those lines had blurred long ago.

It helped that they'd conspired with me to break into Reservation 1. And that Mitch had illegally posted videos for me on the Dark Web.

Ultimately, it was those videos that had resulted in the country voting to free the Kazzies.

WE LANDED IN California a few hours later. Outside, the sun shone brightly. It was balmy and warm when we stepped out of the plane.

I tilted my face toward the sky. *What a change.* I couldn't remember ever feeling warm outside in January. *No wonder so much of the country is moving back here.*

"Did you know that Dorothy lives in southern California now?" I asked Amy.

Our feet clicked on the tarmac as our suitcases wheeled behind us. The rest of the scientists also headed toward the large van that would drive us to Compound 3.

Amy cocked her head. "Have you heard from her?"

"I talked to her recently to tell her that human trials were commencing soon for the potential new cure. She said she's going to be the first to sign up."

Bethany's response when I called her had been similar, but she said it would be a few weeks until she could travel to California. She was still healing from her botched surgery, and Makayla was due to give birth soon. Bethany didn't want to miss welcoming her new nephew or niece into the world, but still, I had felt her excitement strumming through the phone line at the mention of a cure.

Amy's eyes brightened. "What about the other Kazzies from our Compound? Do you know where they are?"

I pulled my suitcase carefully over a large crack in the tarmac. "Sage is waiting for the borders to reopen to Canada while he and Victor live in Colorado, and Garrett returned home to Michigan. Sara, Sophie, and um… Davin… are still in Rapid City."

Amy didn't seem to notice my stumbled words.

Most of my information came from the twins since they spoke to the other Kazzies from Compound 26 regularly, but I'd also called all of them to see if they were interested in the cure. Garrett had wanted to know more, and after telling him what I knew, he said he'd be signing up too.

Amy flashed me a smile. "It's good to know they're doing all right, but I wish they'd return all of our calls and emails, not just yours."

I nodded sympathetically.

It wasn't surprising that Compound 26's Kazzies refused to speak to their former researchers. During the time they'd been imprisoned within the Compound, each Kazzie had been subjected to unethical practices.

Granted, Dr. Roberts had been behind most of that, but the Kazzies still blamed my co-workers for those atrocities. Initially, I hadn't been any better since I'd also gone along with those practices. But it had ultimately led to my rebellion of Dr. Roberts' rule.

Images of my former boss whirled through my mind as we drove to Compound 3. The last time I'd seen him he'd pointed a gun at Davin with the intention of killing him.

"Do you have any idea what happened to Dr. Roberts?" I angled my body toward Amy and winced slightly when my shoulder jarred.

"Last I heard, he was confined to a psychiatric hospital in Minneapolis."

"Do you know how long he'll be there?"

Amy shook her head. "No, but what I do know is that the MRRA is holding him, and you know how they are. Since they follow their own set of laws, who knows what they'll charge him with or if they'll let him walk free."

I bit my lip. So many changes had taken place in our country within the last ten years. *Makanza* had not only changed the face of our nation, but it had shaped new laws and regulations.

Since the MRRA had always been the number one defense against *Makanza*, they carried more power than law enforcement. And since Dr. Roberts had been working for the MRRA on Reservation 1, he was now held under their rule.

It was possible he'd be locked up forever, or he could be freed next week. I shuddered. Only the MRRA knew his fate.

Amy elbowed me. "Meghan! Look!"

I followed her pointing finger and grinned.

Compound 3 glimmered on the horizon. Its large, gray four-story structure rose from the arid land behind the tall perimeter walls. Since Compound 3 was in the southeastern portion of the state, not far from the city of Indio, desert surrounded it.

We weren't the only ones staring at it. The researchers in front of us also craned their necks to get a better view. I guessed many of them had never traveled to this portion of the state. I certainly hadn't.

The structure grew larger the closer we got. The walled perimeter was similar to that of South Dakota's Compound. It rose at least twenty feet high and made a perfect square perimeter around the buildings within.

"It looks just like Compound 26." Amy rested her chin in her hand and propped her elbow against the window. Her childlike wonder reminded me it was her first trip to a new Compound.

"Most of the Compounds are similar. The ones I visited all had a few unique characteristics, but the outside structures are almost identical."

Amy's curly red hair brushed my arm when she pulled back from the window. "I can't believe I'm here!"

When the large, imposing gates filled the front windshield of the van, we ground to a halt. A dozen MRRA soldiers surrounded the vehicle and began the admittance process. It took a while since there were so many of us.

By the time we actually pulled into a parking spot outside of the Compound's main doors, at least forty minutes had passed.

Warm, dry air swirled around us as we walked from the van to the door. The sun beat down and felt more intense than it did in South Dakota.

Amy smiled and closed her eyes. "I could get used to this."

I checked the time on my phone. Davin was probably still in the air. The closest airport he could land into was San Diego, which meant he had over a two-hour drive to reach Indio, the town he'd arranged to meet landlords and view properties. Davin was going to text me the address of our new home after he viewed a few this afternoon and decided on which one to rent.

I bit my lip. My boss still didn't know about my plans to not stay at the hotel the MRI had booked. And since I hadn't told Amy or my boss my plans, I knew I'd have to explain myself eventually. *I'll cross that bridge when I come to it.*

"Ma'am, please place your hand here." The guard's voice startled me. He stood at the main admittance door to the Compound and held out the scanner. The rest of my colleagues were also having their palms scanned before being admitted.

I forced a smile and placed my palm against it. It flashed green.

"Your bag?" He held out his hand.

I handed it over as the MRRA soldiers admitted us one-by-one.

Once we were finally inside Compound 3, I wasn't surprised that the interior was very similar to Compound 26. The main lobby had stone-flecked flooring, grayish blue walls, and a large receptionist desk. Unlike my wing in Compound

26, in which only Carol was seated, Compound 3's main lobby had five receptionists.

Each smiled as our group huddled in the lobby. Their voices echoed in the large ceilinged entry as they took calls. One of them approached and handed all of us new access badges for Compound 3, along with maps of where the labs, offices, and cafeterias could be found.

"Ah! They've arrived!" a voice boomed.

I turned to see a middle-aged gentleman walking toward us from the back hallway. He was short and balding. A large smile covered his face. He held out his palm to shake hands with the first Director he encountered.

I knew who he was from his appearance. Dr. Dornhoff, Compound 3's Director, looked almost identical to his official MRI photo.

But he wasn't alone in greeting us. A woman stood just behind him. She had a pleasant smile plastered on her face and carried a clipboard. I could only assume she was his assistant.

"Dr. Thorson, it's a pleasure to see you here." Compound 3's Director pumped the hand of the Director from Vermont. "This must be quite different from the weather you're experiencing out east. How was the flight?"

They exchange pleasantries before Dr. Dornhoff moved on to the next group.

When he reached Dr. Sadowsky, his smile was still in place. The woman continued to follow behind him.

I observed the two men with my hands clasped. My fingertips felt cool, but my heart still beat evenly. Beside me, I could tell that Amy was itching for her introduction.

"And who do we have here?" The man asked turning to Amy.

She shot her hand forward. "Dr. McConnell, sir. It's an

honor to be here."

"It's our pleasure to have you." He shook her hand and let go.

I swallowed tightly as he turned to face me. His eyes widened for the briefest moment as his smile grew broader.

"And here we have Dr. Meghan Forester. I was hoping we'd see you. Dr. Sadowsky tells me that you've returned to work after a few weeks off. We hope that you're now one-hundred-percent. It's a pleasure to finally meet you. I'm Dr. Dornhoff."

His hand felt warm, so I knew my fingers were still cool. But I kept my head up and held eye contact.

"Yes, thank you, Dr. Dornhoff. I'm feeling fine now and am ready to return to work. I'm very excited to join Division 5."

I bit back a grimace when he pumped my hand so hard my shoulder burned.

"Now, if you'll all follow me." Dr. Dornhoff turned on his heel and strode down the hall. He was surprisingly graceful given his large belly.

Luckily, I was able to keep up with the Director's pace. During the walk, the woman who'd been following him sidled up to me. She was around my height with short brown hair. Smiling, she extended her hand.

"I'm Giselle Warren, Dr. Dornhoff's assistant and research analyst. I've been looking forward to meeting you."

Smiling, I took her hand awkwardly as we walked. "It's nice to meet you too. I'm Meghan Forester."

She let go of my hand and nodded toward the Director. "He's been gushing about you ever since he heard you were coming. You've made quite a name for yourself."

I ducked my head as my cheeks heated.

Giselle nudged me gently. "I've been excited to meet you too. If you need help with anything while you're here, just let me know. I'd be happy to show you the ropes."

Smiling genuinely, I nodded. "Thanks."

Dr. Dornhoff continued to lead us through the maze of corridors and back hallways while Giselle stayed at my side. Compound 3 was like being inside Compound 26—it could have been identical. Wide, bright white halls zigzagged through the maze within the gigantic structure. We passed labs, closed doors, and various other rooms that we didn't have time to look into.

Similar to the other Compounds, signs for an underground railway appeared at times. However, Dr. Dornhoff didn't seem in any hurry to reach our destination since we didn't take the rail system.

Fifteen minutes later, we approached a heavily guarded area. A set of white double doors waited ahead. Four MRRA soldier's stood at attention with rifles held stiffly in their arms.

The sign above them read *Research Bay 13.*

Dr. Dornhoff nodded at the double doors. "This is where we'll be convening every morning. All of you have this area located on your maps. Starting tomorrow, everyone will be working full-time. I hope you're well rested as it will be a vigorous schedule."

His eyes fell on me when he said that last part. I tilted my chin up and made sure to stand straighter.

When the large doors finally hissed open, a rush of cool air swept across my cheeks. It held the stale smell of most labs.

I smiled at the bustling activity within.

Rows of benches revealed liquid handlers, centrifuges, sequencers, thermocyclers, and other standard equipment used to study DNA. MRI scientists in white lab coats bustled about.

It was such a familiar sight that my remaining anxiety melted away.

"Can I have everybody gather around?" Dr. Dornhoff beckoned our group and the group already working within the lab closer.

Compound 3's employees made their way toward us.

There were over a dozen of them. Most of them were men, but a few were women. One woman's eyes fell on me.

She had short black hair, was around my height, and eyed me appraisingly.

"These are the scientists who will be joining Division 5." Dr. Dornhoff proceeded to introduce us.

When it was my turn, my palms were sweaty, but I managed a tight smile and nodded at each scientist.

The dark-haired woman's eyes stayed on me. I felt them needle into my back when I turned to shake her colleague's hand. When I turned to her, her eyes narrowed to slits.

"So… you're Meghan Forester." She didn't use the *doctor* title in front of my name like everybody else had. The woman snuck a peek at the directors. Dr. Dornhoff and Dr. Sadowsky were currently speaking with Vermont's Director. They were out of earshot and didn't seem to be paying us any attention.

Nodding politely, I replied, "Yes, that's me. And you are?"

"I'm Dr. Monica Brown." She didn't hold out her hand to shake.

"It's nice to meet you, Dr. Brown. I look forward to working with you."

She smirked. "Yeah, I'm sure everyone here is dying to work with you as well."

With that, Monica turned on her heel and returned to her bench.

Amy bristled and whispered into my ear, "Something tells

me that one's a bit green… with envy that is."

I frowned. "But why is she so hostile? I've never done anything to her."

"No, but with some people, it doesn't matter. Just the fact that you've succeeded or done better than them is enough for them to hate you."

Amy's comment swirled in my mind when she left my side to join Dr. Sadowsky. I stood numbly and watch Monica. She'd returned to work, her goggles and gloves in place.

It wouldn't be the first time others had worked against me, but it would be the first time anyone hated me with such venom simply because I'd achieved something more than them.

I'm probably making a bigger deal out of this than it is. Pushing my worries aside, I stood straighter when Dr. Dornhoff approached.

"Dr. Forester, we'd like to get everyone up to speed on our research." Compound 3's Director ushered me and the other new scientists to an adjoining room. Since Amy and Dr. Sadowsky had already been seated, I took a chair beside a middle-aged man with a full beard. A twinge of anxiety followed when he nodded hello.

The room fell silent when the lights dimmed. A slide-presentation glowed to life on the wall as a projector above hummed to life. Sitting forward in my chair, I listened intently as Dr. Dornhoff began explaining the research that had been conducted over the past year.

But even though my focus was on the slides that flashed in front of me, I couldn't help but feel a pair of eyes needling into my back. The few times I turned, Monica Brown watched me with slit-like eyes. She reminded me of a snake that wanted to strike its prey.

I shuddered. I had a feeling Division 5 had just become more complicated.

16 – NEW HOME

It was close to 7 o'clock in the evening by the time we wrapped up—much longer than my approved six-hour shifts, but Dr. Sadowsky had been so busy he'd never seemed to notice that I'd stayed on. And the pain meds I'd taken were doing their job. I only felt a little sore.

Davin had texted a few times to let me know that his plane had landed and he'd viewed a few rentals. He'd decided the third rental home was the best, so he'd signed the lease and sent me the address. He'd also asked if I'd eaten and taken my meds.

Sighing, I fished another two pain pills from my purse and dry swallowed them before tapping in a reply.

When the van arrived to take everyone to town, the California sun hung low in the sky. The temperature had cooled, but it was still vastly warmer than South Dakota.

Behind us, the giant Compound loomed as warm air flowed through the breeze. Desert plants and sand filled the open areas around the various parking lots within the perimeter walls. Excited chatter filled the air. Everyone stood in line to step aboard the van. They slowly filed past me one-by-one as I stood by the main doors.

When almost everyone had boarded, Dr. Sadowsky and Amy looked at me expectantly.

A breeze lifted the hair around my shoulders. "I've... uh... actually found separate accommodation so I won't be joining you."

A scuffle sounded behind me. I turned to see Monica standing in the shadows by the door.

Amy stepped closer to my side, pulling my attention back to her. She raised her eyebrows. "What? You're not staying at the hotel?"

Dr. Sadowsky also cocked his head. "If you're not staying at the hotel, then where are you staying?"

I reminded myself that I hadn't broken policy by dating Davin. Standing up straighter, I replied, "Since I anticipated we'd be here for a while I actually rented a small home I found online."

Amy laughed. "Well, someone was certainly thinking ahead. Wish I'd thought of that. But if it's a house, there's probably room for me, right?"

I resisted the urge to tug at my shirt collar. *Crap. I should have said a studio apartment.* While I wouldn't mind living with Amy, Davin was another story entirely. He still carried a grudge against other MRI scientists, but since I couldn't very well turn her away without revealing *why* I was hesitant, I finally nodded. "Of course, there's room."

"Perfect! I'll just grab my bag from the van." Amy hurried to the vehicle.

When it was only me and Dr. Sadowsky, he stepped closer. "Perhaps it's best you have separate accommodation so you can rest as needed. Did everything go all right today?" He checked his watch. "It's been almost a twelve-hour day."

I nodded my head vigorously. "Yes, it all went well. It was a lot to take in, but I'm feeling fine and not at all tired." I forced a bright smile.

"Hmm." I could tell he wanted to probe me with more questions about my injury.

Luckily, Amy saved the day. "All right, I've got my things. Now, how are we getting to this house you rented?" She grinned as she shouldered her purse.

"I called for a cab an hour ago. It should be arriving any minute outside of the main gates."

"Should we walk up there?" Amy glanced in the distance toward them.

Dr. Sadowsky tightened his grip on his briefcase. "Just make sure you're back here by seven o'clock tomorrow morning. We still have a lot of work to catch up on." His questioning gaze alighted upon me, and I once again got the impression he wanted to ask more questions about my condition.

I hurriedly grabbed Amy and pulled her away before he could.

As the van drove off, Amy and I walked toward the gates. Our footsteps tapped on the asphalt as the sun dipped lower. Red blazed across the horizon, setting the desert aglow.

"It's so beautiful out here. And I absolutely love that I'm not wearing a jacket in winter," Amy declared. "So what's the deal with you getting a house anyway? And why didn't you tell me? I would have been happy to pay my half."

"I…" Sweat erupted across my brow.

Amy raised her eyebrows.

I knew I could trust Amy. I should have just told her right away. "The reason I rented a house was to hide something from the MRI." I had the ridiculous urge to look around, as if secret cameras and microphones were stationed throughout the grounds. "Davin and I... we're... uh..."

Her eyebrows rose even higher.

"We're in a relationship." I blurted. "He's actually moved out here to be with me while I'm working."

If it was possible for somebody's eyebrows to reach their hairline, Amy's would have fit the bill. "Holy shit! Are you kidding me? You and *Davin*, as in our former *Kazzie*, are in a relationship? But I thought he was in Rapid City?"

"Well... he was, but now he's here. I'm sorry I lied."

She shook her head. "Oh my God, Meghan. I had no idea! I mean, I knew you were really close with Davin and the other Kazzies, but I never..." Her eyes grew wider. "So all of this time when we've been doing research on him, you've—"

"No, not all of the time. We didn't officially become a couple until recently. However, things weren't always innocent between us when he lived in the Compound."

"I had no idea."

I breathed a sigh of relief as the gates grew closer. "Well, that's good to hear. The reason I kept it a secret is because I don't know what the MRI will do if they find out. What if they kick me out of Division 5?" I lowered my voice as the MRRA soldiers grew closer. "I hope I don't need to say this, but please keep Davin's and my relationship between you and me. I'm in enough hot water with Dr. Sadowsky right now. I don't need to add this complication on top of it."

Amy gave me a scolding look. "Of course I won't tell anybody, Meg. It's not like you're the first person to date someone they met at the Compound. Remember how I was dating a certain someone before it was even allowed?"

I remembered all right. The first time I'd met Ben had

been when he and Amy showed up unexpectedly at my doorstep following my firing from Compound 26. That had been a long time ago, but back then, it had been against the rules for MRI employees to date one another.

It hadn't stopped Amy and Ben. They were still in love and very happy together, and since that policy had changed they no longer had to hide their relationship.

When we neared the gates, we stopped talking as we went through security. Similar to Compound 26, the security measures had lessened here. It only took ten minutes before the giant gates opened to let us exit.

A taxi cab waited outside. It would be the first time I'd ever taken a cab.

"Where to, ladies?" The taxi driver sat in the front and looked over his shoulder at us.

I rattled off the address of the home Davin and I had rented. "Do you know how far away it is?"

The driver nodded. "About half an hour."

I sat back and bit my lip as I tried to figure out the logistics of traveling to and from Compound 3 every day from our temporary home. The MRI provided transportation to and from the hotel for the employees via the van, but I wasn't sure what Amy and I would do.

"Don't worry, Meg." Amy patted my hand. "I can see the wheels turning in your mind right now. We can either rent a car or invest in bicycles."

A laugh bubbled out of me. "I can just see it, two prestigious MRI scientists arriving every day to work on bikes."

Amy's eyes twinkled with amusement. "It would be worth it just to see the shocked look on Dr. Sadowsky's face."

We both started laughing.

WHEN WE REACHED the house that Davin and I had rented, I took in the surrounding neighborhood. Large palm trees lined the road. The houses sat closely together. Browning grass filled our rental home's front yard. Desert plants and shrubs surrounded the perimeter. It seemed that most of the houses in this neighborhood were occupied. Only a few had boarded-up windows and neglected yards.

The cab driver unloaded our bags from the trunk and set them on the curb. Pulling cash from my purse, I stuffed the bills in his outstretched hand and thanked him for the ride.

"So this is home sweet home?" Amy put her hands on her hips as an evening breeze ruffled the long red curls around her shoulders.

I nodded. "This is it. It looked decent enough in the pictures. As long as there are no snakes in the toilets or cockroaches under the sheets, I'm sure it'll be fine."

A horrified look crossed Amy's features. "Snakes and cockroaches? You're joking, right?"

I laughed. "Your face looks almost as terrified as Mitch's would."

She rolled her eyes but chuckled anyway. It was no secret that our co-worker back in South Dakota hated all forms of nature.

The front door opened as we climbed the steps up to the small porch. Davin's eyes narrowed when he saw Amy.

Amy swallowed tightly and gripped her bag harder. Her knuckles turned white. "Hi, Davin. It's good to see you again."

"Um, yeah, you too." He ran a hand through his midnight hair and opened the door wider to let us in. His shoulders were so broad, they filled the doorframe.

The tension between Davin and Amy was so thick I could have cut it, but it still didn't stop my tingle of excitement at seeing him here, in California. However, that excitement would have to wait.

"So, Davin…" I wrung my hands. "I may have invited Amy to live with us."

Silence followed.

Davin glanced between me and Amy.

Crap, I should have talked to him first.

"I mean, I don't…you know… have to stay here…" Amy stammered. "You know, come to think of it, it's probably best if I join the rest of the scientists at the hotel." She picked her bag back up from where she'd dropped it by the door. "I think the cab's still out there. I'll just go check."

She bolted out the door before I could stop her.

When it was just me and Davin in the entryway, he crossed his arms and raised an eyebrow. "Really? A woman who did experiments on me for years is now going to be my roommate?"

I wrung my hands more. "I know. I know. I should have talked to you first, but Dr. Sadowsky was right there, and I couldn't very well give a reason for refusing her without bringing you into it."

A muscle ticked in his jaw.

"She's my friend, Davin." I stepped closer to him and said more quietly, "And she's not bad, really, I promise. She actually sticks up for me and has my back every time I need her. And I know she did some awful things to you under Dr. Roberts' rule, but she hated doing it. Please believe me. She really didn't want to."

Some of the tension eased from his shoulders, but the dark expression on his face remained. With a scowl, he finally shook his head. "Fine. She can stay, but don't expect me to like her."

I nodded. I knew it was the best I could hope for right

now.

Hurrying back outside, I was relieved to see that Amy hadn't left. She currently stood on the curb while tapping a text furiously into her phone. The cab was nowhere to be seen. A warm evening breeze blew hair into my eyes as I rushed to her side.

"Amy!"

Her wide gaze met mine. "Shit, Meghan. That was a mess. I'm so sorry. I should have never asked to live with you. If I had known Davin—"

"You couldn't have known because I never told you." I picked up her suitcase, wincing slightly at the strain. "It's fine. Come back in. Davin's okay with it now."

She eyed me skeptically. "What did you do? Hold a gun to his head and force him to accept me as a roommate?"

I grinned at her sarcastic tone. "Nothing that dramatic. Just... uh... don't expect him to be all friendly right away, okay? He still doesn't know you in the way I do."

Amy rolled her eyes but still followed me back to the porch. "What have I gotten myself into?"

Back inside, Amy and Davin once again faced each other like gentlemen dueling at dawn. Both eyed the other warily yet none seemed committed to making the first move.

I grabbed his hand. His warm fingers closed around mine like a glove that fit perfectly. I squeezed him tightly.

Amy set her suitcase down. "Are there really two bedrooms here?"

Davin clenched his jaw. "Yeah, there are two. Plenty of room for you."

Amy coiled a finger around her curls nervously. "In that case, just let me know which room is mine. I'll get out of your way so you two can get settled."

Since Davin had already been at the home for a few hours, he gave us a quick tour. The largest bedroom lay in the back of the house. It held a queen bed, two end tables, and a large dresser. The other bedroom also held a queen bed but was smaller.

"I'm guessing I'll take this one." Amy slung her purse over the door handle to the smaller room.

Davin eyed her and said cautiously, "That's what I figured too."

As Amy began to unpack, I followed Davin out to the living room. Once we were alone, I said, "Thank you for letting her stay."

Davin ran an agitated hand through his hair. "It's fine. Really, it is. If I'm going to be your boyfriend and a permanent fixture in your life, I guess I need to learn to put the past behind me. Amy's your friend, so I'll have to find a way to accept her whether I like it or not."

I swallowed back my smile. More and more it was beginning to sink in that Davin and I were truly a couple, and that come what may, we were in this together.

"Do you need pain meds?" His hand dropped as he eyed my wound.

"I'm okay for now. I took a dose before we left the Compound."

He pulled me onto the couch. The rental was sparsely furnished and decorated in pale greens and browns. At least everything appeared clean.

After sitting beside him, he asked, "How was your first day? Did it go okay?"

I thought about Dr. Dornhoff, Giselle Warren, Division 5, and Monica Brown. The last thought had me scowling.

Davin tensed. "That bad?"

"I don't know." I told him about Monica and her apparent hatred for me.

His brow furrowed while his electric-blue eyes glittered. "Don't pay her any attention. People like that aren't worth your time."

I nodded in agreement, but worry still plagued me. I had a feeling Monica Brown wouldn't let it be that easy.

17 - DISCOVERY

The next morning, Amy and I called another cab. We still hadn't figured out an economical way to travel to and from work. That was Davin's job. Today, he'd be scouring the area's dealerships for a short-term car lease.

Settling into the back, Amy told the driver where we were headed, and he took off. Dawn sunlight blazed through the front windshield.

Nibbling my lip, I angled my body toward Amy. "Do you think anything will happen if the MRI finds out that Davin and I are romantically involved?"

Amy shrugged. "I honestly don't know, Meg. There's not a policy on that, so you have that to fall back on should you be questioned. *But* it could be seen as a conflict of interest. If they know you're in a relationship with a Kazzie, you may no longer be allowed on the team."

I bit my lip sharply and winced. That was my fear too. That once it was discovered I'd become romantically involved with a Kazzie that my time with Division 5 would end.

Amy patted my hand. "Let's hope it doesn't come to that."

When we entered Compound 3, we went straight to the lab. Inside, energy buzzed in the air. Most of the other scientists were already hard at work. Unfortunately, Monica Brown was one of them.

As soon as I entered the room, I felt her eyes zero in on me. Considering we'd just met, the hostility it carried was crazy. *Just ignore her.*

Amy shrugged her lab coat on. "Don't look now, but your new friend is sending mental daggers your way."

"I know. I can feel it."

I didn't want to look at her, but it was like an invisible hand turned my head. Sure enough, Monica was glaring at me from over her lab station. She sneered before glancing away.

Shallow breaths filled my chest. *Ignore her, Meghan. Whatever her problem is, it's not your concern.*

Doing my best to take my own advice, Amy and I got to work. We still had so much to catch up on. Division 5's most promising lead revolved around targeting a type of RNA that was only produced in cells infected by *Makanza*.

Thankfully, I soon immersed myself in work and all thoughts of Monica fell away. The morning flew by. Before I knew it, Amy was tapping my shoulder.

"Meghan? Earth to Meghan."

I shook my head when I finally realized Amy stood at my side. "Sorry, what is it?"

Amy waved her hand around the lab. It was almost empty. "Um, it's lunchtime. Do you want to join the rest of us?"

Heat rushed up my cheeks. I'd once again become so immersed in my own head that I'd been oblivious to everything around me.

I snapped my gloves off reluctantly. Even though the last thing I felt like doing was stopping to eat, I knew I should. *I should probably take some pain meds too.*

"Yeah, of course."

I had my lab coat halfway off when something pushed strongly against my back. I stumbled. My hands came out instinctively to stop me from crashing into my lab bench. The sudden movement caused pain to course through my arm. I hissed in a breath.

"Watch where you're going!" The words reached my ears just as whoever pushed me strode past.

I stiffened as Amy called after the person, "What did you do that for?"

By the time I pushed myself back upright, Monica was already sailing out of the lab. When she opened the door to leave, she glanced over her shoulder and smirked.

I stared at her open-mouthed as the door closed behind her.

"What the hell is her problem?" Amy said through gritted teeth. Her small hands clenched into fists. "She purposely just knocked you over!"

"I... I know." I rolled my shoulder. The pain quickly subsided, but I knew I should check my wound. Since it had been opened so much over the past few weeks, it wasn't healing well. It was very possible Monica's shove had just reopened it.

"That bitch definitely has it out for you." Amy's green eyes glittered. "You should report her."

Amy had a point. Physically assaulting a co-worker was far from okay. "I will if she does it again."

I pulled Amy toward the door and peeked under my shirt. A dot of fresh blood seeped through the bandaid. A flash of anger coursed through me.

Of course, all of it didn't go unnoticed. A soft scratch

filled the back of my mind. I opened readily to Sara. *Hi. I'm fine.*

Are you sure? I got a flash of... I don't know. Fear and then pain or something.

I scowled in disgust but then caught Amy's raised eyebrow. I quickly smoothed my face. *I'm fine. Really. It was just... an unfortunate incident.*

What do you mean? Sara's curiosity turned into worry.

I told her about Monica. *For whatever reason, she has it out for me. It doesn't seem to matter that I've never done anything to her.*

Unbelievable! You should tell your boss.

That's what Amy said.

Sara and I spoke for a few more moments as Amy walked beside me. I tried to keep my face neutral, but a few times Amy looked questioningly my way. I figured that meant I wasn't hiding my internal conversation as well as I'd hoped.

I better go. Amy keeps giving me weird looks.

Talk to you soon?

Yeah, Davin and I will get in touch with you tonight so we can all talk.

Good, I can't wait to hear what California's been like minus the mean girl.

THANKFULLY, THE REST of the afternoon Monica didn't bother me. I felt certain that was mostly because I was surrounded by people the entire time. However, it didn't stop a few glares from her. But I took Davin's advice and ignored her.

As we were wrapping up for the day, I pulled out my phone to check my messages. My heart stopped when I saw the text from Cate.

We found what killed Zoe. It wasn't *Makanza*. It will be broadcast on the news tonight.

My hands shook as I hurried out of the lab with my phone in tow. I'd been wondering how things were going with Zoe's autopsy but had been too busy to call Cate. And we still didn't have any proof that Senator Douglas was behind it all.

Perhaps we never would.

I quickly dialed Cate's number. When she answered, my heart was pounding so hard I could barely get the words out. "You discovered what killed Zoe?"

Cate's reply echoed disbelief. "She contracted rabies."

"What?"

"Exactly. We were all shocked to discover that."

"But how?"

Cate sighed. "It seems they took a trip down south prior to the Kazzies' release. They'd told investigators about their travels initially during interviews, but it wasn't until we arrived and began to dig deeper that a key detail finally emerged. Apparently, the day before they left Florida, Zoe made a comment about encountering a cat near the beach. Her mother recalled a scratch that Zoe said was tingly and bothering her, but after cleaning it and applying a bandage, her mom didn't think anything of it."

"You're kidding me." I shook my head. "That's incredible. I can't remember the last fatal rabies case our country had."

"It was over three years ago. That's probably why it took so long to pinpoint. It's such a rare way to die."

"And how are her parents doing with the news?"

"Her mom's blaming herself, saying she should have taken her to the doctor after that scratch, but her dad's been acting... odd."

My heart sped up. "How so?"

"For one, he sought me out. He wanted me to tell you that he's sorry for what he did." Cate paused, as if waiting for me to explain that comment. When I didn't, she added, "What would he be sorry about?"

"Um…" I debated skirting the issue but decided Cate deserved better than that. I finally told her about the attack in Iowa.

"He attacked you?" Cate sputtered. "And you didn't tell me?"

I winced at her tone. "I didn't want it causing any more issues for me, and it's in the past now. So what does all of this mean moving forward?"

Cate sighed heavily. "It means that the vaccine is as effective as we said it was. And that fact will be all over the news by tonight."

I was grinning when we hung up. Even though we still didn't have proof that Senator Douglas was behind Zoe's delayed autopsy, at least we had proof that the Kazzies weren't to blame for her death.

On my way back to the lab, I bumped into Giselle in the hall. She held her clipboard and wore an airy blouse. Her small frame was swallowed in it.

"You certainly look happy," she commented. Her eyes twinkled with amusement.

"I am. I just got off the phone with Dr. Hutchinson. They've discovered what killed Zoe Mathison and it wasn't *Makanza.*"

Giselle's smile froze. "Really? What killed her?"

"Rabies. It wasn't *Makanza* at all."

That night, ANN ran the story about Zoe Mathison and what her autopsy revealed. Amy, Davin, and I watched it in our living room on the small rental TV.

I held Davin's hand. When the news anchor explained that rabies had actually been the culprit for Zoe's death, Davin squeezed my hand tightly.

"They can't lock you back up again," I whispered. "They have no proof that you're a danger to anybody."

He merely swallowed tightly and nodded, but he didn't look convinced.

18 - FINDING A CURE

During the next few weeks, Amy and I spent long days working at Compound 3. There was so much to do as we prepared for human trials.

It helped that Dr. Sadowsky was busy. He rarely checked to see if I'd left after six hours which meant I worked *much* longer than my allotted time. And while that led to disapproving glances from Davin and the occasional argument, for the most part, he kept his promise to try and support my decision to work.

It helped that I grew stronger each day. On our twelve to sixteen hour days, I was tired, but not in pain. And since I'd begun working remotely with a physical therapist, my range of motion had improved. I felt less stiff and more like my old self every day.

The one downfall that continued was Monica Brown's harassment. She hadn't lessened in her torment. If anything, it had increased. However, she was subtle which meant I had no proof the harassment was from her, even though I *knew* it was.

Some days, I'd return from lunch to find the contents of

my purse dumped all over the floor, or my research files in a jumbled mess on my lab bench, or chemical solutions splashed on my lab gear which meant I had to venture all the way to the laundry department to find new clothes.

The acts were petty and malicious, which was why I knew it was her. Nobody else hated me.

But Monica was nothing if not clever. She never did anything that could implicate her.

However, the worst part was the afternoon she breezed against me and muttered under her breath, "I know who your roommate is."

That statement had made me grow cold while Monica sailed off with a smug smirk on her face.

I figured she wasn't talking about Amy. No. She was talking about Davin. And if Monica knew about Davin and me, that meant she could report our relationship at any time.

Subsequently, I didn't report Monica's harassment to upper management. It was like Monica knew she held my future in her hands. And while Amy was right, not having an MRI policy against dating Kazzies *was* on my side, I wasn't willing to risk getting kicked out of Division 5.

The one thing that kept me sane was knowing the drug trials were starting soon, and if a cure was found, I'd be leaving Compound 3 and Monica Brown behind me forever.

A PILE OF university brochures sat on our kitchen table when I got home that night. We'd been in California for two weeks. That knowledge had my insides tingling in anticipation. Only one week to go until I was officially, *finally* declared healed.

Which only meant one thing.

I eyed Davin as he cooked at the stove. His broad

shoulders and tousled hair made a deep need clench inside me.

He glanced over his shoulder and caught me watching. A knowing glint entered his sapphire eyes.

During our time here, Davin had already applied for half a dozen schools in the Midwest. Despite the unrest in our country, Davin was planning for a future.

A future I was intent on giving him.

I hopped onto the kitchen counter as Davin stirred some sauce he'd made. From the delicious scents wafting up, it smelled like Italian.

While doing my physical therapy stretches as I sat on the counter, I eyed the brochures. "How's the application process going?"

"I applied for two more today, both in North Dakota."

He nodded toward the newspaper. "Did you see that story?"

The paper sat off to my side. I glanced at the headline. *Woman in Idaho claims she almost died from Makanza.*

I flipped it over so I wouldn't have to see it. "I bet money she made it up for the attention. Either that or Senator Douglas paid her to say it." It still infuriated me that we still hadn't found anything to implicate the senator. Despite Cate digging deeper into the senator's background, she hadn't found anything incriminating.

"He's not going to stop, is he?" A flash of anger crossed his features.

"No, I don't think he will."

While Davin's skepticism over his continued freedom remained, he wasn't as cynical as he'd been a few months ago. Freedom had done that to him. Now that he had a taste of it, I knew he'd fight to keep it.

I hopped off the counter and approached Davin from

behind. Pressing myself against his back, I wrapped my arms around him. His flat abdomen felt as hard as a rock beneath my hands.

"But with a cure, it won't matter what he does." I turned my head and pressed my cheek between his shoulder blades. "He'll have lost his leg to stand on. And since drug trials start tomorrow, the end could be near."

In a blurred move, Davin turned and held me in his arms. "I hope you're right."

WHEN AMY AND I entered work the next morning, a buzz hung in the lab, which wasn't surprising since the drug trials started today. But what I didn't expect was to see all of the researchers huddled in the corner around someone.

"What's going on?" Amy pulled her lab coat off its hook.

I shrugged and grabbed mine too. "I have no idea."

We strode toward the group. When they saw us approaching, they parted so we could join them.

My mouth dropped when I saw who stood among them.

"Dorothy!" I rushed forward.

The Kazzie that had formerly resided within Compound 26 grinned and pulled me into a hug. "Meghan, it's so good to see you!"

Her plump matronly build hadn't changed since I'd last seen her. She felt soft and round in my arms. I felt everyone's eyes on us. It didn't stop my tears of joy. "It's good to see you too. What are you doing here? I thought you weren't arriving until this afternoon?"

She pulled back just enough to look me over. "I couldn't wait any longer. I decided to come early. Now, where's this drug you told me about? I hear I'm going to be the first guinea pig." Her brown eyes shone with excitement. "Ever since you told me about the cure, I've been waiting rather impatiently for it."

Given Dorothy's past behavior, I wasn't surprised by her enthusiasm. Dorothy had strain 8, which meant she had pounds of brown fat that would never disappear regardless of how much she exercised or how little she ate. However, it also meant she'd never die from starvation. She could go for months without eating or drinking and still stay alive.

Before I could respond to Dorothy's question, Monica stepped forward.

I tensed.

"Come with me, Dorothy." Monica waved the Kazzie toward the door. "We have everything ready for you in the Experimental Room."

Dorothy stiffened. "The Experimental Room?" Her voice sounded small.

The rest of the researchers were already heading toward the door so hadn't heard her question, but Dorothy hung back.

Monica didn't seem to realize that the Kazzie wasn't following her.

"Wait!" I yelled at the retreating scientists.

All of them stopped. Monica's hand was on the door to leave the lab when she turned to glare at me. "Yes, Dr. Forester?"

I glanced at Dorothy's terrified expression. "Why do we need to administer the drug in the Experimental Room? Why can't we do it here?"

Contempt dripped from Monica's words when she replied, "Protocol dictates we administer the drug there. Now, do you want to take the drug or not, Dorothy?" Monica's unsympathetic gaze turned to the Kazzie.

Dorothy stood up straighter. "Of course, I do."

"Then follow us. The drug will be administered in the Experimental Room as planned." Monica stormed out the door.

Amy glared after her.

Dorothy shuffled her feet uncertainly. "I suppose that's decided then. Should we follow her?"

I seethed inwardly that Monica was now treating Dorothy as poorly as me. Trying to swallow my anger, I replied tightly, "I suppose."

Amy, Dorothy, and I all marched toward the Inner Sanctum. Similar to Compound 26, the Inner Sanctum consisted of twenty cells that formed a circle around the Experimental Room. The Experimental Room was the epicenter of the Kazzie wing.

"I never thought I'd come back here," Dorothy joked. She waddled down the hall as we approached the first cell, her arm brushing mine.

Despite her lighthearted words, I still caught the edge in them. I squeezed her hand. "You can back out at any time. Remember that."

Dorothy managed a faint smile. "I didn't come all the way out here to back out."

By the time we reached the Inner Sanctum, most of the scientists had convened in the watch room that overlooked the Experimental Room. It was almost identical to Compound 26's.

A huge control panel sat in front of the large glass window that overlooked the four beds within. Large robotic arms hung over each bed. I remembered all too well what it was like to be placed on one of those beds.

When I'd been exposed to *Makanza* and had become sick, I'd lived in the Inner Sanctum within Compound 26. Samples had been taken from me in a bed very similar to the ones before me. I shuddered remembering what that experience had been like—those spidery, robotic arms swishing and swaying above had haunted me for weeks.

I stepped closer to Dorothy. "I'll come in with you."

Dorothy nodded tightly. "Please do."

The door opened with a hiss. My hands balled into fists that we were making Dorothy do this, in this room. The drug we'd been working on was an injection.

A simple injection.

There was no reason that it couldn't be done in an office or in the lab, despite Compound 3's protocols. Even though the full course of treatment required a dozen injections spread out over several weeks, it was still easy to administer. There was no need for all this hoopla.

"Please seat yourself on bed two." Monica's voice rang through the speakers. She sat at the control panel. The technicians who formerly manned it were nowhere to be seen.

"I can administer the drug." I turned to face Monica. "You don't need to use the robots."

Just then, the staff door cracked opened in the corner of the watch room. Giselle slipped inside. She moved as stealthily as a panther and blended into the back of the room. I'd have never known she was there if I hadn't been facing the door directly.

Monica carried on, oblivious to our newcomer. "Protocol dictates all medication administered within the Experimental Room be delivered by the robots. If you have a problem with that, you may bring it up with Dr. Dornhoff. Now, do you wish to proceed, Dorothy?"

Dorothy squeezed my hand from where she lay on the bed. "It's all right, Meghan. I don't want to cause any problems."

The only thing that made me step away from Dorothy was the quiet plea in her voice. I knew she wanted a cure as desperately as Bethany.

Regardless, it didn't make it easier when the robots descended. Dorothy squeezed her eyes tightly shut as her whole body turned rigid. It was sickening to watch. For years, the Kazzies had been subjected to practices like this. Practices against their will.

Thankfully, it was over quickly. The robots injected Dorothy with the first drug treatment. Her breath hissed in when the drug entered her muscle. It probably burned painfully since it was such a potent, concentrated dose.

When finished, the robots placed a bandage precisely over the small puncture site before freezing above her like a suspended octopus.

Dorothy opened her eyes. "Is it over?"

I rushed to her side to help her off the bed. "Yes, it's over for now. Your next injection will be in two days."

"They said I'll need to stay in the Inner Sanctum while I participate in this drug trial."

I nodded sadly. "We need to monitor you. But remember, you're not a prisoner here. You may leave at any time, and if you decide you no longer want to participate in this trial, you don't have to."

Dorothy's brown eyes warmed as she squeezed my hand. "I know, Meghan. I'm free now because of you. And in a few weeks, I won't have *Makanza* anymore."

She sounded so convinced in the cure.

I could only hope she was right.

19 – DRUG TRIALS

Word soon spread that we'd begun drug trials. It seemed every day more Kazzies arrived at Compound 3. All twenty cells in the Inner Sanctum quickly filled—some even held two Kazzies. However, it would still be weeks before we would know if the cure was effective.

When I strode into Compound 3 on Friday morning, concluding my third week in California, my eyes widened when I saw who stood in the main lobby.

His broad-shouldered frame had already captivated the receptionists' interest. Two of them were blatantly trying to capture his attention. Between their demure grins and batting eyelashes, they were practically falling over their feet for him.

Ian Gallager rested a muscled forearm against the desk as he chatted easily with them. He still had the same red curls and a scruffy beard. In jeans and a button-up shirt, he looked just as I remembered him.

Handsome. Strong. And uniquely charming.

I grinned when I approached him. "Ian, what are you doing here?"

Light blue eyes crinkled in the corners when they alighted upon me. He straightened and took a step my way. "I heard you were working here."

"Yeah, but that doesn't explain why *you're* here."

"I've been roped into organizing the drug trials. With so many Kazzies wanting to partake, they needed somebody to oversee its management. I'm the lucky winner."

My mouth dropped. "So does that mean you're working here now?"

"For the time being, yes."

I wonder what Davin will think of that. The Kazzie still had no idea that Ian had previously wanted to date me. I'd turned Ian down. Despite genuinely liking Ian and caring for him, he didn't make my heart race or cause that fluttery feeling in my stomach, not like Davin did.

Out of the corner of my eye, I caught the secretaries enviously looking on. One was leaning so far forward, I was worried she'd topple out of her chair.

Giving them wan smiles, my heart rate ticked up at the attention Ian and I were drawing. I nodded toward the back corridors and said, "Should I show you around?"

His dimple appeared when he grinned. "Lead the way."

I led him through the maze of corridors behind the reception area. Even though Compound 3 was similar to Washington's Compounds, they weren't identical. Ian could easily lose his way until he grew accustomed to the layout here.

"I hear there are over twenty Kazzies participating in the trials." His large feet tapped on the concrete floors as we zigzagged through the halls.

I nodded. "That's right. Dorothy's getting her fourth injection tomorrow. The rest are all in various stages behind her."

Ian's cedar scent fluttered to me in a draft. A large vent hummed overhead.

His head dipped toward mine when he said, "As of now, there are seventy more Kazzies who signed up to participate. We're planning to open Compounds 1 and 2 to accommodate them as well as Nevada's Compound."

"That many?"

He nodded. "It seems a large percentage of Kazzies don't want to stay infected."

"Has someone explained to them they'll be housed in the Inner Sanctums during the trials? And more importantly, do they all understand why?" I stopped walking as I remembered Dorothy's panicked expression when she'd arrived. Nobody had thought to explain to her how the trials worked. She'd been caught unaware and had to learn the hard way. "Because the Inner Sanctum was their prison for so many years, as you know, but should any of them have a severe reaction, they'll have the best medical care on hand. That's why they need to stay here. Not to mention, we can monitor them twenty-four hours a day which helps progress our research. Still, I hate that they're once again held within these concrete cells."

I twisted my hands as Ian placed a comforting hand on my shoulder. "I know, Meg. I know. That's one of the reasons they hired me. I'll go through all of those details with each participant individually."

I breathed a sigh of relief. "Good. And I'm glad it's you. I know you'll treat them well."

Ian dropped his hand and nodded. "You can count on that. Now," he said, nodding down the hall. "Do you want to lead me to the Inner Sanctum? My first task today is to meet every Kazzie here."

I smiled gratefully and began walking again. "Yes. Follow

me."

IAN AND I spent the morning together. I introduced him to the Kazzies who were currently participating in the drug trials. Most of them I'd only met in the previous weeks. However, Dorothy wasn't the only one from Compound 26.

Garrett occupied cell nine. Since he had strain 19, his eyes were as large as eggs, and his brow was unnaturally thick and protruded. He had only just begun the trial, but it wasn't going well for him. He was only two injections in and had been screaming in pain for the past three days.

Ian grimaced when we stepped into cell nine's watch room. Garrett was visible in the corner of the cell. He cradled his head in his hands. Loud moans came through the watch room speakers. He didn't seem to know we were there.

An image of Davin sitting like that, in the corner of a cell, writhing in pain flashed through my mind. It wasn't the first time I'd thought about what Davin would experience if he entered the trials. So far, I hadn't brought up the subject with him. I was too terrified of how the drug would affect him. But more than that, I only wanted Davin to enter the trials if *he* chose to.

The guard stationed in Garrett's watch room swiveled around in her stool. The loud squeak from her chair, intermixing with Garrett's wails, made me wince.

Crossing her arms, the guard shook her head. "He's suffering again."

I swallowed tightly. "Yeah, he looks like he's really hurting."

The guard frowned. "They've tried everything. Narcotics, numbing cream, anti-anxiety medications, heat, ice, you name it, but none of it works."

"*None* of it?" Ian's brow furrowed.

I shook my head, my expression grim. "It was the same when he Changed the first time. They couldn't help him then either."

Ian raised his eyebrows so I explained further.

"When he'd contracted *Makanza*, strain 19 enlarged his skull to accommodate his egg-shaped eyes. The bones around his eyes Changed as did his actual eyeballs. It was a slow process. And now, the cure reverses that. It's the same process all over again, except this time, it's backward." I frowned. "We knew this was a risk going in, that the reversal could be just as painful, and unfortunately, that seems to be exactly what's happening."

"How slow will this process be?" Ian asked.

"We're assuming it will take several weeks, since that's how long it took for him to Change." I stepped closer to the watch room glass.

Garrett had fallen to his side and was rolling back and forth on the floor.

My stomach sank. "Susan's right." I nodded toward Susan, Garrett's guard. "We've tried everything, but no amount of morphine or fentanyl will control his pain. Most days, he lies on his bed, cradling his head and alternates between screaming and whimpering."

Garrett sat back up again. At that moment, he lifted his head. Our gazes connected.

He gave me a pleading look. "Please!" His word came out in a wail. "Please, Meghan. Help me!"

My insides chilled at the agony in his voice.

I turned to Susan. "Will you call the Experimental Room techs? See if we can sedate him for a few hours, just to give him some relief."

Susan nodded and picked up the phone.

I stepped over to the control panel and leaned into the microphone. Pushing the button, I said, "I know you're in severe pain, Garrett. We can sedate you for a few hours if you'd like."

His large, egg-shaped eyes shimmered with tears. All he managed was a slight nod before he winced again and returned to moaning.

Ian and I stayed in Garrett's watch room until the lab techs arrived. They helped Garrett to the Experimental Room where he'd be sedated and monitored.

As we stepped out of the watch room, Ian raised an eyebrow. "Why not keep him sedated the entire time? Surely anything's better than what he's experiencing."

I shook my head regretfully. "It's too dangerous. We'd have to use powerful anesthetics to keep him under which compromises his breathing even if he's intubated. If he's under for too long, it's possible he won't wake up."

Ian sighed. "I had no idea a cure would make them suffer."

I held my hand up to the scanner when we reached the next access door. "They're all experiencing side effects, but it's not excruciatingly painful for everyone. While every Change, and likewise its reversal, has some degree of pain, not all are unbearable."

We stepped into the hallway outside cell ten. The floor to ceiling windows showed the bustling activity within.

Dorothy's eyes shone with excitement as two lab techs escorted her out of cell ten's back panel. When the back panel door slid open, she grinned and waved at me before following the technicians.

I lifted my hand in farewell as she waddled through the

panel. The door slid closed behind her.

Turning to Ian, I nodded toward where Dorothy had gone. "Dorothy's on her fifth injection today. Tomorrow's her sixth. She'll be officially halfway through treatment."

Ian put his hands on his hips. "And the results so far?"

A smile spread across my face. "So far, the drug seems to be working. She's still overweight, but the PET scans show a 40% reduction in brown fat. Her DNA also appears to be Changing. However, it's too soon to tell if it will be 100% effective."

"That seems promising."

"It is. We withheld water from her for the entire day yesterday. Near the end of the day, she complained of feeling slightly thirsty. That's a promising sign. Before, she never felt thirst."

"And her kidneys?"

"Her creatinine clearance has fallen into a normal range. When we biopsied one of her kidneys, the cells appeared almost identical to that of a normal human."

Ian grinned. "In other words, this cure is showing promising results."

"Exactly."

DAVIN HAD DINNER waiting when I got home that night. Since it was the weekend, Amy had flown back to South Dakota to visit Ben. My nerves tingled in anticipation at spending some time alone with Davin. We'd had no time to ourselves in the weeks we'd been in California.

Scents from dinner wafted in the air when I stepped into the kitchen. The sight that greeted me when I rounded the corner made my breath stop.

Davin stood in front of the stove. His broad shoulders

strained against his t-shirt. Worn jeans hung from his lean hips while he stirred something in a pan. Steam rolled around him.

He slung a towel over his shoulder and glanced my way. In a blurred move, he was at my side. Pulling me to him, his arms slid possessively around my waist. "You're finally home."

I stood on my tiptoes and pressed my lips to his.

He tightened his hold even more. Parting my lips, his tongue grazed across mine.

A heavy longing pulsed in my lower belly. My six weeks were officially up. "I've missed you," I breathed.

"Me too. These days are long without you."

Rolling my neck, I again marveled that my injury no longer hurt. I finally felt healed. *But will Davin agree that I'm healed, that's the real question.*

Something splattered on the stove, and in another blurred move, Davin was lifting the pan. "How was work?"

"Good." I pulled out a bar stool at the counter and slid onto it to watch him. "Ian arrived today. He's going to be managing the drug trials."

Davin raised an eyebrow as he began to warm a pile of tortillas. "Ian's here?"

"Yep, he flew in this morning."

"So, do I finally get to meet this mystery guy?"

I smothered a smile at his tone. He was trying to act nonchalant, but I still caught the edge. "You have nothing to worry about. He's just my friend."

His brow furrowed as he flipped a tortilla in the pan. "Perhaps things have changed, but from what I remember, most guys are only *friends* with women if they think there's a chance of being more than that."

I averted my gaze so he wouldn't see my guilty expression. Ian had definitely wanted to be more than friends once upon a time. However, he'd been nothing but a gentleman since I'd turned him down, but I still had a feeling Davin wouldn't be thrilled to hear about Ian's past interest in me.

I quickly changed the subject. "Did I tell you that Bethany's arriving on Monday?"

Davin pulled out two plates and began dishing the food up. "She is? No, I don't think you told me that."

I nodded and stood to help get dinner on the table. "I'm hopeful the drug will help her. While we still don't know if it's 100% effective, it *is* effective enough to reduce physical Changes. Maybe that will be enough for her."

He pulled two glasses from the cupboard and filled them with water. "For now, it will have to be enough." Handing me my glass, he added, "I hope you like Mexican. I'm branching out with my cooking."

I eyed the plates of steaming tortillas, blackened chicken, peppers, and onions. My mouth watered. Stretching my arms overhead, I again marveled that I no longer felt pain in my wound. Every evening and morning, I'd diligently done my PT exercises. It seemed to be helping.

My breasts strained against my shirt when I did another stretch.

Davin's gaze dipped lower. His pupils dilated when my nipples hardened under his stare. Glancing at the calendar on the wall, he said, "You do know what today is, don't you?"

My heart rate sped up. "What?" I asked the question even though I already knew the answer.

His gaze grew hooded. "The last day of your restrictions. Therefore, according to your doctors, you're fully healed."

My heart stopped. *And that only means one thing.*

"Are you hungry?" His hand brushed my hip when he passed me on the way to the table.

My nerves tingled at the contact. "Um, sure," I squeaked.

He sat down and patted the chair beside him. "About *that*... I have a surprise for you."

I sat down stiffly at his side. "A surprise?"

Leaning closer, he brushed the hair from my eyes. His feathery touch shot tingles down my spine.

"Since it's the weekend, and you've worked every weekend since we've come here, I was hoping I could convince you to take this one off."

"Take it off?" The repetitive question was all I could manage as anticipation built up inside me.

"Yeah." His lips brushed my neck. "Can you take the weekend off?"

I closed my eyes and tilted my head to the side. "I suppose I could. What are we doing?"

He pulled back and grinned devilishly. "You'll see."

DESPITE MY CONSTANT questions over dinner, he wouldn't tell me what he'd planned. I knew he had something up his sleeve from the excited gleam in his eyes, but he wasn't letting on.

After we finished eating, in which I barely managed to finish half of my fajita as my nervousness consumed me, Davin disappeared from the kitchen.

Returning with two packed bags, he nodded toward the door. "Are you ready?"

I quickly finished washing the last plate from dinner before drying my hands. "Ready for what?"

"Come with me and you'll find out."

Goosebumps rose along my arms as I followed him onto the porch. Cool wind whipped around the porch. With the sun set, the temperature had steadily fallen.

I shivered.

"Cold?" Davin pulled out my jacket and handed it to me.

I shook my head in amazement. "How is it that you remember everything?"

He shrugged. "Since I've already applied to every school I'm interested in, my days now revolve around trying to make your life easier. If that means having your jacket on hand when I know you'll be chilly, that's what I do."

I laughed. "I think I'm going to miss this when you're in school."

He waggled his eyebrows. "Yeah, don't get used to it. It's not going to be like this forever."

I laughed and slipped my coat on as Davin locked the door behind us. He disappeared from my side and reappeared a second later. Our bags were missing. I knew that meant he'd already packed them.

Sure enough, the car was running with the bags in the back by the time I approached the vehicle. I slid into the passenger seat and buckled my seatbelt.

A tingle of excitement raced along my limbs. "Are you going to tell me where we're going now?"

His midnight hair gleamed in the moonlight streaming through the windshield. Shadows dipped across his features, making his high cheekbones even more prominent. "Have you ever seen the Pacific Ocean?"

IT WAS JUST over a two-hour drive to reach the coast. Stars shone overhead. Since it was a dark drive, I wasn't able to enjoy the view. However, I knew when we reached the ocean.

Salty air whipped through the surrounding hills. The sound of crashing waves lapped the shore below.

Davin pulled into a small motel off Interstate 5.

When we stepped out, our slamming doors were the only sound in the quiet night. It was cooler here. I wrapped my arms tightly around me. "How did you find this place?"

In an instant, Davin was at my side. He pulled me closer to him, his body heat warming me. "It came up on an Internet search and seemed like the best place for our first romantic weekend together."

Romantic weekend. I knew exactly what he meant when he said *romantic.* My stomach fluttered at what tonight would bring. I was currently a twenty-four-year-old virgin, but come morning, I imagined I wouldn't be.

Davin checked us in as I stood nervously behind him. The small motel was similar to our accommodation in Texas. It was run by a couple who had returned when the borders reopened.

"I have you in our best room. There's a balcony that overlooks the ocean, and it's very private." The older innkeeper winked after she said that.

That small gesture had me blushing like a schoolgirl.

The woman showed us to our room, her skirt swishing around her knees. Like most accommodations, the room she led us to was simple yet clean. However, it was obvious it wasn't the room that drew people here.

It was the view.

My breath sucked in when I looked out the large windows overlooking the coast. A huge glimmering ocean of water moved below. Moonlight reflected off it. Stars hung above. Dark waves rolled and dipped all the way to the horizon.

"I hope you're happy with it." She smiled pleasantly. "This was always our most popular room."

I nodded. For a moment, I couldn't speak. It was too breathtaking. "Um... Yes, yes, of course," I stumbled. "It's beautiful."

Davin stepped closer to me and wrapped his arm around my waist.

The innkeeper's cheeks were rosy when she turned. "I'll leave you two alone then. Just let my husband or I know if you need anything."

The sound of the door closing behind her filled the quiet room. The next thing I knew Davin's warm hands were removing my jacket. He tossed it aside and set his hands on my shoulders.

I turned in his arms and tilted my chin up to meet his gaze.

"Do you like it?" His voice was husky.

"I love it."

"Do you want to go out on the balcony?"

I knew he'd sensed my nervousness and was trying to put me at ease. I nodded and tried to stop my hammering heart. It felt like a thousand butterflies were flapping within me.

It was silly. Davin and I had been sleeping in the same bed for weeks now. However, he'd refused to budge in the sex department. But now that I was officially healed, that rule had changed.

I shivered in the cold wind outside. He stood behind me and pulled me against him. His tall body felt like a rigid plank. Already, the hard bulge below his waist pressed into my back.

Pushing my hair aside, he bent down and pressed soft kisses against my neck. I closed my eyes and let the familiar aching desire wash through me. Between the cool wind and his kisses, goosebumps rose along my skin.

"I brought a bottle of wine," he murmured between kisses. "Do you want a glass?"

"Wine?" I kept my eyes closed when he nibbled on my earlobe. "Where did you find that?"

"I may have been scouring southern California while you

were at work."

Smiling, I turned in his arms. "Um... sure. I've never had wine before."

He disappeared in a blurred move. The rush of air chilled me even more. Turning back to the ocean, I draped my forearms over the railing.

Below, pounding waves crashed against the rocks as the tang of salty air whipped through the breeze. Moonlight glimmered off the vast water as thousands of stars twinkled above.

Davin reappeared at my side as if out of thin air. Wine from the glasses he held sloshed over the sides.

A wry smile lifted his lips. "Whoops. Forgot that could happen."

I laughed and took the glass. In the dim light emitting from our room, the wine appeared deep red. I lifted it up. "Red wine?"

He raised his glass to mine. "Yeah, a cabernet. It's from before the First Wave."

My eyes bulged. "That must have cost a fortune!"

Shrugging, he clinked his glass against mine. "Perhaps, and don't ask how long it took me to find it, but it seemed worth it for the occasion."

Hearing that made nerves flutter again in my belly. I hastily took a sip. The dark fruity flavors rolled across my tongue. "Hmm... it's different from anything I've drunk before."

Davin sipped his too. "Some say wine is an acquired taste."

I took another sip and then another. "It's not... bad."

He chuckled. "You'll get used to it, if we keep buying it."

Davin placed his free arm around me and drew me to his side. Standing next to one another, we gazed out over the balcony at the ocean below.

Leaning into him, warmth from his hard side kept the chill away, and as the alcohol spread through my veins and swam in my mind, I became more at ease.

Seeming to sense the change in me, he took our empty glasses and set them down. "Are you feeling more relaxed now?"

I nodded and entwined my arms around him. "Yes, that was exactly what I needed. Thank you."

He pulled me closer and leaned down to kiss me. The familiar throbbing and steady need began to fill my belly.

"I've been waiting for this for months," he whispered.

"Me too."

He lifted me in one of his lightning-fast moves. My head spun. The next thing I knew, we were back in the room and I was on the bed.

He left me just long enough to dim the lights. Then, he was back at my side, his weight sinking the mattress. He kissed me again as we slowly shed our clothing piece by piece.

My eyes drank in the site of him. His shoulders were so broad they seemed to fill the room, and his chest was as hard as steel.

And what happened next became a flurry of desire and spiraling need. Hands everywhere. Skin on skin. Limbs entwined. Davin took me to a realm I didn't know existed. The galaxy exploded behind my eyes when I shouted my release. His crushing embrace followed as his shout filled the room.

Minutes, hours, days later, I didn't know—my eyes fluttered open as his heavy arm lay across my abdomen. The night sky bathed the horizon out our window. Sweat licked my body as Davin hauled me against his chest. Time stood still. I trailed a finger along his forearm, the soft hair tickling my fingertip.

He pressed a kiss against my neck. "I love you," he whispered.

Contentment rushed through my veins as a feeling of absolute completeness settled within me. "I love you too."

THE NEXT MORNING, I snuggled into Davin's hard length as he spooned me from behind. My entire body ached in the most delicious way. Muscles I never knew I had felt sore and stiff, but my shoulder and chest felt fine. I wouldn't have traded it for the world.

Davin pushed up onto a forearm and smiled down at me. The morning sun glowed outside our window while the Pacific lapped below.

"How do you feel?"

I trailed a finger across his chest. "Sore but in the best way."

He chuckled. "Was it as good as you'd hoped for?"

I tenderly brushed a stray lock of hair from his forehead. "Better. I can't believe we waited that long. Now that I know what I've been missing, you won't be able to keep me off you."

He laughed deeply. "Good."

In the morning sun, his bronze skin glowed, reminding me of the powerful warriors he'd descended from.

"What are you thinking?" He trailed his finger along my jawline.

"Just you. How much I love you and how I'll never get sick of this."

His finger stopped. "I meant it at the hospital the other week, when I told you I'd never leave you. I'll stay with you forever if you'll have me."

Tears formed in my eyes as a strong surge of love filled my

chest. Sometimes, I loved him so much it was hard to breathe. "You're it for me too, Davin. I'll stay with you forever if you'll have me."

He smiled cheekily. "I suppose that's settled then." He leaned down and pressed his lips against mine.

I closed my eyes thinking he would draw it into a long, morning kiss. However, he pulled back and began pressing soft kisses against my jaw and then down my neck.

When he reached my collarbone, he paused. My eyes fluttered open to see him staring at the scar on my chest.

Instinctively, I reached up to cover it.

He gently clasped my wrist and pushed my arm away. "Don't."

Pulling the sheet down farther, he studied the wound before drinking in the rest of me, his gaze growing hungrier by the second. For the most part, my skin was smooth and soft, thanks to him. From my recent weight gain, I'd developed curves in areas I'd never had curves before. His pupils dilated while he looked his fill. But when he reached my thighs, a flash of anger crossed his features.

Two small scars marred the skin on my outer thigh. More battle wounds from my time within Compound 26, when samples had been taken from me to ensure I wasn't infected with *Makanza*. That was after my exposure, when I'd been confined within the Inner Sanctum.

"I hate what they did to you." His finger trailed along my scars before he kissed each tenderly.

"What about what they did to you?"

Scars littered his abdomen like a cross-stitch. Some of the scars were thin and fine. Others were ragged and wide. It was like they'd butchered him.

My hand shook when I reached for him. I traced my finger

along a prominent rigid scar.

His breath sucked in. "I'm not pretty anymore." His joke fell flat when I saw the pain on his face.

I quickly shifted so I was looking squarely in his eyes. I brushed a lock of hair from his forehead and cupped his cheek. "You'll always be beautiful to me. Even with the scars that the damned Compound inflicted on you, you're still the most breathtaking human I've ever met."

"I'd have more scars now if it weren't for you. I'd still be locked up in a cell under Dr. Roberts' rule—a lab rat he could do with as he pleased. It's because of you that I'm out here. Free."

A tear spilled onto my cheek at his heartfelt admission.

He brushed it away. "Don't cry. I never dreamed I'd be as happy as I am right now."

He pulled me closer as our arms wrapped around one another. For the first time since he was free, I dared to dream of a future together. A future that spanned decades. A future in which our love only grew.

A future in which he was free forever.

20 – PRODUCTION BEGINS

The weekend came to an end faster than either of us wanted it to. However, I couldn't revel in Davin's freedom quite yet. We still didn't know if the cure was 100% effective, but each day, it was looking more and more like it was. Because of that, drug production had been ramped up.

Dorothy would receive her last six injections in the coming week. The others Kazzies would soon follow. Most would be done with their treatments within the month. And if this drug was as effective as we hoped it was, the end of *Makanza* ruling the world was on the horizon.

On Monday morning, Amy and I drove to work. The dawn sun lit the wintry desert aglow. We were both quiet. Amy's thoughts seemed to be on Ben and South Dakota as a content, faraway look filled her gaze.

My thoughts shifted between the magical weekend with Davin and Bethany's impending arrival. I couldn't wait to see Bethany's face when she received her final injection. If this drug truly was as effective as we hoped, her wings would disappear on their own as her body reverted back to human form. I imagined it would be an extremely painful reversal for her, but I knew Bethany would still willingly suffer through it.

Luckily, one of the Kazzies had agreed to share her cell with Bethany so Bethany could stay at Compound 3. The list of Kazzies waiting to partake in the trials had doubled. Ian was busy readying California's other Compounds for them. And there were plans to open Nevada's Inner Sanctum too.

A smile spread across my face at what the future held.

"So what time is Bethany arriving?" Amy asked as we pulled into a parking spot outside Compound 3.

"Her flight's due at nine into San Diego. An MRI car is picking her up, so she should arrive no later than noon."

"It's hard to believe that things are going so well. I thought for sure it would be months or years before we found a cure." Amy cocked her head thoughtfully. "But I suppose that means we'll be returning to South Dakota soon." Her eyes shone with excitement.

My heart filled at the thought of returning home. "Did you have a good weekend with Ben?"

Amy clicked off her seatbelt as we stepped out of the car. Cool winter wind washed across my cheeks as our footsteps clicked on the pavement. Neither of us had bothered putting jackets on since it was already in the fifties. As we'd come to learn, the temperature would rise steadily during the day.

"We had a great weekend. We watched a few movies and caught up with his friends. I had no idea I'd miss him so much."

"Maybe he should come to visit." I winked.

"That's a great idea!"

As we approached the guards, our conversation stilted. It was only when we strode into our wing that Amy said under her breath, "I wonder what Monica will be like today."

I rolled my eyes. "With any luck, she's lost interest in tormenting me." Just last week, she'd made a snide comment about me wanting special treatment for my injury. All because I wore a V-neck shirt that revealed the edge of my jagged scar. As if I'd worn it simply to show off my old wound.

"She really has it out for you."

I bit my lip as our feet tapped in the hallway. Most likely, my time at Compound 3 would be drawing to an end in the next few weeks. Things were progressing so nicely with the drug trials, that I didn't think we'd be needed much longer. And then I'd never have to see Monica Brown again or worry about what she knew of Davin and me. Her words from the other week still haunted me. *"I know who your roommate is."*

When we reached our lab, my eyes darted around as I looked for her. Thankfully I didn't spot any short dark hair. *With any luck, I won't see her today.*

Amy and I worked side-by-side for most of the morning. Monica never showed up. When noon approached, I snapped off my gloves and shrugged out of my lab coat.

"Are you going to greet Bethany?" Amy asked.

"Yes. I want to be at the front doors when she arrives."

Amy continued working as I slipped out of the lab. My footsteps echoed in the long halls as I hurried to the front of the Compound. When I reached a fork in the hall that offered two alternative routes to reach the main entrance, I debated which way was quicker.

Probably left past the Production Room.

A few minutes later, I was sailing down the hall when the large windows appeared that overlooked the factory-like monolith within Compound 3. Within the Production Room, drugs were manufactured that the MRI created.

I smiled while gazing into the industrial-like area.

The Production Room was like a giant, mechanical assembly line intermixed with advanced robotic technology. The machines within shifted and moved at impossible and precise speeds. The vaccine that Compound 3 had produced had been manufactured here.

Now, it was producing the cure.

This room held every chemical compound known to man, which the robots handled expertly. Those chemicals and the hydraulic machines made this room fascinating but also incredibly dangerous.

My smile grew as I watched. The robots whizzed and moved like metal dancers in a perfectly coordinated waltz. If production continued as it was, we'd have doses for a thousand Kazzies within the month. And if production began at every other Compound nationwide, we'd have doses within a few months for the entire world's Kazzie population.

The implications of that were mind-blowing.

If *Makanza* was wiped off the globe, the world would truly become as we'd once known it. Of course, it would never be the same, but world trade would begin again, borders would reopen, and we'd reunite as a global community.

I grinned.

I was so lost in my own daydream, that I almost missed the figure that darted by the corner inside of the room. My gaze snapped in that direction.

Frowning, I stepped closer to the window and peered in. *I swear I just saw somebody who wasn't suited-up dash by.*

I checked my watch. Bethany was due to arrive in fifteen minutes.

But if someone's inside the Production Room without the required gear, he or she could potentially be contaminating the entire chemical process.

That wasn't something I could ignore.

Instead of continuing down the hall, I hurried to the entry doors and scanned my badge. The doors hissed open.

Inside, the loud machinery was deafening even though another set of sealed doors stood in front of me. I quickly donned the full-body suit, goggles, mask, and ear protection.

Not wasting any time, I entered the large room and searched again for the figure I'd seen. I knew there was no point in calling out. If someone *was* in here, they'd never hear me.

I stood on the large metal platform overlooking the monstrous room below. Nothing appeared remiss. *But I know I saw someone.*

I checked the clock on the wall. Ten minutes until Bethany arrived. *Better hurry.*

Taking the steps down at a jog, I headed toward the corner where I'd seen the person. Large machinery crisscrossed my path. Once I reached the corner, I gazed around at the various walkways that intersected the area.

I didn't see anyone.

"Hello?" I called out even though I knew it was unlikely anyone would answer.

Just do a quick search. Then go greet Bethany.

Picking up my pace, I wandered deeper into the gigantic room's interior, but the farther I traveled the more I realized how easy it would be for someone to hide in here. There were so many crevices between the machines. *But why in the world would anyone want to hide in here?*

Although, it would be hard for somebody to venture back this way. The machines sat so tightly against one another, that only a small person would be able to squeeze through them.

A small woman could. I gazed at the opening in front of me.

I'd be able to shimmy through it even though it would be tight, but a grown man certainly wouldn't.

I bit my lip and glanced over my shoulder. I'd been searching this room for at least ten minutes. *Bethany's probably here and wondering where I am.*

Pipes, whirring machines, spidery robotic arms, and conveyor belts filled my vision every which way I looked. In the far distance, the viewing platform was barely visible. I'd gone much farther than I'd realized, and when a moving arm shot back from a conveyor belt and almost nailed me in the face, I realized it wasn't entirely safe.

I better get out of here. Another area ahead came into view between the machines. *Just check back there and then go.*

Stepping carefully over several large drains that crisscrossed the floor, I was about to hop over one when something shoved me in the back.

Shrieking in surprise, my arms windmilled as images of a robot nailing me between the shoulder blades filled my mind. But try as I might to stay upright, I lost my balance.

Falling forward, I landed hard on top of the drain. The rough movement shifted the grate that covered it. Liquid beneath splashed my face. The goggles I wore protected my eyes, but a spackle of liquid splattered my exposed cheek. Burning immediately set in.

Alarm bells warned within my head. *I've just been exposed to a potentially toxic substance!*

Scrambling, I tried to stand upright but winced when I straightened my knee. I'd hit it hard on my way down. Bracing my hands on the floor, I caught sight of two feet leaping over the drain to my side. The assailant disappeared as I darted my gaze up.

With wide eyes, it sank in that it wasn't a machine that had hit my back. *Someone purposefully shoved me to the ground!*

My heart thudded as I finally managed to stand. Once upright, only machinery filled my gaze.

Forget about that right now. You've just been exposed to a chemical. Find the emergency station, now!

More than anything, I wanted to scan my surroundings to see if I'd be attacked again, but I didn't have time.

I ran back the way I'd come while searching for whoever had pushed me. I still didn't see anyone. The burning in my cheek increased.

It took several frantic turns before I saw the emergency signs.

The station sat along the wall. I had to duck under several pipes to reach it. When I skidded to a halt in front of it, I slammed my hand against the button that triggered the emergency cleansing shower.

A waterfall poured down on me.

I gasped.

It was freezing cold.

The gushing liquid soaked me completely and was so heavy that I struggled to breathe.

When the gallons upon gallons finally ceased, I stood like a drowned rat as the machinery continued to whir all around. My cheek didn't burn as much, but I still needed to assess it. Leaning forward, I rinsed my mouth a dozen times from the fountain even though the shower had filled my mouth already.

Once certain that any chemical residue had been washed off, I hurriedly scanned my surroundings again. No one was about.

A shiver struck me. Then another. The freezing shower had soaked me to the bone.

Drenched, the sterile suit sucked onto me like a leech.

Water sloshed in my shoes, and my teeth chattered so loudly I could hear it in my head. *I need to get out of here.* Whoever had pushed me could still be in here.

"Whoa! Meghan, are you all right?" The words barely penetrated my earmuffs.

With wild eyes, I turned to see Giselle hurrying toward me. She wore the same white suit as me along with all of the other protective gear. For a second, I flinched back. *Is she the one who pushed me?*

When she reached my side, her confused expression grew. Forcing myself to relax, I reminded myself she'd only ever been kind to me.

"What happened? Were you exposed?" She reached gently for my arm.

I nodded numbly.

Her eyebrows knit together in worry. "Come with me. You'll need to be checked over."

She latched onto my elbow and led me toward the exit bay. It was only as we exited the room that I saw a figure standing in the corner, watching us.

Monica.

I almost tripped. When I righted myself, my gaze snapped to the corner again.

She was gone.

Swallowing tightly, I struggled to keep up with Giselle's pace as something solidified in my mind: whoever had been in the Production Room had been up to something and hadn't wanted to be caught.

And it hadn't been above them to hurt me in the process.

IT TOOK OVER ten minutes before anybody would listen to me about what I'd seen. Giselle was so intent on ushering me to the medical bay that every time I tried to tell her that somebody had shoved me to the ground and was unattired in the Production Room, she merely nodded complacently.

I was so frustrated I almost stomped my foot. "Giselle! We need to call security, now!"

"Meghan, we need to get you to medical first. Your cheek isn't looking good," she replied soothingly, as if I were a small child speaking irrationally. "Then we can call security."

Despite digging in my heels, she still gently forced me along. It was only when I entered the medical bay and hurried to the receptionist that someone finally heard what I was saying.

"Security needs to be informed that somebody unauthorized was in the Production Room." Water dripped onto the floor around me as I gazed down at the seated receptionist.

Her eyes grew wide. "I'm sorry?"

This time I *did* stomp in frustration. Annunciating each word carefully, I said, "We. Need. To. Call. Security. *Now!*"

The receptionist picked up a phone. "What should I tell them?"

"Somebody was in the Production Room who wasn't properly attired. They intentionally shoved me to the ground, and it's possible that they've contaminated the entire process."

Giselle gasped. "You mean they hurt you on purpose?" Her eyes grew wider with every word that I uttered.

The receptionist dialed security's number as the door in the corner of the room opened. A nurse stepped through. "May I help you?"

Giselle nodded toward me. "Dr. Forester was exposed to an unknown chemical in the Production Room. She needs to be checked over."

The nurse hurried forward. "Of course."

I spent the next hour in the small clinic. My clothes were ruined even though I'd been wearing the required protective suit. Consequently, I was given a pair of MRRA guard pants and a top to wear. It was the only clothing the Compounds readily stocked.

My heart pounded with each minute that passed. Bethany was no doubt wondering where I was.

By the time everything finished, anxiety strummed along my limbs in solid, steady waves. I had no idea if security had found anything, but that would have to wait. I needed to find Bethany.

The physician that had attended to me handed me a salve. Despite hurrying to the cleansing shower, the chemical I'd been exposed to had burned my cheek. Luckily, it had only eaten away the top layer of skin.

"What were you doing in there anyway?" He eyed me through his metal-rimmed glasses. A clipboard sat in his hand that contained the medical information I filled out.

"When I was passing by, I saw somebody in there who wasn't properly attired." I hopped down from the examination table and searched for footwear. A pair of MRRA boots sat in the corner. I hurriedly slipped them on.

They were at least a size too big.

"You saw somebody in the Production Room that wasn't supposed to be there?" He raised an eyebrow.

I nodded emphatically. "I'm sure of it. It's the only reason I went in."

"Why didn't you call security right away?"

I sighed. He had a point. "In hindsight, I should have called them immediately, but at the time I was more worried about getting the person *out* of the room so acted first."

He nodded, looking only partially convinced. "I suppose that makes sense."

I glanced at the clock on the wall. It was almost two in the afternoon. "I really need to get going. Someone was expecting me earlier."

"Make sure you apply that salve for the next week. If it doesn't heal, come back to see me."

I thanked him for his time and hurried out of the medical bay.

The oversized clothing and large boots made walking difficult. It didn't help that my knee still hurt from my fall. I tripped repeatedly which got a few smothered smiles when people passed me in the halls.

Feeling my cheeks flush bright red, I made my way back to the lab, limping occasionally. Once there, I searched for Bethany.

I didn't see her.

"Amy!" Hitching my pants up, I walked carefully toward her. The last thing I wanted was to face-plant in front of my co-workers.

Her eyes widened. "Meghan! What the heck are you wearing?" Her gaze alighted on my cheek. "And what happened to your face?"

"No time to explain right now. Do you know where Bethany is?"

Amy shook her head. "No, I thought she was with you."

I groaned in frustration. "I need to find her. I promised her I'd be here when she arrived."

Before Amy could ask any further questions, I left the lab and went in search of Bethany. It took over twenty minutes before I finally found her with Ian and Dr. Dornhoff in the

Director's office.

"Dr. Forester. We've been wondering where you were." Dr. Dornhoff's gaze widened as he looked up and down my frame. He'd obviously never seen a researcher in MRRA cargos before.

"I'm afraid there was an incident." I smiled sheepishly at Bethany. She lifted her head only long enough to nod in understanding. After that, she dropped her gaze back to the floor.

I frowned. Her ebony skin was barely visible in the layers of clothing she wore. Once again, she seemed intent on hiding her appearance from the world.

I stepped closer to her. "I'm sorry I wasn't able to meet you at the front door like I promised."

Bethany nodded while Ian's eyebrows drew together. He gave me a baffled look.

It suddenly occurred to me that I would probably have to explain why I was late and why I was dressed the way I was. "Somebody was in the Production Room. A report is being written about it."

Dr. Dornhoff's brow furrowed. "What do you mean?"

I eyed Bethany and gave him a pointed look.

Luckily, he seemed to catch my unspoken concern.

"Perhaps we can step out for a minute to discuss it?" He pushed up from his chair. His large belly brushed against his desk.

Ian stood too. Bethany barely seemed to notice when we stepped out.

Once in the hall, Dr. Dornhoff crossed his arms while Ian waited with his hands on his hips. Ian's gaze drifted to my burned cheek.

"What happened?" the Director asked.

Annoyance flashed through me that the Director hadn't been alerted to my concerns. I quickly filled them in.

"You're saying somebody was unattired in the Production Room?" Ian's brow furrowed.

"I can't be certain, but that's what it appeared to be. And whoever it was, may have also shoved me to the ground."

Ian's jaw clenched and unclenched as he processed my words.

Dr. Dornhoff's expression looked just as grim. "Thank you for informing me. I'll look into it."

I nodded in relief. "Good. I'm glad to hear it."

Ian dipped his head down. "Would you like to accompany Bethany and me to the Experimental Room? She's ready to begin the drug trials."

"Yes, of course."

Bethany was twisting her hands when the three of us entered the room again. Fear filled her eyes as her gaze shuffled between me, the Director, and Ian. "Is everything okay? Can I still take the drug?"

"Yes, everything's fine." I smiled for good measure which made my cheek tingle in pain, but I could tell she wasn't convinced. "And of course you can still take the drug. If you'd like to come with Ian and me, we can get started."

The loose skin under her arms flopped against her knees as she followed us into the hallway. Despite her cloak, it was still visible.

Her posture stayed folded and hunched over as we traveled through the halls. The few times we passed other MRI employees, she kept her gaze averted or on the floor.

My heart sank at how dejected she looked. I had no idea if that had been her personality before she contracted *Makanza*, but it certainly seemed to be the person she was now.

I stepped closer to her when we rounded a corner. "How's Makayla doing? And how's the baby?"

A smile lit her face as she finally looked up. "They're both doing so good. Little Oliver was over ten pounds when he was born, and he's already gained another two. Makayla said he came into the world ready to eat."

I laughed. "Do you have any pictures?"

Bethany fished her cell phone out of her bag and proceeded to show Ian and me photos as we walked down the halls.

"He's a beautiful boy." Ian's dimple showed through his beard when we reached the Inner Sanctum. "And I'm sure you'll be the best aunt he could ever have."

Bethany dipped her head. "I'm certainly going to try."

When we were in the Inner Sanctum and walking toward the Experimental Room, I said to her, "The drug we've been working on is showing great potential, as I'm sure Ian's told you. All of the Kazzies have shown a significant decrease in physical Changes. Many of them have begun reverting back to their prior forms."

A glimmer of hope shone in Bethany's eyes when we reached the Room. "That's what the Director and Mr. Gallager said. I hope it will work for me." She grabbed my hand and squeezed it tightly. "I don't know what I'll do if it doesn't."

I frowned at the desperation in her tone and led her into the Experimental Room.

I spent the rest of the afternoon with Bethany while Ian managed her entrance to the trials. I stayed with her despite the lab techs taking over. I knew I didn't have to, but each time I stepped out of her view, she watched to see where I'd gone.

When I assured her again that I would stay, the tension in her shoulders eased.

"Does this drug hurt?" she asked as the tech hooked her up to the monitoring equipment.

I shrugged helplessly. "To be honest, for some it does. For others, not as much. We won't know until it's administered to you."

She nodded tightly. "I don't care if it hurts. I still want to do it."

I hoped that the process would go smoothly for her. It certainly wasn't going that way for Garrett. At times, his screams could be heard through sealed doors.

21 – SABOTAGE

I told Amy about the Production Room incident on our drive home that night. Her eyes widened more with every sentence.

"You mean somebody *intentionally* pushed you to the ground?" Outside, the setting sun set the desert aglow.

I nodded. "I saw them run past me after I fell."

"Do you have any idea who it was?"

An image of Monica standing in the corner of the room flashed through my mind. *She's the only one who hates you.*

I bit my lip. Hating me didn't mean she'd intentionally hurt me. But then I remembered how she'd shoved me a few weeks ago.

Coincidence?

Sighing heavily, I replied, "I'm not one-hundred-percent certain who it was, but Monica was there when I left the room."

Amy angled her body to face me better. "Seriously? So is anything being done about it?"

"Dr. Dornhoff said he'll look into it. I can only hope he does."

Amy's cheeks were flushed in anger when she turned her attention back to the road. The desert shimmered in the fading sun, sending the sandy hills aglow. "The whole situation is crazy. And Monica is such a bitch to you. It totally could have been her." She sneered. "You could've been really hurt." She eyed my cheek. The skin was bright red and raw. "Davin's gonna flip when he sees that."

I sighed. "I know."

Sure enough, after we stepped into our small rental home and Davin scanned my cargos with a raised eyebrow, his gaze immediately fell on my burned skin.

"What happened?" He stepped closer and reached for me.

I eyed Amy. She merely mouthed *good luck* and retreated to the kitchen.

Pulling at the uniform I wore, I tried to say casually, "I was exposed at work today."

"Exposed to what?"

"We're not entirely sure." I knew his questions would continue until I divulged every detail so I added, "There was an incident in the Production Room." I pulled him to the couch and explained what happened.

With every word I uttered, his expression grew darker and darker as if a storm cloud brewed just above him. "You mean somebody *purposefully* attacked you?"

"It seems so."

"And do they know who it was?"

"Not yet."

"Meghan…" His large hand settled on my thigh. The heat from him penetrated the thick MRRA pants. "Maybe you should stay away from the Compound until they figure out who did it."

I shook my head. "I can't do that. Besides, there's no

reason to believe whoever it was targeted me directly. I may have been in the wrong place at the wrong time. If somebody else had gone searching for who I saw, they may have done the same thing to them."

Davin sighed harshly and ran an agitated hand through his hair. His cobalt eyes flashed. "What are they doing to prevent something like that from happening again?"

"I imagine the first thing they're going to do is figure out who it was. There are cameras in the Production Room. Surely, they picked up something."

He growled and pulled me closer to his side. I sighed in contentment at the feel of him so close.

"They better. If anything happens to you, they'll have to answer to me."

THE NEXT DAY, I hurried to the Inner Sanctum as soon as I entered the Compound. Amy had stayed in our lab, saying she was going to nap on the lab bench since I'd woken her so early. Since we shared a car, she didn't have much choice other than to come in with me.

Even though I felt a twinge of guilt about getting her out of bed at the crack of dawn, I was glad we came in early. So much was happening today, and I'd been unwilling to wait at home while Amy slept.

Bethany had just spent her first night in Compound 3's Inner Sanctum, Dorothy would receive another injection, and Ian was busy arranging for more Kazzies to enter the trials.

With any luck, Dorothy would be *Makanza*-free by the end of the week and Bethany would be on her way to looking more human.

Tapping from my feet echoed in the large, wide hall as I raced through the corridors. It was still early. Not many scientists were around, but that would change soon.

An access door appeared at the end of the hall when I rounded a corner. I lifted my badge to have it ready to scan. *Only two more doors to the Inner Sanctum.*

I grinned. I'd soon be able to hear how Bethany was fairing after her first injection.

Hurrying forward, I held up my badge, but I never made it to the scanner. A loud *BOOM* rocked the walls and knocked me off my feet. Shrieking, my hand instinctively reached for the wall as dust fell from the ceiling.

On the floor, I looked around in a daze. *What the hell was that?*

For a moment, the lights dimmed before flickering back on. My heart thudded as I gazed around the empty hall. Slowly, I pushed to standing as adrenaline pounded in my veins.

Tapping in the back of my mind indicated my reaction hadn't gone unnoticed. I opened up to Sara. *I'm okay, but something just happened here at Compound 3.*

What?

I have no idea. Whatever it was knocked me over. Can I let you go so I can find out?

Her nod penetrated our bond. *Sure, I'm just glad you're okay. The reaction I got from you... It was pretty powerful.*

The price of telepathy, eh? I tried to joke, but it fell flat. My heart still pounded with whatever had caused that event.

We shut down our connection after I promised to talk with her soon. Guilt flooded me that I'd been so consumed with work that we hadn't spoken more often. Luckily, the twin seemed to sense my busy schedule. She'd only been in touch a few times a week since Davin and I moved here.

Pushing my guilt away, I hesitantly stepped toward the access scanner again. Whatever had caused the boom had been so loud and powerful that it shook the walls. Dust coated the floor. It seemed the ceiling material had loosened in the blast.

The blast? I shook my head. *Was it really a blast?*

But that didn't make sense. It had to be something else.

An earthquake?

Fear made my stomach flip. Earthquakes could be deadly. I waited for rumbling and shaking, but it never came. Whatever it had been, seemed to have been a singular, powerful event.

With an unsteady hand, I lifted my badge to the scanner and then laid my palm against it. Green light flashed. The door hissed open.

On shaky legs, I stepped through it and rounded the corner. A voice carried to me from the end of the corridor. Ahead, a guard was frantically speaking into a hallway emergency phone.

I caught the end of his conversation just as he was hanging up. "Yes, sir. I'm on my way, sir."

"What happened?" I asked as he started to rush past me.

"It seems there was an explosion, maybe two. Please evacuate immediately. It's not safe."

He ran down the hall before I could ask anything further. His heavy pounding footsteps filled the quiet until he disappeared from view.

With wide eyes, my mind raced with what he implied. *An explosion? Possibly* two *explosions?*

I had no idea where an explosion could have occurred, but considering thousands of gas lines ran throughout the Compound, an explosion was feasible. And an exploding gas line would be powerful enough to shake the entire building.

That must be what it was.

A female robotic voice suddenly sounded through the hallway speakers as the lights dimmed. An emergency red light flashed overhead. "Please head to your nearest exit. Mandatory evacuation has ensued."

My breath caught in my chest. *They're evacuating the entire building? But what about the Kazzies?* They were still locked within the Inner Sanctum. *Surely an emergency evacuation means their cells will open.*

But what if they don't?

For a moment, I waffled. I knew emergency protocol dictated that I immediately travel to the outer wing and exit the building, but something made me rush toward the Inner Sanctum. When I reached the unmanned access door to head deeper into the Compound, I scanned my palm.

The scan flashed red.

Red.

I just stared at it before trying again. The same color appeared.

That's never happened before.

The overhead voice again penetrated the air as the red light flashed. "Please head to your nearest exit. Mandatory evacuation has ensued."

I gritted my teeth in frustration. It seemed the access doors leading into the interior of the Compound had been closed. I could only hope that my friends were being evacuated safely.

Turning around, I picked up a jog as I headed toward the exit. The halls grew more crowded the closer I got to the perimeter. A flash of bright red hair caught my attention just as a frantic researcher bumped into me.

"Amy!" I yelled to my co-worker.

Her green eyes were as round as saucers when I finally reached her side. I'd had to push through a dozen scientists to catch up to her.

"Oh, Meghan, I'm so glad to see you. What the hell is

going on?"

I shook my head as more and more employees joined us on our walk to the exit. It became so crowded in the singular hallway, that we were all pressed tightly together. I took a deep breath as my heart pounded. I was surrounded on all sides by dozens of people. *Stay calm, Meghan. Just stay calm.*

In a shaky voice, I replied, "There was an explosion, apparently. A guard told me."

"An explosion?" Amy moved closer as we were funneled through a door in the hall. She yelped when someone stepped on her foot. "Watch where you're going!" she yelled after him.

"What else do you know?" she asked.

I didn't get a chance to tell her as guards appeared ahead. They began directing people and issuing orders. Their voices drowned out ours.

It didn't help that the female robotic voice continued above—repeating over and over to head to the nearest exit as mandatory evacuation had ensued. I swore I was going to have dreams about that robotic voice for the rest of my life.

It was only when we stepped out of the Compound into the parking lot, that I was able to take a deep breath. Cool air filled my lungs. The temperature felt like it was in the high fifties. It was still so early that the daily warm temps hadn't set in.

A shiver struck me, then another, but thankfully my anxiety abated. Even though my heart still pounded from how close I had stood to everybody, it no longer felt like the world was closing in.

I searched for any Kazzies in the parking lot. None. I swallowed the lump in my throat.

Amy grabbed my arm. "Meghan! Look!"

I turned back around to the Compound and gasped. Black

smoke rolled into the sky from the center of the building. The outer Compound appeared intact, but the interior was another story.

Murmured whispers erupted in the crowd as everyone became aware of the damage. Amy grabbed my hand as the guards yelled for us to retreat farther into the parking lot. "Let's not lose each other."

We followed the other scientists and Compound employees as flashing lights and sirens wailed in the distance. They sounded far off. With a start, I realized they came from outside of the Compound's walled perimeter. It occurred to me what I was hearing. Emergency responders.

"Do you know anything else about what happened?" Amy wrapped her arms around herself and stepped closer.

"No, nothing more than what I've already told you. I was on my way to the Inner Sanctum when the explosion occurred. It shook the walls."

Amy's hair brushed my shoulder when she nodded. "I was in the lab and the same thing happened. My lab bench shook."

I circled my arms around myself to ward off the chill and told her about the guard on the emergency phone. "He's the one who told me about the explosions."

The sirens grew louder as a fleet of firetrucks reached the Compound's perimeter. In the distance, the large gates opened to emit the emergency personnel. Never had I ever thought to see something like that happen. The Compounds had always been so indestructible. So formidable.

To think an actual explosion had occurred was unfathomable.

THE NEXT FEW hours passed in a slow, frustrating haze. Guards appeared handing out blankets to ward off the chill, but we didn't need them for long as the sun climbed the sky. Another warm day loomed.

But the morning chill was the least of my worries. None of us knew yet what happened. And despite multiple employees asking the guards for more information, they all shook their heads. It didn't seem we would have any answers today.

Those who were lucky enough to have their car keys in their pockets had tried to drive home.

They were all stopped.

When demanding answers, the guards simply told them that nobody was allowed to leave until more information was acquired.

"Do they think that one of *us* caused the explosion?" Amy huddled closer to me and asked the question under her breath.

"Possibly," I replied. My stomach growled. I hadn't eaten breakfast, and it didn't seem we'd have an opportunity for lunch. But food was the furthest thing from my mind. I kept thinking about the Production Room incident yesterday. I was attacked and now an explosion today.

Are they linked?

I shaded my eyes from the overhead sun and scanned the crowds for what felt like the hundredth time. There was still no sign of the Kazzies. So far, I hadn't seen anybody from the Inner Sanctum. "Do you think they're okay?"

Amy patted my hand. "I'm sure they're fine. They're probably in the parking lot on the other side."

Even though I knew she was right, worry still clawed my gut. If anything had happened to Bethany, Dorothy, Garrett, or any of the other Kazzies…

No, don't think about it. Just the thought, made me sick.

BY LATE AFTERNOON, MRRA soldiers and law

enforcement had divided the hundreds of workers huddled in the parking lot into smaller groups. Each and every one of us had been questioned and photographed. I knew it wouldn't be the end. We'd all hear from them again as it was only the beginning of their investigation.

I thought for sure we'd be allowed back inside to collect our things, but that never happened. Instead, hours passed while the sun made its lazy trail across the sky. The heat wasn't helping. The chilly morning had turned into a sweltering afternoon. And despite asking the tense and anxious-looking guards for answers multiple times, they refused to divulge any details.

To pass the time, I imagined that Davin was with me. I wanted nothing more than to feel his comforting arms around me. Closing my eyes, I pretended his unique scent flooded my senses and his deep voice soothed my worries.

"Meghan?"

I was so lost in my daydream that for a moment I thought it had come true. *Davin.* Smiling, I opened my eyes.

"Ian!" My head snapped back.

He stood only a few feet away with his arms dangling at his sides. A heavy expression covered his face, his dimple nowhere to be seen.

My heart sank. "What happened?"

He stepped closer and reached for me. His fingers brushed my forearm. "Come with me. We still haven't officially released anything to the public or the employees, but I wanted you to know before we did."

Amy's gaze traveled between the two of us. When she tried to follow, Ian stopped her. "Sorry. Meghan only. They're not allowing anybody else in."

Amy hung back. I felt her gaze on me as Ian and I hurried

through the crowd. Murmured whispers erupted as we passed everyone. Even here, I was a familiar face.

"You're worrying me. What happened?" I said the words in a low tone so nobody but Ian would hear.

He glanced over his shoulder, his expression grim.

He never replied.

My heart fluttered when an MRRA guard admitted us inside. A somber expression covered his face too.

I stepped closer to Ian once we were inside the familiar lobby. He towered above me like a giant redwood. His fiery hair stood up on all ends as if he'd been running his hands through it.

My breath caught in my throat. "Ian, tell me what's going on. *Please.*"

His gaze wouldn't meet mine. He shuffled his feet when he said, "There were two explosions this morning. One was in the Production Room, and the other was in the Inner Sanctum."

My hands turned to ice.

Ian finally looked up. When he saw my stricken expression, he reached for me.

His hands felt as hot as lava. They scorched me in his grasp. But it was the look in his eyes that fired my anxiety full-throttle.

It was a look I'd seen before.

When the MRRA soldiers had arrived at my parents' doorstep to tell us about my brother.

"No." I shook my head "No. No. No! Please tell me what I'm thinking isn't true!"

He took a step closer. "I'm sorry, Meghan."

I swallowed tightly. "How many?"

"Over half are dead. The other half are badly injured."

Tears filled my eyes. "Bethany? Garrett? Dorothy?"

From the expression on his face, I already knew the answer. He replied quietly, "They're all dead."

"No!" My knees gave out. I fell to the ground.

Dead.

The word was so definite. So finite. It was a word I'd heard too often.

Ian's word pounded at my heart. It felt like a boxer beat everything inside of me until I was nothing but a bloody pulp.

A sob wracked my chest. Then another. The tears fell next. Hot and steady, they trailed down my cheeks.

Ian crouched at my side. "I'm so sorry. I know they were your friends, but there's something else..." He laid a large hand on my shoulder. "Someone obviously sabotaged us. It's not just the Production Room and Kazzies they targeted. All of the research is gone. The database has been wiped clean. Any hope of producing a cure blew up in the explosions. And the Kazzies who had volunteered for the drug trials, they..." He took a deep breath. "Even the ones that survived will most likely carry permanent injuries."

My mind reeled with all that he implied.

"How..." I wiped a hand unsteadily across my cheek. "How did this happen? How *could* this happen? Nothing like this would've happened a year ago. Security wouldn't have allowed it!" My voice rose with each word as burning rage brewed inside me.

The pain and fury blended into one until it felt like an animal clawed in my chest, demanding to be let loose. I wanted to howl in frustration.

In the back of my mind, I felt Sara trying to get in touch, but I couldn't talk to her. Not now. How could I tell her what had happened?

Bethany's dead. Garrett's dead. Dorothy's dead.
And all because of me.

I'd encouraged each and every one of them to come here and join us. If I hadn't done that, they'd still be alive.

Images of Dorothy's round figure and comforting smile filled my mind. She'd always been so kind even when the Compounds had beaten her down. Even then, she'd been a gentle soul.

And Garrett. He'd always been so quiet, so content to draw his art. He'd only ever wanted to be free.

And Bethany. The withdrawn Kazzie who'd come to *me* to help her. All she'd ever wanted was to look normal. Images of her proud smile as she showed us pictures of Oliver flashed through my mind. She'd singled me out and trusted me—she thought for sure I could help.

And now she was dead.

How am I ever going to tell Makayla?

Fresh tears filled my eyes. "Take me to them. I need to see them. I need to know that they're really gone."

Ian's hands stopped me when I tried to push past him. "I can't. The entire Compound is on lockdown. Nobody will be allowed in or out of this building until the investigation concludes. And… there's something else—"

"But they were my friends!" I gripped his shirt and dug my fingers into it. The fabric balled in my fists like a crumpled rag. I pushed against him. "They were my *friends*, and now they're dead! All I'm asking is to see them!"

His eyes softened. "I know, and I'm so sorry. But Meghan, you need to listen to me. I wanted to be the one to tell you because I know it's bullshit."

His words were like a fog filling my mind. Images of my dead friends, burned to death and exploded into a thousand pieces, kept pummeling me. Another tear streaked down my face.

I wiped it away. "What are you talking about? What's bullshit?"

He paused. When he said his next words, he looked away. "Right now, they think it's *you* who did it, Meghan."

"Me? What do you mean *me?*" Confusion rained down on me just as Dr. Dornhoff, Dr. Sadowsky, and four MRRA guards marched around the corner.

Shock covered Dr. Sadowsky's face while anger and indignation filled Dr. Dornhoff's.

I turned wild eyes on Ian. "What's going on? Ian, what's happening?"

The guards reached for me and slid smooth, metal cuffs around my wrists.

"Ian!" I struggled against them, but it was no use.

"I'm sorry," Ian replied quietly. "But I thought it was best coming from me."

Another sob wracked my chest as my world began caving in. "But I didn't do anything! What's this all about?"

Dr. Dornhoff stepped forward. "What's happening is that you're being arrested, Dr. Forester. We managed to extract video feed from the Production Room yesterday before the explosion destroyed the rest, and the video shows one thing. *You* planted the bombs in the Production Room."

"Me?" *But that's impossible!*

The Director's icy gaze shifted to the guards. "Take her away."

"But it wasn't me!"

My words fell on deaf ears. I felt Ian's sad gaze follow me as I staggered on shaky limbs behind the guards. They yanked me down the hall, their grip unforgiving.

My mind reeled with everything that happened. My friends were dead. Our research was gone. And I was being blamed for it all. But despite the gravity of what I faced ahead, only one thought filled my mind.

Any hope we had of discovering a cure just vanished in a single afternoon.

Which meant that Davin and every other Kazzie in this country were at risk of imprisonment once again.

22 – HE RETURNS

The guards took me to a narrow hallway that led to another door. Bright white walls filled this space. It was so typical of corridors in the Compounds. That crazy thought was the only thing that penetrated the fog in my mind.

At the end of the hall, the guards opened another door, and I realized what it was.

A discreet exit from the Compound that employees knew nothing about. Outside, a patrol car waited.

The sun was on its downward descent which meant the end of the workday had almost come. I knew Davin would be expecting me home soon. He probably had no idea of all that had transpired today. And I still hadn't opened up to Sara's persistent knockings. I just couldn't.

I eyed the cop car as anxiety strummed along my limbs. It wasn't the first time I was going to be placed in the back of one. And it wasn't the first time I'd been arrested.

Following my illegal break-in to Reservation 1, I'd also been arrested. *And now those charges, while dropped, coupled with these charges…*

I knew it didn't look good.

"When do I get my phone call?"

The guard opened the patrol car door and forced me inside. I peered up at him. Behind him, shadows from the monstrous Compound filled my view.

A hard edge lined the guard's features. It was impossible to decipher his emotions. "You'll have to ask the police officers." With that, he slammed the door.

The police officer driving the vehicle pulled away. In the distance, the MRI and Compound employees still stood in the parking lot. Except now, at least five buses lined it. It appeared that the employees were being herded onto the buses one-by-one. Apparently, they were finally letting them go.

I snorted quietly. *Now that they have me locked up, the apparent bomber, of course they'll let them go.*

It still hadn't fully sunk in that I was being blamed for the explosions and deaths of the Kazzies. Anger fired within me at the absurdity of it. It didn't make any sense! I'd only gone into the Production Room to find the unauthorized person. I'd never planted any bombs. Surely, the videos showed that. Not to mention, my incessant work to *help* the Kazzies. *How can they possibly think it's me?*

An image returned in my mind. It was of feet leaping past me after I'd been pushed to the floor. I closed my eyes and concentrated on the memory. My eidetic memory created a slideshow in front of me. I slowed the image down until I could make out every detail on those shoes.

They were small and covered with booties. *So the assailant was properly suited up.* Most likely, the feet belonged to a woman. If I had to guess, I'd say she wore a size seven. The shoes poking above the booties were simple and black. From the angle, I couldn't make out a brand.

I opened my eyes as a howl of frustration threatened to overwhelm me. *It's imperative I discover who wore them.* Most likely, that person was the true criminal.

I nibbled my lip.

Monica?

She'd been just outside the Production Room after the incident. I closed my eyes again until my memory brought back that day. An image of her there and then gone flashed in my mind. I slowed the image.

Monica had been standing in the corner. She wasn't suited up. My gaze traveled down the image in my memory.

Booties covered Monica's feet.

My eyes flashed open. The suspicion that Monica had been the one to attack me had been rolling around in my mind since the incident. She'd always been so vicious. Not to mention, from day one, I'd been her target. *Who's to say she's not behind all of this?*

I leaned forward in my seat. "Where are you taking me?"

We'd just exited the Compound. Behind us, the buses were still being filled with other employees.

"To the police station." The officer said the words in a monotone voice. He never glanced in the rearview mirror. Instead, he calmly drove forward.

I chewed my lip as I debated my options. I knew I'd be allowed a phone call once I reached the station. I also knew I'd go through the booking procedure.

Davin's going to flip. As much as I wanted to call him and reassure him that I was all right, my phone call couldn't be to him. I needed to call an attorney.

But I don't know any attorneys.

But Cate would. Perhaps she could give me some advice. Once again, I knew who my phone call would be to.

WHEN WE REACHED the police station, everything passed in a blur. Similar to Rapid City, I was searched before I donned prison garbs. I watched mutely while they took inventory of my meager possessions. After that, I recited my medical history, signed forms, and had my fingerprints and mugshot taken.

And finally, I was given my phone call.

I stood in a drab, concrete hallway with a guard standing at my side. The phone was at standing height, so I stood while I called Cate. This time, she picked up.

"Meghan? I just received word that there were explosions at Compound 3. Is that true?"

I clutched the receiver tightly. Voices rumbled around me from other inmates and guards. I plugged my other ear so I could hear her better. "Yes, it's true, and I'm being blamed for it."

"*What?* They're blaming *you* for the explosions?"

"Yes." Relief filled me at Cate's disbelief.

I quickly summed up what had happened yesterday in the Production Room. I told her about the person who shoved me and the shoes they'd been wearing. "I'm sure that's who planted the bombs but, for some reason, Dr. Dornhoff thinks it was me. He said something about video feed showing me planting the bombs. But that can't possibly be true. I never did it!"

"Of course, you never did it. We need to sort this out and get you out of there. Do you have an attorney?"

"No, I was hoping you could help me with that."

Rustling sounded from her end, as if she were shuffling papers. "I'll contact my attorney in Washington and see if he has any referrals in California. Just hang tight for now. I'll have an attorney come directly to you at the jail. Is there anybody else you want me to contact in the meantime?"

"I'm sure Amy's told Davin by now that I was taken away, but could you call him and fill him in?"

"Davin?"

I almost smacked myself. Cate had no idea that I was dating a Kazzie. "It's a long story, but Davin's here with me in California. Neither he or Amy know that I was arrested." I rattled off both of their phone numbers to her. "Will you call them and tell them everything? And if you don't mind calling my parents as well, I'm sure they'd want to be informed."

Scratching sounded from Cate's end. I knew she was writing down the phone numbers. "I'll call all of them," she said briskly, "and don't worry, Meghan. We'll get to the bottom of this."

I felt slightly better after Cate and I hung up. However, my stomach still twisted into knots when the female guard gripped my bicep and tugged me down the hall. Concrete walls and floor greeted us, along with a stale smell. My hands were cuffed behind me, and the pants they'd put on me were too big.

It was all too familiar.

The pant hems dragged across the floor as I shuffled to a cell. The guard pushed me inside, undid my cuffs, and locked the door behind me. The sound of that key twisting caused a surge of panic to race through me. More than anything, I wanted to bang my hands against the door and demand to be let out.

But I knew it was useless. The only silver lining was that unlike Rapid City, I was alone in this cell.

At least I won't be harassed by other inmates.

Wrapping my arms tightly around myself, I surveyed the small prison cell. It was barely eight feet by ten feet. It held a single toilet, sink, bed, and a lone tiny window.

I sat down on the bed and hung my head in my hands. The hard mattress pressed against my thighs. A part of me wanted to curl up on my side and cry again.

In the chaos of the afternoon, I'd managed to forget that Dorothy, Garrett, and Bethany were dead. But now, it all came rushing back.

Tears again filled my eyes. It was such a horrible way to die. And all of them had been so hopeful at their futures to come.

A future that no longer exists.

The tears fell down my cheeks like hot steady raindrops. My throat tightened as a sob wracked my chest. It all felt so helpless. So unbelievable.

How could this have possibly happened?

AN HOUR LATER, I finally opened up to Sara and was talking telepathically to her as a guard brought me supper. Sara had tried to keep me calm, but it was no use.

The twin sounded just as tormented as me. Garrett, Dorothy, and Bethany had been her friends too.

I picked at the food, unable to eat. *Sara? You better talk to Davin. I'm sure Cate's talked to him by now, but I don't know if she'd have told him about the deaths.*

She sniffed in her mind. I knew she was crying. *Do you want me to channel him to you later?*

Yes. I breathed a sigh of relief at the thought of hearing his voice. *Please.*

Just then, the guard returned. "Someone's here to see you."

Um, Sara, I gotta go. Someone's here. Tell Davin I'll talk to him soon.

We shut down our connection just as the guard cuffed me

and pulled me into the hall. From there, I followed her to a small room.

The room was filled with small tables and chairs. I figured it was some kind of visiting area, but at this late hour, it was empty except for a man in a business suit.

He sat at one of the tables and appeared to be middle-aged but fit. Short, brown hair covered his head. With precise movements, he wrote on a small tablet. A briefcase sat at his side.

The guard pushed me toward him. The hem on my too-big pants continued to drag on the concrete floor.

When I reached him, he glanced up and eyed me coolly. "Dr. Meghan Forester?"

I nodded.

"Have a seat." The female guard pulled out a chair.

I did as she said, but when she shoved the chair under the table with me on it, the chair leg caught the hem of my pants.

I gave the guard an annoyed look and rearranged myself. That was difficult considering my hands were cuffed in front of me.

The guard merely retreated to the corner and stood watch.

Once it was only me and the businessman at the table, he held out his hand. "My name's Kevin Pratchett. I was contacted by a friend of yours. She said you needed legal counsel."

I nodded emphatically. "Yes, I do. I'm being accused of a crime I didn't commit."

"I see." He pulled something out of his pocket and set it on the table. "If you don't mind, I'd like to record our conversation."

I eyed the small recording device and shrugged. "Sure."

The attorney proceeded to ask me everything and anything

that had happened during the past twenty-four hours. I divulged every detail, including my suspicions about Monica. He listened tirelessly and took meticulous notes along the way.

"So you believe that the person in the Production Room yesterday, possibly this Monica Brown woman, is the true criminal? Whoever pushed you over may have also planted those bombs?"

"Yes. I know I certainly never planted any explosives. It had to be her or someone else."

Kevin turned off his device and put his papers back in his briefcase. "I'll obtain a copy of the video from the Compound. You'll see the judge tomorrow. From there, we can post bail so you can go home."

I breathed a sigh of relief. "Thank you."

"Don't thank me yet. The charges being pressed against you are incredibly serious. You're potentially facing a lifelong prison sentence."

Kevin left shortly after delivering that blow. When he departed from the room, it was just me and the guard. I waited for her to tell me what to do. When she did nothing, I glanced over my shoulder.

"Will I be staying here?"

Her eyes didn't meet mine when she replied, "You have another visitor. He's on his way in."

My eyebrows knit together as I tried to figure out who else could be visiting me. A smile lifted my lips at the thought of Davin coming to see me when the door burst open.

My smile vanished.

Senator Douglas strode in. With the flick of a hand, he dismissed the guards who'd accompanied him. When the female officer stationed in the corner made no attempt to leave, he addressed her too.

"You may step out. I'll only be a few minutes."

My mind was still trying to process him being here when she departed. It was only then I wondered how he did it. *Aren't the guards supposed to stay in here with me?*

Fear coiled in my belly. My hands began to shake so I clasped them tightly together as Senator Douglas pulled out the chair across from me. It squeaked on the concrete.

The senator wore a crisp suit and tie. His heavy jowls jiggled when he grinned.

"Wha... what the hell? How are you here?" I whispered.

"I warned you to not mess with me."

His words washed over me. *Mess with him?* Never mind that. I was still trying to process him here. In the jail. Gloating.

He leaned back and crossed his arms. His paunch belly pushed against the table. "If only you had listened and stopped fighting for those Kazzie scums, things could have turned out differently."

My eyes widened. *"You* framed me in the bombings?"

"Framed?" He chuckled. "Oh, no. Of course not. I would never do anything illegal." Sarcasm dripped from his words, like venom beading from a snake's fang.

And then it hit me.

He was behind this.

He was behind all of this. *Including Monica's involvement?*

"But..." I shook my head as the implication of what he said sank it. "You murdered them! You murdered innocent people! And for what?"

"People?" he scoffed. "They don't look like people to me. More like virus-infected filth. The world is better off without them."

My entire body began to shake. Rage like I'd never felt before coated my skin, like a hot film scorching me in its intensity. "You bastard! They were my friends! They were innocent *people!*"

The jovial glee left his expression. Nothing but cold hate glimmered from his irises. "Enjoy the rest of your life, *Dr. Forester.* I wish I could say it was a pleasure meeting you, but it wasn't."

He abruptly stood and walked away, his jowls jiggling with the movement.

"You won't get away with this!" I screamed after him. But my empty words fell on deaf ears.

He didn't even look back.

When the door closed behind him, I sat frozen. Only my harsh breaths filled the room. Everything else around me was eerily silent.

I dropped my head into my hands and hissed in pain when my palms grazed the burn on my cheek.

This could be the end.

The door opened again when the female guard returned. "Let's go, Forester."

I numbly stood. My chair caught on the pant hems again, and I almost fell. But not even that penetrated the fog in my mind. The reality that lay ahead of me suddenly seemed even more daunting.

If the senator had it out for me, it may not matter that I was innocent.

No one would believe me.

23 – UNLIKELY ALLY

The numbness wore off more and more with every step back to my cell. In its place, sheer panic began to build. I was shaking by the time the guard sealed the jail cell door behind me.

From there, I collapsed to the floor. A sudden rush of terror clawed at my nerves, like electric jolts shooting down my arms.

No words formed in my mind. Only emotions. The urge to run was strong. It became an inhuman need that was almost impossible to ignore. Gripping my arms tightly around my knees, I clung to my shins, burying my head between my thighs.

A mewling sound filled my cell. It took a second before I realized that sound came from me.

Frantic knocking came from the back of my mind.

I barely had the wherewithal to open the telepathic connection to Sara. Words refused to form in my mind to enter hers.

I'll get Davin. Her clipped tone disappeared. A moment

later, I felt him.

The deep, comforting presence of the man I loved more than life itself entered my mind.

Meghan? Babe?

It took a full minute before the shaking stopped. During that time, Davin's increasing fear and furious protectiveness surged into me at regular intervals, like waves pounding the shore.

Just take your time. Talk to me when you can. While his words were calm, his emotions betrayed him. The rage building inside of him was barely kept in check. It transferred to me. A hot, pulsing, fire that seemed to take on a life of its own.

Did someone hurt you? His words came through clenched teeth.

In that question, I knew he assumed the worst. Shaking my head, I managed to get one word to him. *No.*

He waited quietly for me to continue. Despite his rage, his never-ending patience and love pulled me back to the surface. I clung to the life raft his connection threw. Using that, I finally felt like I broke through the drowning void.

Breathe.

Inhale.

Exist.

Words finally came to me after I took a shuddering breath.

Senator Douglas came to see me. He's framed me. He's the reason I'm in here.

Davin's reaction was swift and absolute. I imagined if he and I were in the same room, he'd be punching a hole through the wall.

He framed you? He admitted that?

My shaky response took a moment to get out. *More or less. He told me this is what happens from defying him. I don't know how he framed me, but I'm certain he did.*

Where is he?

No. Davin, just no. You can't go after him. That will only make it worse.

With each word that left my mouth, I felt more in control. More like myself. I pushed to standing from the cold, concrete floor and moved to the bed. My legs still shook, but I was standing and walking. And my heart no longer felt like it would beat out of my chest.

The mattress sagged when I sat. Hard springs poked into my butt. I ignored them.

Slowly, bit by bit of myself began to return. I was stronger than this. I wouldn't let the Senator beat me. Anxiety and panic attacks... They were essentially who I was. But they didn't define me.

They never would.

He can't get away with this. Davin's teeth grated, as if he were grinding his teeth in my mind.

And he won't. I met with an attorney tonight too. He's coming back for my hearing tomorrow. I'll tell him about Senator Douglas' involvement then.

Sara abruptly interrupted. Apparently, the emotions raging off Davin were making her head spin. We closed our connection with promises to talk soon. And once they were gone, I was completely alone. In my cell. In the dark. While coldness seeped into the walls behind me.

I DIDN'T SLEEP well that night. Everything warred within me. The death of my friends. The incident in the Production Room. The explosions. Me being held accountable. And Davin's rage.

The worries refused to leave me and did little to quell the

anxiety strumming inside me like disjointed music chords.

Everything my attorney and the senator had said kept turning over in my mind like a thousand tiny sand particles sifting back and forth through an hourglass. I was innocent. Even if the senator had set me up, that fact didn't change.

I just had to find a way to prove it.

I knew there had to be more clues to the explosions—clues that would solidify it *wasn't* me who planted the bomb.

Now, it was a matter of finding them.

By the time morning came, my eyes felt gritty and bloodshot. I spent most of the day pacing in the small cell until they came and took me to court. Kevin's professional demeanor and no-nonsense attitude helped put me at ease, but when I told him about my visit from Senator Douglas after he'd left yesterday, his gaze turned pensive.

"I don't recall seeing any visitors on the roster yesterday other than myself."

My mouth parted. "But he was here! You can ask the guards. He was here and he practically admitted to framing me."

Kevin frowned. "He admitted that?"

"More or less." I summed up my conversation with the senator.

Kevin tapped his chin. "I'll look into it, but right now, we need to concentrate on getting you out of jail."

He ushered me into the courtroom while I followed his lead. Sitting on the hard wooden chairs before the judge, my nails dug into my palms. It was all surreal, like something out of a movie, but when the judge set my bail for one hundred thousand dollars all hope crumbled within me.

I hung my head. "I don't know how I can possibly raise that kind of money."

Kevin merely leaned over and said quietly, "You don't need to. It's been taken care of."

"What do you mean?"

"Cate Hutchinson began a fund for you last night. It's already raised $150,000."

"A fund?"

Kevin smiled. It was the first time I'd seen him as anything but stoic. "It appears you have quite the fan base in this country."

While I didn't fully comprehend what he was telling me, it soon became apparent that I wouldn't be spending another night in jail. I was given back my clothes and belongings, and before I knew it, I was ushered out the door while Kevin promised to look into Senator Douglas.

As soon as I walked through the exit doors of the courthouse, a dozen cameras and reporters rushed toward me. Luckily, the guards from the jail stepped forward. They formed a circle around me, but it did little to help.

Flashes from cameras, and reporters yelling questions, came from every which way. It was only when the guards pushed past them that my eyes alighted on the figure running up the stairs.

Davin.

His midnight hair fluttered in the breeze. He wore jeans and a short sleeved t-shirt as the warm sun beat down. His intense blue eyes immediately zeroed in on me as he strode through the reporters, pushing them back as if they were inconsequential flies.

He did it all so deftly, so easily. Even though he could have knocked all of them over like bowling pins, he took care to not use excessive force. Still, they didn't stand a chance pushing him out of their way. A few tried, but it was like trying to move a concrete pillar.

"Meghan." His single word was my undoing.

The guards parted, allowing him in. He rushed to my side and put a protective arm around me. I used his strength and unbending will to get me down the stairs. I knew he could have scooped me up and whizzed us out of sight, but that would have caused more of a spectacle. I was glad he didn't.

He rushed me to the car. It felt like hours before we were safely inside, buckled, and driving away. The reporters continued to chase us, but Davin didn't look back.

It was only when we rounded the corner and were alone on the street that fresh tears filled my eyes. A sob came next.

"Oh, babe…" Davin gripped my hand tightly as he accelerated down the road. "I'm so sorry, Meghan. I'm so sorry about what happened."

"Senator Douglas has framed me. I may never get out of this, and not just that…" Another sob wracked my body. "I can't believe so many of the Kazzies that were staying in Compound 3 are dead. Not just Dorothy, Bethany and Garrett… Half of them died in the explosion."

His face tightened as tears filled his own eyes. "I know."

Twenty minutes later, we pulled up to the curb outside of our rental home. My gaze widened as I wiped the tears from my cheeks. Three additional vehicles sat in our driveway.

"Are other people here?"

He nodded. "We've had a few visitors since you were arrested."

I DIDN'T KNOW what to expect when I stepped into the house, but when I saw Ian and Cate sitting in the living room, relief billowed through me. Cate stood and rushed forward. Before I knew it, her arms were around me.

"This is absolutely ridiculous. I'm livid that you're being accused of anything like this. And Davin tells me Senator Douglas is involved again. That lying, conniving, son-of-a-bitch!"

Ian placed a hand on her shoulder.

Cate took a deep, unsteady breath. It took her a full minute to compose herself.

When she finally pulled back, her cool blue eyes traveled up and down my frame. She looked exactly as I remembered her—lean and fit, with short blond hair that swayed on her shoulders.

Ian shoved his hands in his pockets as I dried more tears from my eyes. "I'm so sorry about yesterday, Meghan." His expression fell. "I don't for a moment think that you're guilty of what they're saying."

I smiled gratefully. It was good to know I had people on my side.

I felt Davin's presence just behind me. It was the first time he'd met either of my Washington friends. And while a tense air hung between Davin and Ian, they seemed to be getting along.

"What time did you arrive?" I asked Cate.

"This morning. I took the first flight that I could find."

A shuffle sounded in the hallway and my eyes widened when I saw who stood there.

Amy, Sharon, the twins, and my parents.

Amy flew into the living room. "You're back!"

She barreled into me, practically knocking me off my feet. "Hi, Amy."

"Jesus Christ, Meghan. One minute I'm in the parking lot with everybody else, the next second you're hauled off, and then they're shuffling us onto buses and sending us home. And it's only when I showed back up here and was told by Davin that you'd been *arrested* and sent to jail that I knew what was going on. Are they seriously blaming *you* for those explosions?"

I nodded. "It seems so. Senator Douglas has it out for me."

Amy's mouth set into a grim line. "I heard. That bastard."

The twins, Sharon, and my parents came forward next. One-by-one, they hugged me as tears poured down everyone's faces.

"I can't believe it, kiddo." My dad patted my shoulder. "Those conniving cons. How dare they say that about my little girl."

His fierce anger and my mother's protective arm around my shoulders helped keep my anxiety at bay.

"It's so crazy," Sophie wailed. "You'd *never* do anything like that!"

Sara still held my hand despite my parents standing so close. It felt like she was afraid to let go.

Cate nodded toward the couches. "How about we all sit?"

The ten of us sat down as best we could. Since there wasn't enough furniture, the twins, Ian, and Amy opted to sit on the floor.

Davin sat close to my side and put his arm around me. My parents flanked my other side.

A few times, I caught Ian glancing my way. It was hard to gauge how he felt since his expression gave away nothing. After all, only two months ago he'd been making a pass at me in a hotel room in North Dakota. But even then, I couldn't forget Davin. I couldn't move on despite Ian being a good guy.

I glanced up at the Kazzie at my side. His expression was grim, but he gave me a reassuring squeeze when our gazes met.

Cate sat forward in her chair and clasped her hands.

"Okay, Meghan. Fill me in on everything that's been happening here. I need to know all of the details. If Senator Douglas wants to play with fire, I'll give him a fucking inferno."

The afternoon quickly turned into the evening as I told them everything I knew. Now that I knew I had been set up, it was a matter of figuring out how to undo it.

"Kevin said he'll receive a copy of the video by the end of today," I concluded. "I have a meeting scheduled with him tomorrow morning to review what he's found. He also said the investigation is still underway at the Compound. No definitive conclusions have been made yet."

"So they suspect you, but they don't have solid proof?" Sara asked.

I shrugged. "Maybe. I don't actually know." I glanced at Amy. "Have they said when everybody will be allowed back in?"

She shook her head. "Everybody's on indefinite leave until the investigation finishes."

I leaned into Davin's hard side. His warmth surrounded me. I bit my lip as I tried to figure a way out of this, but no matter which way my thoughts turned, there were no pretty outcomes.

CATE, IAN, THE twins, Sharon, and my parents stood to leave just before nine at night with promises to return first thing in the morning. All of them had booked hotel rooms despite my insistence they could all stay.

"There are not enough beds, Meg." My dad patted my shoulder as he and my mother gathered their things. "But don't worry about us. You just worry about yourself right now."

I hugged him fiercely and then my mother. For the first

time in my entire life, I felt like I could lean on them. They'd stayed by me through everything since the Kazzies had been released. And not once had they questioned the science behind the vaccine or doubted my ability to continue this fight. Other than their worry over my injury, they'd been behind me one-hundred-percent.

My throat tightened at that realization.

"My meeting with my attorney is scheduled for ten tomorrow morning. Will you come?"

My mother squeezed my hand. "Of course. We'll meet you there."

Cate, Ian, the twins, and Sharon all said their goodbyes. When the door finally closed behind everyone, the house seemed unnaturally quiet.

Everything felt so surreal. The entire last forty-eight hours felt like a bad nightmare that I would surely wake from at any moment.

Amy retreated to her room to call Ben.

That left Davin and me alone in the living room.

He pulled me from the entryway and tugged me down the hall. "You look exhausted." His words were worried and his eyes bright. I'd felt him watching me all night.

"I didn't sleep very well last night," I joked.

His mouth tightened. "Come here."

He pulled me into our room. Moonlight bathed the carpet and furnishings. Closing the door behind us, he crushed me to his chest.

His soap and aftershave scent washed over me as I closed my eyes. It was so easy to lose myself with him. When he and I were alone like this, with his strong hands around my waist and his achingly familiar body pressed against mine, it was tempting to forget the outside world.

"I wish we could stay like this. I wish it could be this simple. This easy. All I've ever wanted is for you to be free and to be with you," I whispered.

"And we will be. I won't let them take you from me."

His tone held a steely edge that made a shiver run through me. He tilted my chin up and pulled me closer. When his lips descended over mine, a fierce longing exploded inside me.

I wrapped my arms around his neck and threaded my fingers through his silky hair.

He groaned.

In a blur of movement and need, our clothes were off and we were on the bed.

Our lovemaking was frantic and raw. Every moment felt precious and precarious, as if the next minute could be snatched away from us.

When we were both sated and spent, we lay in a tangle of sheets. With our limbs entwined, Davin held me close and pulled the covers up around us. He traced a finger up and down my back as moonlight bathed his fiery skin.

"I'll always love you," he whispered. "From now until the day I die."

"I love you too. Please know that. If anything happens and I don't—"

He put a finger to my lips. "Nothing's going to happen. We'll figure this out and we'll have a normal life. Any alternatives are not something I'll accept."

I smiled at his firm words and absolute conviction that he could fix this. But deep in my heart, I knew it wasn't that simple. I knew that come tomorrow, reality would come crashing back and our love for one another may not be enough.

CATE, IAN, MY parents, Sharon, and the twins met us at Kevin's office the next day. I felt as pale as a ghost when his secretary ushered our group into the conference room.

A crumbling five-story building lay directly across the street. It was visible through the boardroom's expansive windows. Several large bird nests sat on decaying window fixtures that were splattered with bird poop.

"Please have a seat." Kevin waved at the chairs around the large board table.

Despite having everyone at my side, I still felt like a cornered mouse.

Even though I knew my friends and family would fight for me until the end, I also knew against the law, it didn't matter. If the courts deemed me guilty of the explosions, my innocence was inconsequential.

I'd lose my freedom, I'd lose my friends, and I'd lose Davin.

A part of me wanted to laugh hysterically at the irony of it all. I'd spent months upon months working to free my Kazzie friends. Now, they were working to free me.

"I have a copy of the video." Kevin picked up a remote control and flicked on a TV hanging from the wall. "I figure we'll watch that first."

The ten of us swiveled our chairs to face the screen. Kevin hit another button and the video turned into a blur as he forwarded to a specific scene.

When he pressed play again, the image stilled. It showed the Production Room with its numerous mechanics and machinery. For a moment, nothing happened. Since the video was silent, all we could see were the machines turning and moving, but everything else was still.

I leaned forward in my seat as I waited for the

incriminating scene to unfold. I didn't have to wait long. A second later, a person entered the frame.

It appeared to be a woman from the person's small build. She was fully suited up.

I frowned.

From the camera's distance, she *did* look like me.

Davin and I shared a puzzled look before turning back to the video.

The scene wasn't long. It showed the woman rushing toward one of the machines with a device. She crouched down and taped what I assumed was the bomb to the machine.

A few minutes passed. It seemed that she was programming something into the bomb.

When she finished, she stood and darted away.

Kevin stopped the video. "This is a video they claim shows you planting the device."

I turned to him with wide eyes. "But you can't see the individual's face. That person just has a similar build to me."

Kevin raised an eyebrow. "Exactly. However, they are claiming that when you zoom in on the feed that person looks like you. Not to mention, the time stamp matches when you were in the Production Room."

Cate snorted. "I've seen plenty of videos firsthand from our security feed, and I can tell you that zooming in on an individual does *not* give a clear picture. That person could be any woman the same size as Meghan and just because her time stamp shows she was in the room doesn't prove she planted the bomb."

Kevin nodded. "True, but there's more. Your fingerprints are on the bomb remnants, Meghan."

"What?" The word exploded out of me.

Kevin continued on, his tone unwavering. "That coupled

with this video, is their evidence that you're the one who planted the bomb."

I couldn't believe what I was hearing. "But... surely that's not proof. If I've been framed, then I could have been set up to touch that material before it was turned into the bomb. Senator Douglas visited me in jail. He gloated and more or less told me that my arrest was because I defied him. He practically admitted that he framed me!"

Kevin nodded. "Even if he did say that, we don't have proof of it. I'll check the visitor's log at the jail again, but a visit from him doesn't prove that he framed you."

I slumped back in the chair, my heart thundering in my chest. "What about the video feed showing me being attacked? Surely, that would help them understand it wasn't me?"

Kevin steepled his hands. "There is no video of that."

Davin tensed as my mouth dropped. "How can there not be?"

"It was either in a blind spot that the cameras didn't pick up, or it was destroyed in the explosion."

Or Senator Douglas removed it before the explosion so he didn't leave any loose ends behind.

Even though I felt like dropping my head into my hands, I didn't. Straightening my shoulders, I asked, "So now what?"

"Exactly, now what?" My dad turned a stern gaze to my attorney.

Kevin replied calmly, "I continue to build our case while the investigation continues."

"And if we can't find more evidence that Meghan is innocent?" Cate demanded. "Despite her little visit from Senator Douglas in which he practically admitted to framing her?"

Kevin raised a hand. "Without proof that he was there,

and without proof that conversation took place, that's not something we can use in our case. I suggest we cross one bridge at a time."

That non-reassuring comment left me chilled to the bone. *If we can't prove that I'm innocent, I'm going to jail.*

EVERYONE RETURNED TO our rental home after we wrapped up with Kevin. More than ever, I needed to go for a run. I hadn't run in weeks, not since Dr. Roberts had shot me in Mobridge. But now I was healed, and I desperately needed to blow off steam.

I retreated to Davin's and my bedroom to change into my running clothes the second I walked through the door. Tense energy seemed to hang every which way I turned. It was driving me crazy.

Cate and Ian were currently in the living room. They'd pulled out their laptops with shaky hands so they could work remotely. Amy had picked up the phone to call Ben, while the twins and Sharon had popped a movie into the DVD player after trying unsuccessfully to get me to watch it with them. Only my parents weren't in the house.

My mother had the foresight to realize we didn't have much food. Whisking Amy's, Davin's and my Food Distribution Center cards from our wallets, she'd pulled my dad from the home with promises to come back soon with a mountain of groceries.

Davin appeared at our bedroom door and crossed his arms. "What are you doing?"

I twirled my hair up into a ponytail and slipped on my running shoes. "I need to run. Do you want to join me?"

"Are you sure you're up for it?"

"More than up for it. If I don't run, I'm going to scream."

Stepping into the room, he slipped off his sweatshirt in one swift move. Despite the gravity of my situation, my breath stopped at the sight of his bare chest and rippling muscles. Scars littered his honey-hued abdomen and legs, but it didn't deter from his magnificent physique.

After donning shorts and a t-shirt, he nodded toward the back door. "Let's go."

We slipped out before anyone knew what we were doing. I led the way down the driveway with Davin at my heels. The only other time we'd run together had been at the Compound when I'd been contained within the Inner Sanctum.

Other than that, we still hadn't had time to enjoy anything as simple as an evening run together.

My muscles protested as I set a vigorous pace. Warm evening air flowed across my cheeks as our feet pounded the asphalt. I knew I'd be sore tomorrow. It had been weeks since I'd run, and I already felt it in every muscle in my body.

"Are you doing okay?" Davin ran steadily at my side. His words were even and deep. I knew this run would be like a Sunday afternoon stroll to him, but I loved having him with me.

"I'm going to feel this tomorrow that's for sure." My breath was labored, but I didn't slow. Even though it was my first run in over two months, I wasn't going easy on myself.

Right now, I needed the solace running brought. It was the only time I felt still. The only time I felt at peace. It had been my therapy for so many years, and at the moment, I needed therapy more than anything.

We ran in silence as the miles ticked by. Every now and then, Davin's arm brushed mine. The feel of him, and his towering form, helped clear my mind and still my quivering nerves.

It was his calming presence that freed my mind. As each mile pounded beneath us, I turned more inward. I scanned my memories again and again, looking and searching for anything that may help my case against the Compound.

By the time we looped back to the house, sweat poured from my face and ran in steady rivers down my back. It was only as I stopped to walk in circles to cool down, that a memory flashed to life inside me.

I gasped and closed my eyes.

The memory solidified in my mind, like a movie playing on the big screen. It showed me with Dr. Roberts in the interrogation room on Reservation 1. It had been right after I'd returned from Washington D.C. following Davin's and my friends' imprisonment on the reservation.

I'd met with my former boss in hopes of securing my friends' safety. It was during that meeting that I'd made the deal to never talk to or contact them again.

But it wasn't that deal that triggered the memory. It was what Dr. Roberts had said.

"And just so you know. I've heard you've been busy. Just yesterday you were in Washington D.C. From what I hear, you were once again trying to sabotage my career. This time you were asking the president herself that I be removed from my position."

My eyes flashed open. "Davin!"

Davin's tall form turned my way. Worry grew in his liquid cobalt gaze. "What's wrong?"

My hands shook. "Dr. Roberts... He..." I gasped for air. It was more than just the run that made it hard to breathe. If I was right, if my hunch was correct, my former boss may be the key to keeping me out of jail.

Davin's gaze hardened at the sound of Dr. Roberts' name. "What is it?"

I explained to him what I'd just remembered. If Dr. Roberts had known about my meeting with the president then he had insider contacts in the nation's capital. It was possible, but not probable, that his contact had been Senator Douglas. They both hated the Kazzies. They'd both worked to keep them imprisoned. And if the two men were connected, it was possible my former boss may have information about the senator's illegal activities.

Davin's eyebrows knit together, his mouth tightening into a line as hard as granite. "You're saying that Dr. Roberts may have dirt on the senator."

I nodded my head vigorously. "And if he has any incriminating information, it's possible he may share it in return for a shorter prison sentence."

Fury emanated from Davin as he balled his hands into fists.

I laid my hand on his forearm. "It's worth pursuing. If I can prove that the senator is behind not only my framing, but the debacle behind Zoe Mathison's death, the charges may be dropped. I know it's grasping at straws, but we have to do something."

Breathing deeply, Davin gave a curt nod. "As much as I hate that bastard, you're right. So now what?"

"Now, I call him."

DAVIN AND I rushed into the house and informed everyone of what I'd remembered.

Thankfully, Cate hadn't left. While the MRRA may have allowed me to contact Dr. Roberts in their psychiatric facility before my arrest, now I knew they wouldn't. However, as a former Director, Cate held more power than most generals within the MRRA. After one call from her, I was now on hold while waiting for a guard to retrieve Dr. Roberts from his cell.

My hands shook. Within minutes, I'd be speaking to the man who'd tortured my friends and personally sought to destroy me.

There were no guarantees he'd talked to me even if he had information that could exonerate me.

The line clicked.

"Dr. Forester?" the guard asked.

"Yes?"

"I'm putting you through now."

Another click followed and then breathing could be heard from the other end. My heart rate increased.

"Hello?" I asked tentatively.

"Dr. Forester. I have to say it's quite a surprise to hear from you." My former boss' words rolled through the connection.

My grip tightened on the phone. "Thank you for speaking with me."

I expected a sarcastic or scathing reply. Instead, Dr. Roberts said, "What can I do for you?"

I eyed the people around me. Cate, Ian, Davin, the twins, Sharon, Amy, and my parents all leaned forward, hanging off my every word. Closing my eyes, I tried to calm my rapid breathing.

"It's about Senator Douglas. I'm calling to discuss a few things with you."

Silence followed.

My heart slammed against my ribs. "Hello?"

"What do you want to discuss?" he finally replied coolly.

I relayed the encounter my boss and I had on the reservation. "You said you already knew of my meeting with the president, but how did you know? Who told you?"

Dr. Roberts cleared his throat. "So what you're really asking is if Senator Douglas told me? You're wondering if he's the one who relayed that information to me?"

I swallowed tightly. "Yes."

"And why would I tell you if he had?"

Breathing harder, I replied, "Because he's framed me for a crime I didn't commit, and I need proof of his involvement and his illegal activities." I gripped the phone harder, my palm a sweaty mess. "I know that you hate the Kazzies. I know that a Kazzie killed your wife and child—"

His breath sucked in.

I paused for the merest second before adding, "But if you know about Senator Douglas, if you know anything about his illegal activities or involvement with these crimes, please, Dr. Roberts. *Please*, for once, do the right thing and tell me. Help me prove my innocence. I'm begging you!"

He didn't say anything. Only his breathing came through the line.

I closed my eyes, willing him to have the answers, willing him to help me, but knowing the chance of any of it were as slim as winning the lottery. He'd shot me only weeks ago. His hatred for the Kazzies had driven him to a criminal act. Who was to say anything would be different now. It was possible he'd gloat over my current state, even happier to hear of my demise.

"I'll have to think about that."

His reply had me sitting up straighter. "You'll…" I took a deep steadying breath. "Do you really know something?"

He cleared his throat again. "Perhaps."

"So you'll tell me?" My voice rose higher.

"I told you, I need to think about it. I need to speak to my attorney before I make any decisions."

"What if you revealing information results in an earlier release for you?"

"Like I said, Dr. Forester, I need to speak to my attorney first."

I didn't press my luck. The fact that my former boss may have information and was even considering telling me was more than I'd hoped for.

"Of course. I'll wait."

We hung up after Dr. Roberts promised to be in touch soon.

However, I had no idea how soon that would be. But I did know one thing, a jail cell waited for me if my former boss refused to divulge whatever information he had.

24 – REVELATIONS

I spent the evening pacing and worrying. My parents, Sharon, and the twins were no different. My call to Dr. Roberts seemed to heighten the anxiety in the house.

From what I could gather, my former boss had information that may help me, but there was no guarantee he'd relinquish it.

"Is there anything we can do to pressure him to talk?" Sara frowned heavily. Her and Sophie's skin had shimmered continually during the evening. I knew they'd been speaking telepathically since I'd hung up with Dr. Roberts. However, it didn't seem they had any intention of sharing whatever they'd discussed.

I could only guess they were filled with doubt and didn't want me to know. Their experience under Dr. Roberts' rule had solidified him as a monster in their minds.

Cate crossed her arms. Steely authority rang in her tone. "I'll make more calls. If we can pressure the MRRA to make a deal with him, it's possible he'd be more likely to talk. Ian?" She glanced his way. "Come with me. We have work to do."

Cate and Ian retreated to Amy's bedroom to make calls in private. More than ever I was grateful for Cate's continued support. With all of us working together, it was possible we'd get Dr. Roberts to talk.

"What about the psychiatrist treating him?" Amy asked. "What if he can convince Dr. Roberts to reveal whatever dirt he's got?"

I nodded. "I thought about that too. Is there any way we can speak with him?"

Amy's red hair swished over her shoulders when she turned. "It's worth trying. Let me get a hold of Dr. Sadowsky. We'll see if he has any favors to cash in with the MRRA."

I hadn't heard from my boss since being arrested. Despite the shock that had covered the Director of Compound 26's face when I'd been hauled away, deep in my heart, I knew Dr. Sadowsky didn't believe I was guilty.

He knew me too well.

While Amy, Cate, and Ian were busy making calls, I wracked my brain for any further information that could help my case.

Unfortunately, I came up short. The only hope we had was if Dr. Roberts pulled through.

Now, it was a matter of waiting to see if he did.

BY MORNING THE next day, I was an anxious mess. Despite Davin's soothing presence the night prior, nightmares had plagued me.

For the first time since beginning my quest over a year ago to free the Kazzies, the nightmares weren't about them being imprisoned. The nightmares were about jail cells surrounding *me*.

Amy had only just begun brewing coffee when a sharp

knock came on the door. Without waiting for a reply, Cate and Ian strode in.

"We have a deal." Dark circles lined Cate's lower eyelids, but her irises glowed with excitement. "The MRRA has agreed to reduce the charges against Dr. Roberts if he agrees to share whatever information he has."

I dropped the coffee mug I held. It clattered to the counter before dropping into the sink. Coffee sloshed everywhere.

Rushing around the counter, I reached Cate's side.

"They have?" I asked breathlessly. My heart pounded like a bass drum in my chest.

"Yes. It seems you're not the only one Senator Douglas has screwed over in his attempts to climb the political ladder. A few officials within the MRRA were more than happy to oblige."

My lips trembled as hope blossomed inside me.

"How do we get the information?" I asked.

Cate held out her phone. "You ask him for it." She eyed the bullet scar that peeked out from under my shirt. "It seems most fitting coming from you."

DR. ROBERTS AND I were on the phone for over an hour. He divulged details that I could only hope to have acquired. The information he had was mind-boggling.

It implicated the senator and Giselle Warren in the explosions and deaths at Compound 3.

When he said Giselle's name, my first reaction was disbelief. Giselle had never done anything to me. She'd always been friendly and accommodating. Only Monica had shown hostility toward me.

But the more he revealed, the more I realized it *could* have been Giselle. Everything else fell into place after that.

My mind reeled as I connected the dots together. All along, I suspected it was Monica who had planted the bombs, but it never was. She hated me, that hadn't changed, but she wasn't a criminal.

My memory fired to life as flashes of my previous encounters with Giselle turned over in my mind. Like a spinning carousel, they flipped by one-by-one.

I remembered how her smile had frozen when I revealed it was rabies that killed Zoe Mathison and not *Makanza*. Or how she'd moved so stealthily the first time Dorothy entered the Experimental Room. It was like she knew how to remain unseen. And the day I'd been assaulted in the Production Room. She'd been there immediately after the incident because *she'd* been the one to shove me to the floor.

She hadn't been working in the Production Room that day, she'd been planting the bomb. And she and I were about the same size. The person in the security video had been her. Not me.

More memories surfaced. How Giselle had always been happy to help me over the previous weeks, including having me help her assess equipment. Several times she'd had me inspect lab machines. It was my guess that one of those "machines" had actually been part of the bomb. Little had I known that she was actually having me hold things to get my fingerprints on them.

My former boss went on to say that Senator Douglas had planted Giselle in Compound 3 after the senator had learned of the MRI's progress toward a cure. Even though the cure would revert Kazzies back to normal humans, it wasn't what the senator wanted. He wanted to keep the public afraid.

A cure would stop that terror.

With fear running rampant, the senator planned to

continue ascending to higher positions of power. The senator had so effectively instilled fear in so many citizens, that they turned to him for help.

Dr. Roberts divulged that the senator planned to run for president in the next election. With the public looking for a strong leader to support our country during this tumultuous time, who better to turn to than the man who'd permanently jailed the Kazzies and posed himself as the protector of those unharmed.

It all made me so sick.

Bile rose in my throat as I realized the depth of Senator Douglas' acts. His beliefs were selfish and twisted, but if there was one thing I'd learned in my time within the Compounds, it was that the depths of human ambition knew no bounds.

Dr. Roberts further explained how he acquired all of this information. As I suspected, he and Senator Douglas had been in cahoots with one another ever since our breakthrough over a year ago. And that long relationship with the senator had resulted in months' worth of information passed back and forth.

Information that my former boss had kept stored on his online hard drive which we now intended to use as evidence. Luckily, unbeknownst to the senator, Dr. Roberts had recorded every conversation he and the senator had shared, and he'd saved every email.

When I'd asked how he'd still been in contact with the senator during his imprisonment, Dr. Roberts had merely said he'd had help. However, my former boss refused to divulge which guard was helping him access his email and files stored on the web, but I didn't care. All I wanted was his information.

His information proved that Senator Douglas had coerced Chicago Children's CEO. Once again, my suspicions had been right. All along, it had been the senator demanding they don't conduct the autopsy.

When Dr. Roberts and I finally hung up, I leaned my head back against the wall as months of information filtered through my mind.

"Do you have enough evidence now to implicate the senator?" Davin hunched at my side. I'd retreated to the living room during the phone call. Davin had remained steadfast during my entire conversation.

"Yes. He said everything he has on the senator should be sitting in my inbox. All I have to do is open my email."

"Do you think you'll speak to him again, after he's… out." Davin's face hardened at the mention of Dr. Roberts walking free.

I shook my head. "No. It wasn't that kind of conversation."

My former boss and I hadn't ended our phone call with flowery affirmations or promises to connect again. He'd called to ultimately secure his release. He hadn't called because he wanted to be in the Kazzies' lives or because he wanted to mend things with me. He hadn't even apologized for shooting me.

But I was okay with that. I'd accepted who my boss was a long time ago—an evil man.

His view toward the Kazzies may have been shaped by the death of his family, but he'd probably always had prejudices against others. His family's death had simply been his excuse to mistreat those who were different.

I shifted closer to Davin.

He put his arm around me.

"I don't want Dr. Roberts in my life any more than he wants to be in it. Despite him helping us, I don't trust him, and

I never will. But at the same time, I'm grateful that he's chosen this current path versus a darker one."

Davin helped me stand. We moved into the kitchen. Everyone else followed. They all watched me with wide eyes.

I pulled out a chair and sat down. My legs were shaking so badly I was afraid I'd fall over if I didn't.

Davin sat at my side. He placed a comforting hand on my back. I could tell that a thousand different emotions were swirling through him.

While I didn't think he would ever forgive Dr. Roberts, I could also see a hint of gratitude in his gaze. A man who had spent years torturing and tormenting him had now just helped the entire Kazzie population—early release or not.

That was something Dr. Roberts had never done in the ten years he'd ruled Compound 26.

"So what did he tell you?" Sharon tucked a strand of auburn hair behind her ear.

"Yes, what did he say?" Cate leaned forward, her expression shrewd.

I told them everything, including how all of Dr. Roberts' information should be sitting in my inbox. When I finished, Cate pushed back from the chair and stood. "We're going to the police with this. Right now."

KEVIN JOINED US at the police station. I showed the officers the multiple files that my former boss had sent me. Their eyes grew wider and wider with every revelation.

It was crazy to think that an elected official was the center of all of this. And while that didn't surprise me, I was surprised at the lengths at which he'd gone.

Senator Douglas had willingly murdered innocent people. It was probably his intense hatred for the Kazzies that had bonded the senator and Dr. Roberts.

I didn't know what fate had in store for Senator Douglas, just like I didn't know what they would do with Giselle Warren. I could only hope they received the punishment they deserved. The two of them, along with whatever network of supporters had helped them, were the reason my friends were dead.

My throat constricted at the thought of never seeing Garrett, Dorothy, or Bethany again. Each of them had been a light to this world. I had never seen a mean bone in any of their bodies. If anything, they were goodness and kindness wrapped into one.

We spent hours at the police station. Davin stayed at my side the entire time. When we finally finished, Cate and Ian said they were going to the Compound to address the situation more. The building still wasn't open, too much damage had been done, but upper management was still there daily with the investigators.

"We'll get this sorted out." Ian smiled, his dimple appearing in his cheek. "Sooner or later, this will turn out okay."

I didn't tell him how much it still hurt that our research was gone. It felt like my friends' deaths had been in vain. Over a year's worth of research had gone up in smoke with the explosions and Giselle's careful destruction of Compound 3's backup servers.

All of it was gone.

We'd have to start all over, and there was no guarantee we'd recover everything we'd lost.

I FELL ASLEEP that night with Davin's arms around me. Vivid dreams plagued me through the night—bombs, explosions, the Kazzies' faces filled with hope at the drug we'd created. But those dreams morphed into something else.

They showed a woman behind a glass wall, knocking on it and pleading with me to open my eyes. She was pointing at something behind me and begging me to turn. With her long brown hair, hazel eyes, and slim build, it was like looking in a mirror.

That's because it's you.

With a start, I woke up.

I bolted upright.

Darkness filled the room as Davin's arm rested across my belly.

My heart hammered in my chest as I took deep gulping breaths. The house was silent. I glanced at the clock. 3:16 a.m.

Rubbing my face, I tried to wipe away the effects of the dream, but I kept picturing myself behind that glass wall.

What does it mean?

I'd been pointing at something behind me, begging me to see what the dream me saw so clearly. I closed my eyes and returned to that vision in my dream. Forcing myself to take steady, even breaths, I concentrated on what my subconscious was trying to tell me.

It's all there. Just open your mind.

My eyes flashed open as I realized what I'd known all along.

Lifting Davin's arm off me, I sprang out of bed. "Amy!"

I dashed into the hall. The sound of Davin's feet hitting the ground came next just as I opened her door.

"Meg?" he called. "What's going on?"

But I ignored him and barreled into Amy's room. "Amy! Wake up!"

I nearly fell onto her bed in my haste to wake her. Long,

red curls spread across her pillow as she woke with a start.

"Jesus, Meghan!" Her eyes flashed open as she pushed hair from her face. "What the hell? What time is it?"

"You need to wake up, Amy. The cure isn't lost! I have the data. I have *all* of it!"

She sat upright just as Davin appeared in her doorframe. "What do you mean?"

"I mean, that I *remember* all of it!"

Understanding dawned on her face as dim moonlight filtered in through her window. "You remember everything Division 5 showed us."

"Yes! Exactly!"

She pushed back the covers and quickly twirled her hair into a ponytail. "Then let's get to work."

When I spun around to face Davin, a shocked expression was on his face. "Of course," he said quietly. "Your memory. You remember it all."

I nodded and stepped closer to him. He automatically put his arms around me. A grin spread across my face as my eidetic memory roared to life. I closed my eyes. One-by-one, the research Dr. Dornhoff had shown us in the slideshow on our first day at Compound 3 turned over in my mind.

I saw it all clearly. Every chemical compound, every equation—all of it.

Turning to Amy, I said, "What if I recounted all of that information to you, do you think you could record it all?"

"Yes. I'll turn my computer on right now." She skipped around us to collect her laptop in the living room, her hair a mess around her head.

We followed her. "I better make coffee." Davin squeezed my shoulders. "Something tells me that today's going to be a long day."

When we reached the kitchen, Davin turned on the lights and shook his head in amazement. "So the research isn't lost after all."

I smiled. "No, it's not. It's been in my mind the entire time."

AMY AND I spent the next sixteen hours going over every detail of research that had been told to us after we'd arrived at Compound 3. It took hours upon hours for me to go through every conversation, every slideshow, every computer screen that I'd ever looked upon.

I was exhausted by the time we went to bed that night, but it didn't stop us. First thing the next morning, Amy and I woke up and did it all over again.

And the next day, we did it again.

I recounted the research to her as she recorded it. By the end of the weekend, we had hundreds of computer files that held the chemical secrets to the cure that Compound 3 had discovered.

"Do you know what this means?" Amy leaned back in the chair. Fatigue lined her eyes. We'd easily been working sixteen-hour days. "The cure *isn't* lost, Meghan. We can put this into production at another Compound. Those that don't want to be Kazzies anymore can still take this drug. And we can still produce it and give it to the world. Because of your memory, we truly can wipe *Makanza* off the face of the earth."

A smile grew on my face at all that she implied. My heart hurt at the devastation that had occurred, but I knew she was right.

All was not lost.

We still had the research, which meant we still had the cure.

I met Davin's gaze from where he stood against the wall by the kitchen. He'd been silent most of the weekend while keeping my parents, his mom, and the twins occupied so Amy and I could work. But now, our gazes met as the enormity of what we'd done set in.

A smile spread across his face. Happiness radiated from him like rays from the sun. It was like we both knew the future we dreamed of, the future we'd been clawing our way toward for months on end, was *finally* coming true.

25 – END OF AN ERA

To say Dr. Dornhoff was surprised when Amy and I showed up at Compound 3 with our files, would be an understatement. But his incredulous expression was worth our surprise arrival.

When Amy and I unloaded the numerous computer files to him that contained all of the research he and his colleagues had spent countless months working on, a look of wonder, guilt, and confusion crossed his face.

"I'm so sorry I ever doubted you, Dr. Forester."

Before I could reply, Amy said tartly, "You should be sorry. If this doesn't convince you that Meghan had nothing to do with the explosions, I don't know what will." Amy crossed her arms.

My eyes widened at her bold words.

However, Dr. Dornhoff seemed more interested in our files. Already, he was busy scanning the information we'd given him.

A few minutes later, he looked up with disbelief.

"But... how..." His gaze traveled between us as he sat behind his desk in his office. Similar to other Compounds, his office was huge and situated on the top floor. It overlooked the warm winter desert below. "How did you get all of this? The backup data was wiped. All of our research was lost."

"Surely by now, you've heard of Meghan's memory." Amy leaned back in her chair. "She's a bit known for it. It's why she's the youngest one working for the MRI." Amy winked at me after she said that.

Dr. Dornhoff cleared his throat and removed his glasses. "It seems that I owe you endless apologies." He met my gaze. "Things were rather tense after the incident in the Production Room and Inner Sanctum. We may have been a little rash in our judgment."

Amy snorted. "I'll say."

I gave her a smile and folded my hands in my lap before addressing the Director. "I understand why you reached that conclusion, but anybody who knows me knows I would never have done anything like that."

The door opened behind us. Footsteps shuffled in. Before I could turn, a voice spoke that had me tensing in my seat. "So, she's finally returned."

Monica Brown stood by the door. She had her usual look of contempt for me, but her next words had me gawking. "I told him it wasn't you."

Amy's eyebrows rose as high as mine.

Monica sauntered to the empty chair beside me and sat down. She barely looked my way when she said, "You weren't the only one in the Production Room looking for someone, Meghan. I'd had suspicions for weeks that Giselle was up to something, but I had no proof so I started following her to see if I was right. And when I saw her sneak into the Production Room, when she was supposed to be working in Lab Four, I knew something was up."

So that's why Monica was there when I left! I angled my body toward her. "Was that you I saw unsuited before I entered the room?"

Monica scrunched up her nose. "Yeah. I know, I know. I messed up. But in my haste to catch up with Giselle, I didn't put on the suit, all I managed was the booties. And since I knew I'd be punished for that, I kept my mouth shut initially about seeing Giselle in there, but then when you got arrested, I finally told the police what I saw. Of course, nobody believed me."

Dr. Dornhoff leaned forward in his seat. "We've already spoken about the incident. Monica knows she broke protocol by her actions but, given the gravity of the situation, we've looked past that."

Monica leaned back in her seat and crossed her arms. "I would probably be fired right now if I hadn't been right about Giselle."

I listened startled as Monica described the subtle actions and hints she'd seen in Giselle over the previous months. Monica stated she'd tried going to upper management about her concerns initially but had been brushed off. Following that snub, Monica knew nobody would listen to her unless she had proof.

"So I started collecting information about her."

Dr. Dornhoff sighed heavily. "Everything Monica found has been turned over to the police."

"So where's Giselle now?" Amy asked.

"If all goes to plan, she's being arrested at this very moment along with Senator Douglas," the Director replied.

"There's something else I've uncovered." A gleam grew in Monica's gaze as she swung a smile my way. "Meghan's romantically involved with a Kazzie. They're living together."

My stomach dropped.

Amy leaned forward in her seat. "What the hell, Monica? Do you spend your free time stalking people?"

However, Dr. Dornhoff didn't seem to hear her. He continued scanning what Amy and I had given him.

Monica fidgeted in her seat. "Dr. Dornhoff? Did you hear me? Meghan's romantically involved with a Kazzie."

He barely glanced up. "I heard you. This isn't new information to me."

"It's not?" I sat up straighter.

He met my gaze just long enough to say, "When you refused to use the MRI's provided accommodation, Dr. Sadowsky and I decided to look into why that was. It wasn't hard to discover your involvement with Davin Kinder."

Amy and I shared a surprised look.

"So... you've known the entire time?" I swallowed tightly.

"We have."

"And... it's obviously fine if you know?"

Dr. Dornhoff returned his attention to the computer files. "Since there's no official policy against MRI employees dating Kazzies—yes, you're in the clear."

I leaned back, breathing a sigh of relief. It was silly. I knew I'd always had that lack of policy on my side. Still, the MRI wasn't known for being reasonable.

Monica, however, fumed. In one swift move, she stood from her chair and stormed out of the room.

Amy arched an eyebrow and leaned closer to me. Under her breath, she said, "Just ignore her. That chick has issues."

My hammering heart slowed down as the rush of adrenaline subsided. I gazed out the window behind Dr. Dornhoff. Obviously, Monica still hated me despite her willingness to admit that it wasn't me who'd caused the explosions. Amy had probably been right about her from the beginning. Monica didn't like me—whether that stemmed from jealousy or another reason—I'd probably never know, but as far as I was concerned, that was her problem—not mine.

The desert sun shone brightly in the sky as puffy cotton ball clouds drifted by. My mind reeled with all that had transpired.

It still boggled me that ultimately, the person we had to thank for the information that implicated Senator Douglas and Giselle was Dr. Roberts…

It was unfathomable.

"So where do we go from here?" I eyed the Director and nodded at the data. "We have enough information there to start over. And there are 71 Compounds in the U.S. If we finish the drug trials and every Compound begins production, we'd have enough doses for every Kazzie in the world within months."

Dr. Dornhoff smiled as an excited gleam entered his eyes. "You're right, Dr. Forester, and that's exactly what we're going to do."

DAVIN AND I flew back to South Dakota a few days later. Both of us were eager to return home and put everything that happened in California behind us. The trials would resume next month, so for the time being, I had a few weeks off.

Winter still blew in full force as piles of snow covered the ground. It was a harsh welcome back to our home state following the warm and dry winter in Southern California.

That night, we lay in bed together facing one another. We hadn't bothered to keep the light on. Instead, soft light from the moon poured through my window.

It had been such a whirlwind of a month. Now that we were home, it felt like decades worth of tension oozed out of me, like water being squeezed from a sponge.

"So what are you going to do?" I broached the subject we'd tiptoed around for weeks. "Do you want to be cured or do you want to stay as you are?"

The unreadable expression on his face didn't change. He traced a finger along my cheek and tenderly pushed a lock of hair behind my ear. Just that simple touch sent shivers to my toes.

"Do you want me to take it? Do you want me to be like everybody else?"

I shook my head. "Of course not. I love you as you are. But I also know there's a stigma against you, and probably always will be, but that doesn't matter to me. I just want you to be happy, Davin. That's all I've ever wanted for you. If staying as you are is what makes you happy, that's what I want. But if you want to return to the person you were before your infection, then I'll support that too."

He turned onto his back. The covers fell to his waist, revealing his hard chest and bronze skin.

With a brooding expression, he gazed at the dark ceiling. "To be honest, I don't know what to do. A part of me wants to take the cure so I can forget about the last ten years and try to move on with a normal life. Even though I've been living like this for so long, I'm still conscious every single moment of everything I do. Every time I touch you, I have to be careful to not exert too much pressure. At times, I'm terrified I'm going to hurt you without meaning to. I've had a few nightmares where I've accidentally killed you when I hugged you too tight. I'd never forgive myself if something like that happened."

I inched closer to him and cupped his cheek. "You're

afraid that one day you'll lose control and hurt me. I get that. I'd be lying if I said the thought never crossed my mind, especially when we first met."

He chuckled at my teasing tone and turned to face me once again. His broad shoulders pushed into the mattress as his hand rested on my hip.

His brow furrowed when he asked quietly, "If it didn't matter to me how I was, if it honestly didn't mean anything to me one way or another, how would you want me to be? Like this? Or as the person I used to be?"

My mouth parted. Davin was asking me to choose. *But it's not my choice.*

I shook my head. "I can't. I'm sorry, Davin, but I can't. This is your choice. It's truly *your* choice. If I took that choice away from you, it would go against everything I've fought for. From the first day I met you, I wanted you free. I wanted you to have the same rights as every other person in this country. But if you ask me to choose for you, I'll have taken away everything I fought for."

He sighed heavily. "You're really not going to give me any indication one way or another, are you?"

I smiled tenderly. "No, I'm not. I want this decision to be completely yours. Just know that I'll love you no matter what. If you stay like this, or if you turn into the man you once were, it won't matter. I meant it when I said I'll stay with you till I die. That will never change."

He inched closer and wrapped his arms around me. I turned my head so my cheek pressed against his hard warm chest. His strong, steady heartbeat sounded within.

"I'll have to think about it." His voice rumbled in his chest. "Because it's not just you and me I need to consider. If we ever begin a family, who's to say I wouldn't pass this virus onto our kids. Who's to say they'd survive it? And since nobody knows how this virus would affect a child conceived from a Kazzie, that would be a huge risk."

My breath stopped.

Considering I was the scientist, it was crazy that I'd never considered what he was saying. I pulled my head back to look him in the eye. "I never thought of that."

He ran a finger along my chin before pressing his lips softly to mine. When he pulled back, emotion as deep as the Pacific swam in his irises. "I could potentially be putting our unborn child at risk if I stay this way."

"Or our child could be just fine."

He crushed me to him and kissed me again. An urgency rushed up inside me at all that we had to consider. But right now, I didn't want to think about having children or the implications of a sick child because of the virus. Right now, I just wanted him.

Our lovemaking that night was fast and urgent the first time, but slow and tender the second. Each time we joined as one, love burst inside of me for how much this man affected me. He'd become so ingrained within my heart and soul, that at times I didn't know where I ended and he began.

But I did know one thing. No matter what happened to us in this life, we would figure it out together.

26 – A NEW DAWN

Compound 3's Director held good to his promise. After the drug trials resumed and concluded, we had proof the cure was effective. Following that, every Compound in the U.S. opened their Production Rooms and began producing the cure.

When word reached ANN of what we'd achieved, a shift once again began in our country.

The violence and protests that had ruled the streets for so many months began to die down. When summer came, we had the cure available. As Kazzies lined up outside Compound doors to be administered the cure, the fear truly subsided.

However, due to the Post Wave Rehabilitation Act, each and every Kazzie still had their own rights. None of them were forced to take the cure.

It was their personal choice.

AT THE END of August, I sat in Sharon's living room in Rapid City. The twins were with me while Sharon busied herself with gathering refreshments in the kitchen. Scents of fresh-baked cookies hung in the air as the tea kettle whistled.

Since the twins were busy on their smartphones, I used the moment to process all that had happened in the previous months.

The borders had opened to Canada and Mexico on June 1. That was all thanks to the Compounds' Production Rooms running nonstop for months on end.

Over eighty percent of Kazzies in North America had chosen to take the cure. Considering each of the forty-one strains was affected differently meant different reactions by all. Some Kazzies had incredibly painful transformations back to normal human form, others found the transformation more bearable. But the most important aspect was that the cure worked and nobody was harmed from it.

Of the Kazzies who'd resided at Compound 26, Sage and Victor opted to take the cure. Davin and the twins did not.

It was still painful for me to think of Garrett, Dorothy, and Bethany. Their bodies had been laid to rest, but my memories had not. Forever, I would remember Garrett's screams as he endured the cure. And it had all been in vain.

I would never forget that.

The only solace I took was watching Senator Douglas and Giselle Warren punished for their crimes. The day ANN showed them being hauled away to prison, after being given a life sentence for their involvement in the death of Compound 3's Kazzies, was bittersweet. It would never bring my friends back. It would never repair the hole in Makayla's heart at the loss of her sister.

But at least it was justice.

Taking a deep breath, I smoothed my denim shorts and forced myself to focus on the present. Turning to Sara, I asked, "Have you heard from Sage?"

The twin finished tapping something on her phone before

dropping it at her side. She lounged on the end of the sofa, her lithe blue legs dangling over the side. Whereas Sophie sat on the armchair in the corner, her legs crossed demurely.

Sara sat up straighter to face me. "He receives his last injection tomorrow. After that, his plan is to head straight back to Canada."

Rustling sounded from the foyer just as Victor entered the room. Sophie dropped her phone and jumped to a stand.

The former Kazzie had arrived in Rapid City the week after his final treatment. He was officially *Makanza*-free. And now that he and Sophie were a couple, after the quieter twin had *finally* taken her sister's advice to visit him, he was a constant fixture in Sharon's home.

Victor's skin, that had once been fire-engine red and able to withstand intense heat, was now olive toned with a smattering of freckles. If he touched a hot stove, or ran his finger through a lit match, he would burn like the rest of us.

Sophie's blue cheeks turned pink when Victor pulled her into a hug before smacking a kiss on her mouth. The twin giggled.

Turning to Sara and me, Victor asked, "Are you sure you two don't want to join us for the movie?"

"Nah." Sara shook her head. "You two have some time alone. We can see it later."

"No time, as I'm sure you know." I glanced at the clock. Davin was due to pick me up any minute.

"Enjoy the movie!" Sara called as they strolled out of the room.

"I'll let you know how it is," Sophie replied over her shoulder.

Excitement glowed in Sophie's eyes. A new blockbuster Hollywood movie had just released this week. It was the first

A-list new release to have graced the screen in over ten years. Tinseltown was officially up and running again. The entire country was celebrating it.

"It's nice to see them together," I commented after they left.

"And it's about time." Sara's legs continued to swing from their dangled position.

Sophie and Victor had been dating for over a month now. In that time, I'd never seen Sophie happier.

It warmed my heart that Victor didn't seem to care that Sophie had chosen to stay infected. Both of the twins were still on the fence about whether or not they'd take the cure even though it had been available all summer. I wasn't surprised.

They'd spent the majority of their lives sharing a telepathic connection. In a way, it was what bonded them. Taking the cure meant they'd lose that. It also meant Sara and I would lose our link.

I'd never voiced my opinion to Sara about the cure. In all honesty, I didn't have one. I felt so strongly that each Kazzie should have their own free will, that I only wished for Sara to do what was right for her.

Still, I was terrified of unintentionally saying something that would sway her. So I kept my lips sealed, and anytime Sara brought it up, I simply listened to her internal debate.

The sound of Victor's car pulling away carried through the open window just as Sharon rounded the corner from the kitchen. She wore jeans and a short-sleeved blouse. Her auburn hair was swept up into a bun with the familiar tendrils framing her face. Held within her grasp was the ancient tea tray holding her rosebud and cherry blossom tea set.

"They already left?" Sharon glanced out the window as Victor's car pulled away.

"Yep." Sara's feet dropped to the floor as she leaned forward and snatched a cookie from the tray. "I think the movie starts in half an hour. Hopefully, they'll still get good seats."

Sharon poured tea into three cups as I eyed the small pile of cookies next to them.

She must have noticed because she picked up the plate and held it toward me. "Want to try one? I just made these, and I plan to make a batch of gingersnaps tomorrow. Now that food isn't rationed in the grocery stores, I stocked up on baking supplies. I have enough chocolate chips and flour to last me a year!"

I laughed at the gleeful expression on her face and grabbed a cookie.

Since all borders had opened throughout the world, now that a cure was available, farming was on the rise, and world trade was back in action. Sharon was in heaven. Her entire kitchen was stocked with so many food items I often didn't know what to do when I opened the cupboard. Usually, items fell out.

It didn't help that most of them puzzled me. I had no idea how to cook with the majority of her ingredients. Luckily, Sharon and Davin seemed perfectly happy to keep me fed.

Chirping bird sounds came through the window. Outside, yellow finches sat on the birdfeeder. It was another of many changes happening in the world today. Last year, buying seed to feed wild birds was unfathomable. Those seeds would have been used for planting or to feed livestock. One would never have considered using it to attract birds simply for viewing pleasure.

I smiled in contentment as the birds chirped away. Taking a bite of the cookie, my contentment grew as the soft doughy goodness coated my tongue. Sugar and chocolate had recently become two of my favorite foods. I closed my eyes and enjoyed it.

Just as I was about to reach for another cookie, someone cleared his throat.

My eyes flew open.

Davin stood leaning against the wall by the entry. His arms were crossed while his electric blue eyes twinkled in amusement. In his fitted t-shirt, his broad shoulders strained against the fabric.

"Are you ready to go?" he asked. The amused expression stayed on his face as I downed half of my tea. "Our flight leaves in two hours."

"Is it already time?" My stomach flipped as excitement coursed through me. Davin and I were about to embark on our first true adventure together.

"Yep. Time to get moving."

I hastily stood and grabbed a second cookie for the road. Davin and I had flights booked for the afternoon. We were flying to British Columbia to spend a week on the coast. It would be the first time either of us had left the country.

"Oh my God! Have fun!" Sara squealed. "I can't wait to see pictures when you get back. Make sure you take at least a hundred, and if anything exciting happens, you have to fill me in."

She jumped up to hug me. Her warm slight form pressed against me.

Sharon stood next to bid us farewell.

Brushing the cookie crumbs from my top, I took Davin's outstretched hand. The feel of his hard, warm fingers closing around mine made my heart flip.

He grinned wickedly. "Ready?"

I nodded as tingles of anticipation caused goosebumps to erupt along my forearms. "Ready."

27 – A FUTURE IS BORN

One year later

My hands fluttered nervously over the long white dress. Lace and pearls covered the full-length gown. The train extended several yards behind me. It was a frivolous purchase even though it was my wedding dress.

"You look so beautiful, Meghan." Tears moistened my mother's eyes. She'd helped me pick out the dress on our numerous trips to antique gown stores.

"Davin will be speechless when he sees you," Sharon said from my other side. She dabbed the corner of her eyes with a tissue. Her eyes had been moist for most of the morning.

I glanced back at the six-foot mirror and couldn't believe the image that stared back at me. My long brown hair was swept up into an intricate arrangement of swirls and twists. Sunlight reflected off the pearls and gems woven into the beaded belt that cinched at my waist.

I felt elegant and special—the way every bride should feel on her wedding day.

"Just a few more buttons and then you'll be all set." The twins fussed behind me finishing with last-minute details. Considering the dress had over a hundred tiny buttons trailing up the middle of my back, I felt thankful for their assistance.

"Almost done!" Sophie smiled as her blue fingers swiftly finished the last few buttons.

"There. You're ready!" Sara's excited exclamation came next. Her skin shimmered as she said something telepathically to her sister.

It had been over a year since the Kazzies had been given the option of taking the cure. So far, both twins had decided not to. Because of their decision, they were still harassed periodically, but it seemed that they'd grown used to it over the months.

And every week, those taunts seemed to grow less and less as the fear in our country continually subsided. Since the vaccine had proven so effective, and so few Kazzies remained, for the most part, the public turned a blind-eye to the Kazzies who'd chosen to remain infected.

"We're missing something." Amy's voice snapped me out of my reverie. She stood on my other side and tapped a finger to her mouth. "What are we missing?"

My friends surveyed my appearance as sunlight poured in through the windows. We were currently in an old church in Mobridge that had been abandoned long ago, but it wasn't where Davin and I would be married. It was simply the most suitable place to get ready.

Davin and I were going to be married outside on the South Dakota prairie on the land his ancestors once roamed. Our wedding guests were already out there waiting, while my friends, mom, and Sharon helped me get ready.

It was almost noon which meant the ceremony was due to

start soon.

"Let's see," Sara said. "We have something new." She pointed at my dress. "Something old." She nodded toward my earrings which had belonged to my grandmother. "Something borrowed." She fingered the tiny diamond bracelet on my wrist that belonged to Sharon. "And… that's it! We don't have anything blue. Where's that necklace we bought, Sophie?"

Sophie's eyes widened. "Oh my gosh, it's still in my purse! I can't believe we almost forgot!"

The twin raced to her bag and pulled out the tiny sapphire pendant nestled in the middle of a ring of pearls. When the twins had presented it to me as an engagement gift, I'd fallen in love with it. The sapphire was the exact shade of Davin's eyes.

Sophie rushed back to my side. Placing the necklace carefully around my neck, Sophie secured the tiny clasp.

When she finished, the tiny little pendant sparkled in the sunlight.

Sara smiled. "That's better."

My heart fluttered a hundred miles an hour as my friends, mother, and soon to be mother-in-law, helped me from the room. We ventured down the dusty, forgotten halls to the front of the church. Outside, the limo waited that would take us to the ceremony.

It was only a twenty-minute drive to the area within the Cheyenne River Reservation where Davin and I were getting married. Reservation 1 had ceased to exist. Once again, this land was called as it had been before the First Wave.

In the back of the limo, my long dress spread everywhere. Sophie giggled when she had to push it aside so she could sit down.

"I can't wait to see Davin's face." Sharon dabbed her eyes again. It seemed like she'd been crying on and off all morning.

I squeezed her hand. "Me too."

My mother and Sharon both gazed at me with contented expressions. Over the previous year, they'd become friends in the intermittent times they'd spent together. I imagined they'd grow even closer in the coming years.

Twenty minutes later, when the limo pulled up to the vast South Dakota prairie, I gazed in wonder at the beautiful scenery. This land had been abandoned since Reservation 1 closed, but that only emphasized its natural beauty.

Miles and miles of tall prairie grass swayed in the summer breeze. Wildflowers grew in abundance, dotting the land in a plethora of color.

In the distance, small areas of the fence that had once surrounded Reservation 1 still existed. A brief memory of cutting through the chainlink fence flashed through my mind. It had been so many months since Ian and I had dared that break-in to find Sara with hopes of saving Davin and my friends.

Now, the fence was mostly gone. It had been torn down throughout the months by locals who'd been scavenging for building supplies. The government had never bothered to dismantle it, so locals had taken that task upon themselves.

Only bits and pieces of the fence remained. It was the same with the watch towers. Even though our country had been slowly growing and becoming prosperous once again, goods and services were still hit or miss. As a result, people still foraged and collected items as they found them. The watch towers had proven valuable resources for wood and metal.

All eyes turned on me when I stepped out of the limo. Bright sunlight streamed around.

Our ceremony would be simple. There were no chairs for our guests, carpet for me to walk down, or a fancy trellis for

Davin and I to stand under. It was simply a gathering of friends and family on the wild South Dakota land.

Everyone parted to make room for me as I stepped forward and, in that coordinated movement, I saw Davin standing at the end.

He stood solemnly in a new suit and tie. His jet-black hair flowed around his shoulders. Even from the distance, his sapphire eyes shined.

I saw his breath hitch before a smile spread across his face. My heart fluttered at the sight.

It was hard to believe that only three years ago he'd been a prisoner within Compound 26. At that time, I hadn't known he'd existed. I hadn't known of the atrocities he and the other Kazzies had been subjected to. It had all been a nightmare that I had not yet lived.

Now, seeing him standing tall and proud, the last Sioux warrior to roam this land, my heart filled with so much pride and love I thought I would burst.

Sara and Sophie brushed against my sides. Each reached down to squeeze my hand.

"You look beautiful, Meghan. And Davin looks fantastic. I'm so happy for you." Sophie whispered the words into my ear just as I felt a scratch in the back of my mind.

Sara's telepathic voice came next. *I'm so thrilled for you. I love you like a sister and Davin like a brother. You'll always be my family.*

Tears filled my eyes despite trying to blink them back. It didn't help that Sharon and my mom were already crying. It was going to be an emotional day no matter how much I tried to control myself.

My dad stepped forward from the crowd and extended his arm. His brown hair and brown eyes shone in the summer sun. A simple suit and blue tie adorned his frame.

The twins and Amy stepped into position in front of me just as Victor, Sage, and Mitch appeared to escort them down the grassy aisle. The women wore simple flowing dresses of various cuts and colors. The men wore various degrees of suits, although I caught a peek at Mitch's t-shirt under his suit jacket. *Dear, Math. I'm not a therapist. Solve your own problems.*

I bit back a smile.

The days of coordinated, luxurious weddings with frivolous decorations and thousand-dollar dresses had died with the First Wave. Now, most people were simply happy to have survived and be allowed to spend the future with the one they loved.

Charlie and two of his friends sat in chairs off to the side. The three of them picked up their instruments and began to play the wedding march. My friends walked down the grassy trail in front of me. Davin's smile grew.

And at that moment, it all hit home.

It became real what I was about to do. I was going to marry the only man I'd ever loved, and everything I had ever dreamed of was happening right before my eyes.

"Are you ready, kiddo?" My dad looped my arm through his and placed his other hand over mine. He squeezed.

"I've been ready ever since I met him. He's the one, Dad."

"Then let's go."

My dad walked me to Davin's side as our friends and family watched on. When we reached him, my dad handed me off.

Davin's grip was firm and warm. He was always so warm. That was something I'd never grow tired of. Since he'd opted to stay a Kazzie, despite our initial concerns over him passing the virus to our unborn child, his warmth was permanent and absolute.

"You look beautiful," he whispered.

"So do you."

He smiled, his white teeth flashing in the summer sun.

My breath felt shallow and tight. It had nothing to do with my ever-present anxiety and everything to do with the dashingly handsome man that was about to become my husband. It felt like a thousand tiny butterflies fluttered in my stomach.

Out of the corner of my eye, I saw Sergeant Rose, his wife, and his two sons looking on. I'd never seen the guard smile as wide as he was right now. To his side, stood Cate and Harper. Next to them were Sharon and my parents.

Everyone held tissues in their hands.

"Shall we get started?" Ian stepped forward to conduct the ceremony. His reddish hair curled in the wind, and his dimple appeared when he grinned. He'd become an officiant for the very purpose of marrying Davin and me.

Ian unfolded his papers and began the ceremony. And before our friends and family, as the sun shone down on us on the wild South Dakota prairie, Davin and I promised to have and to hold each other, to love one another, to stay with and cherish each other, until the day we died.

Never had words felt so true and complete as we pledged our commitment before our friends and family. Tears of happiness rolled down my cheeks.

Davin wiped them away as tears moistened his own eyes.

And in that moment, everything was so perfect. So complete.

Only one thing was missing.

I tilted my chin up and gazed at the expansive sky above. Somewhere, somehow, I knew that my brother lived on. He may not be in this world, or even in the universe we called home, but I knew that he still existed and one day I'd see him again.

I wish you could see this, Jer. I wish you could see everything that has happened since you died. I'm so happy, and the only person missing here is you. Know that I love you, brother, and I always will. Wherever you are, I hope to see you again one day. But right now, I'm happy, Jer, and I'm okay. I'm truly okay for the first time since you died, and I know I'll stay that way.

When Ian finished the ceremony, Davin pressed his lips to mine. And in that kiss, I came home.

Pulling back, he tenderly wiped another tear from my cheek. "We did it," he whispered. "It's you and me now, together forever."

I squeezed his hand as love and hope filled my heart. "Yeah, we did it!"

THANK YOU FOR READING!

If you enjoyed *Division 5*, please consider posting a review on Amazon. Authors rely heavily on readers reviewing their work. Even one sentence helps a lot. Thank you so much if you do!

♥ ♥ ♥

If you enjoy Krista Street's writing, make sure you visit her website and join her newsletter to stay up-to-date on new releases. Links to her social media are also available at the bottom of every page.

www.kristastreet.com

THE LOST CHILDREN TRILOGY

Krista Street's bestselling series on Amazon.com

Four months ago, Lena woke up in a dark alleyway with no recollection of who she is. The only clues to her past are a mysterious tattooed symbol and a supernatural power: the ability to see evil in people.

While struggling to regain her memory, she follows a strange guiding instinct to a small Colorado town. There she finds other young men and women with similar stories, similar tattoos, and a multitude of superhuman powers. Among them a man she's intensely attracted to, yet with no memories of him, she has no idea why.

As Lena and the others explore their powers and try to figure out who and what they are, they make a frightening discovery. Those who know the answers to their questions are hunting them. And if they find them, these superhumans may not survive.

FREE E-BOOK!

Join Krista Street's Newsletter and receive a FREE copy of *Siteron.*

A YA Sci-Fi Short Story

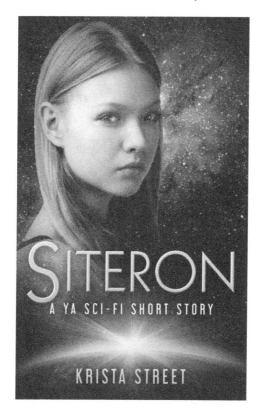

www.kristastreet.com

Made in the USA
Coppell, TX
20 August 2021

60865213R10204